How Not To Lose Your Virginity

ANNE WOAPPI

HARVEST PUBLISHING HOUSE

Library of Congress Control Number (LCCN): 2025919952
International Standard Book Number (ISBN): 9798993179100
Printed in The United States of America. 2nd Edition Printing

Book Cover and Design: Anne Woappi
Book Editor: Elise Woappi

Acknowledgments

To Christelle,
thank you for showing me how to fly,
and to Maman,
thank you for catching me.

Author's Intro

Each girl has a season of her life where she questions herself, where she learns to deal with everything going on around her, where she makes mistakes and grows up.

That one season, where she finds herself.

I hope you can discover her.
I hope you can forgive her too.
I hope you can have your own revolution.

Love,
Anne

Prologue

"I LOVE YOU."

Jordan whispers in my right ear. When he leaned in just seconds ago – a mere centimeter from my face – I thought he meant to remove something from it like a fallen eyelash and to tell me to make a wish.

He's never been this close to me before. Not once during our nightly chats. Our *friendly* nightly chats. It was only three years ago, at his family's lake house, when we started them. Everyone was asleep except us, so we stayed up all night talking. When we got home that summer, one night turned to two and four, and well, here we are. We've been friends our whole lives. He must mean he loves me as a *friend*.

I quickly glance at him, "I love you too."

He shakes his head and slowly tilts his face towards mine. "I'm in love with you."

I can get lost in this preposition all night. *In* sounds nice. In sounds final. In sounds like his decision has been made, against all our odds.

"I mean it." Jordan stares at me, "I'm in love with you." He leaves me no room to doubt his words, not even space between us to feign a lack of hearing. After a moment, he leans his head back against the foot of my bed and rubs his forehead with shaking hands.

I don't recognize this Jordan. He's always well composed. He's captain of the soccer team. He's smart and does AP calculus like he's doing basic math. Jordan Cooper is *not* the nervous kind. But I am, very much so. I've gone mute despite him being the only boy I've ever gotten close to.

He slowly moves his right knee so that it touches my left and a jolt of electricity wakes up each cell in my body. I finally turn to face him, but my words won't escape my lips. *How do I say something in five seconds that I've wanted to say for five years?*

I watch him pull out a small jewelry box from his pocket.

"My farewell gift to you," he hands it to me. "I hope you like it."

"Jordan...this is..." *found my voice.* "Thank you." I slowly untie the silk blue ribbon off the box.

He chuckles as I place the ribbon around my wrist. "That can be yours too."

I stare at the silver heart necklace with the carving of a flower stem on top of it. "It's beautiful," I tell him.

He turns his body to face me then removes my glasses. "Move a little." He pulls my braids to the side and slides the necklace around my neck before clasping it shut. With one swift motion, he moves my shoulders back around to face him.

"Can I?" he asks. This is it. My first crush. My first love and now, *my first kiss.*

I simply nod with closed eyes. I let him lead as his lips caress mine. At first gently, then passionately. I guess this is the irony of life. We're finally confessing our feelings to each other, and he has to leave for college in two weeks.

"Is this, okay?" Jordan asks, pulling away from our kiss.

I want to tell him I can't control the platoon of butterflies taking territory in my stomach. Instead, I inch closer to him. He kisses me more intensely, sliding his hands up my top.

"Not now." *Not like this.*

We kiss again, his hand slides back up.

"I can't." I tell him despite my entire being not wanting to. "I promised myself I would wait."

He leans in closer, our lips touching but not kissing. "One day, I'm going to spend the rest of my life with you."

"I'm going to call you every day I'm at MGU," he adds. There's an intensity in his eyes I've never seen before.

"Promise me you won't be with anyone else?" he asks.

"That's impossible, Jordan."

"Promise me."

I drape my arms around his neck, "I promise."

"I'll honor your wish, Annabelle," he says. He's one of two people that knows it.

He whispers it to me. "Fall in love once, get married, and never get a divorce."

"Like your parents," he adds.

It's not a platoon of butterflies taking territory in my stomach anymore. It's an entire army.

One

One

TWO YEARS LATER

"Follow me, Warren said we can skip the line."

Amanda said to me and Halle and grabbed my hand in front of Warren's house. *No*, his *cousin's* house. *Or was it both?* I had yet to meet Warren or his cousin, but I already knew what to expect when we walked up to their four-story mansion downtown.

"Who are you?" The guy seated on a stool by the front door stared at the three of us. He wore all black and looked our age yet older at the same time.

"We're friends of Warren," Amanda said.

He kept his attention on Halle. "You don't say."

Amanda placed a hand on his shoulder and gave him her smile. In high school, her cheerleading friends called it her *Cooper smile* because everyone in her family had it. It was the kind of smile that helped you get whatever you wanted. The kind of smile that always worked, no questions asked. Except tonight, it wasn't working on this guy, at least not yet.

His eyes were fixated on Halle. "Why should I let you girls in?"

Amanda removed her hand and took out her phone while he moved his prying eyes away from Halle to stare at my shoes.

"It's her first college party," Halle said.

"She's right," Amanda looked up from her phone, "cut my friend some slack."

"It is," I added. It's not like I truly cared, but I really didn't want to be the reason we weren't allowed in. I told Amanda and Halle I'd go out with them tonight on three conditions. One, it was my eighteenth birthday the weekend prior and they said it was unfathomable for me to keep staying in my dorm. Two, freshman orientation just ended, and we had three whole days to watch the student body trickling in. And three, we left by midnight and saw a movie.

"She looks good and you know it," Amanda said, annoyed.

"Listen," he responded, "there's a hundred of you in line, y'all are looking good in those heels, but she's in −" he looked at me with contempt, "sneakers. I'm not saying you don't look good; I'm just saying Warren won't allow anyone to dress down for these parties."

Amanda looked at her and Halle's matching shoes. "These are wedges," she looked back at him, "they're totally a step down from the heels the girls in line are wearing and only a step above my friend's sneakers."

Halle pointed her eyes at him. "I've been here before, what's the big deal?"

"I know," the guy raised a brow and looked her up and down.

"So...what's the issue?" Amanda asked. "Don't you want pretty girls at your party?"

Amanda, with her doe blue eyes, golden blonde hair, and bombshell presence had yet to meet a guy she liked who didn't like her back. She never had to compete for any guy's attention. That is, until she met her roommate, Halle Mitchell. Halle's trailblazing fashion sense, unbreakable confidence, and the constant *you look like Naomi Campbell* meant she didn't just turn heads everywhere she went; she always looked like she stepped off some runway. Together, they were too dynamic of a duo to stop.

The guy gave us another glance then shook his head. *It was only a matter of time.*

"Y'all are wild, get in."

* * *

A loud gasp escaped Amanda's mouth when Halle opened the front door to let us in. "This place's a castle!"

Halle smiled at her. "Tell me about it."

Amanda wasn't exaggerating so we hovered in the entryway, taking it all in. The interior walls were painted in earth tones with shades of white, red, and muted auburn. It was your quintessential New England house, if you took an entire neighborhood block and called it a house.

Scanning the crowd, it wasn't hard to figure out why the guy out front would barely let me in. I *was* in jeans, and I looked nothing like the girls inside.

"Why are you making that face?" Amanda asked me.

"I'm thinking of all the outfits I considered wearing tonight before this one."

She winked. "See? I knew it."

Amanda brought to campus what she called our *going to college wardrobe* in two separate suitcases – one for each of us. In true Amanda fashion, she made sure to give me mine once we were already on campus.

I looked down at the jeans I was wearing. I assumed pairing it with my signature look, hair ribbons, and the red lipstick I borrowed from Halle, would help me look sexy. Looking at all the girls around me, including Amanda and Halle, I barely touched the surface of sexy.

"DJ's too loud," Halle said to Amanda, "text Warren to meet us in his kitchen."

She led us across the crowded living room, past a long and narrow hallway, and eventually into the less-crowded kitchen.

Amanda gazed around, "is this a fine dining restaurant or..."

Halle laughed, "I told you they were rich-rich." She looked at both of us, "I need a drink." She walked past the girls huddled near us and grabbed red cups from the stack on the kitchen island, right next to the oversized keg.

"Take one," Halle handed us each a cup.

"Pour water into yours," Amanda said to me.

Halle stopped pouring from the keg. "Don't tell me you're still not drinking," she looked at Amanda then back at me, "you haven't done anything all of orientation. Are you ever going to?"

I simply shrugged, "I don't drink."

"You're totally missing out," Amanda said.

I couldn't blame them for wanting to have fun. We were in *fun town* after all or Greenspring, Massachusetts. They were both excited to be freshmen at MGU, otherwise known as Massachusetts Greenspring University – one of the most prestigious universities in the state. MGU was known for a lot of things, mainly its frat culture, wealthy heritage, distinguished network, and slew of international students. Amanda and Halle fit here seamlessly. But there was another kind of student, me, who didn't know where I fit in.

Amanda looked up from her phone, "I texted Warren, he said to come outside."

"No, tell him he's meeting us here," Halle reached into the fridge, "jello shots?"

"Now we're talking!" Amanda said.

"Feel free to join us at any time...Annabear," Halle said to me.

Amanda coughed a laugh. "Only I get to call her that."

As far as Halle was concerned, only Amanda and I got to call each other by our nicknames. We were childhood best-friends thanks to our moms who also were. They swore their only girls would be inseparable like them and timed their pregnancies to conceive in the same year. I, *Annabelle Lucille Wilson*, was named after Amanda's mom, Lucy. *Amanda Mariebelle Cooper* was named after my mom, Marie. Our similarities started and ended at our height because we were both under five feet six inches. Amanda was fun, outgoing, always the life of the party. I was friendly but slow to warm up to new people. We were opposites yet very close, and we wouldn't have it any other way.

"I'm kidding," Halle smiled at me and handed the shots to Amanda, who was checking her phone for the third time.

Normally, I'd be more stressed about being at this party, but there was one more reason we were here. I had to meet Warren and approve. I mentally browsed through every guy I met before him and what my initial reaction usually was. If there was one thing about Amanda, her taste never changed.

"Yooo you guys made it."

Must be him.

By the look on the other girls' faces in the kitchen, I knew it had to be Warren or his cousin. I turned around to face him just as Amanda was giving him a hug.

"Hey," he nodded at me then raised a fist-bump. He wore khakis, a button-down shirt, and a smug grin on his face.

"Bring it in," he said to Halle who eagerly gave him a hug.

"Nice to meet you," I quickly looked at the two other guys next to him.

"Not a bad house huh?" Warren asked Amanda.

She brushed a hand through her hair, "not bad for sophomores."

"Speaking of." He looked at the guy to his right. "This is my cousin Gabe, I share the house with him and a couple guys from our frat." Warren nodded at Halle, "You two already met."

Gabe and Halle gave each other one of those looks that told you they already knew each other well.

The two guys were practically dressed the same, but Gabe's blond hair was trimmed. If he grew his hair a little longer, he'd look just like Warren.

"Tell them about your cruise," Warren told Gabe. I glanced at the third guy, who they weren't acknowledging

"I'll get to it," Gabe looked at Halle, "long time no see."

"You only graduated last year," she said, "already miss me that much?" Warren and Gabe grinned, but the third guy didn't. He just kept standing there, observing everyone, not saying anything. He was lanky with curly dark hair and thick eyebrows. His light brown skin also made it that he looked nothing like the frat guys at the party. I was too busy wondering who he could be when he noticed that I was staring at him. I looked away.

"Ben grew up here too," Warren said to us.

"Hi." Ben nodded at us. He looked at me, "nice meeting you."

Halle stared at him. "You graduated from Greenspring High? Why don't I remember you? I knew everyone."

"Cause he was homeschooled," Warren said.

Ben placed his hands in his pockets, "I didn't go out much."

"Enough of this small talk," Gabe looked around, "you girls wanna have fun?" I noticed the rest of the girls were nodding their heads too, so did Amanda.

"Totally," Amanda said, "what girl doesn't want to?"

"It's way too loud up here." Warren looked at Gabe. "We can go to the basement, play a game or something."

"Aren't you renovating it?" Halle asked him.

"It's done," Gabe said.

Warren walked over to the closed door by the kitchen entrance and opened it. A few other girls tried to follow.

"Y'all can stay up here," he said. They looked upset and walked off.

I sighed quietly and watched them walk downstairs before immediately turning to Amanda.

"I don't think we should go down there." I said. "You just met him this week and this is my first time meeting them."

That's when I noticed Ben looking over at us. He was the only one of the boys who hadn't gone down. He waited a little longer then walked downstairs. When he was out of our sight, I turned to Amanda again.

"Seriously Amanda, it's not the best idea."

"That's Warren and Gabe *Vandersant*," she leaned in closer to me so no one could hear us. "The richest family in town, probably this entire state."

I stared at her for a moment, wondering if she forgot she was rich herself. Our families weren't the *Vandersants*, but we certainly did well for ourselves.

"They may be, but I don't feel comfortable going down there."

"We're fine," Amanda said. "You don't feel comfortable doing much of anything so trust me."

"They know Halle," she added.

"She told us she didn't know them that well."

"I'm getting to know Warren and Halle's had a crush on Gabe since forever," she looked around, "look at them, these girls are dying to trade our places."

"Can you try to like them? For me? Please?" She grabbed my clutch and pretended to look for something. "There's not a book in here somewhere, is there?"

I took in a long drag of breath. "Fine, but you said we'd leave by midnight." I walked over to the sink to refill my cup.

"We'll *try* to leave by midnight," Amanda said. "Who knows where the night will take us?"

* * *

"Mi casa es su casa," Warren said to us when we joined the group downstairs. Like the rest of the house, the basement looked like it cost our entire college tuition combined.

We walked over to the lounging section they were huddled in just in time to see Gabe hit the black ball with a cue stick, which went into one of the pocket holes on the pool table.

"Nicely done," Halle gave him a high-five. "One more round?"

"Nah, let's grab a drink," he looked at me, "sit wherever."

I walked over to where Ben was and sat in the empty loveseat next to him.

"Do you watch football?" Ben asked me.

I looked at the game on the screen. "No, not really."

"Anything to drink?" Gabe asked us.

Ben lifted his cup, "I'm good."

"Shots for me and Halle," I heard Amanda say from the bar area.

"Water?" Ben asked me.

"Umm," I looked down at the cup I was clutching onto, "yes."

"That makes two of us," Ben said.

Gabe walked over and plopped himself at the end of the sectional couch across from us and lowered the volume on the TV. Warren sat down on the other end. Amanda and Halle sat in the middle.

"What game should we play?" Warren asked Amanda to his right.

"Last time I was here we played..." Halle looked up, "never have I ever! That's what it was," she looked at Amanda, "best party I've ever been to hands down."

She pointed at Gabe. "This one was a sore loser."

Gabe looked at her. "We had a blast that night."

"What do I get for winning?" Warren asked Amanda.

"Who says you'll win?" Amanda asked him back.

"I don't like to lose," Warren responded.

"Sure, I'll play that game," Gabe said, "if we keep it at sex and dating, otherwise it's a bore." I took a sip of my water.

Ben slouched. "We don't need to add those rules."

"Majority rules," Gabe said without voting.

"Loser takes three shots," Warren added.

Amanda looked at him. "That's bold of you considering you or Gabe are about to lose."

"Shots fired," Gabe clapped his hands. "Let's go!"

"I'll start," Halle slapped Gabe's thigh. "We're going clockwise."

I crossed my arms over my chest. On the bright side, someone else was staying sober. The few times I'd accompanied Amanda to one of her high-school parties, I was the designated driver. I could wait in the car and get lost in a book I was reading. I'd camp there until she was ready to go. I never had to play any games, certainly not this one.

A few deep breaths later, I followed their lead and placed one hand near my chest with my fingers lifted like they were doing.

Halle kicked off the game. "Never have I ever spent money on a date." Each guy put down one finger.

Amanda went next. "Never have I ever been dumped."

"Think highly of yourself, don't you?" Warren asked her.

"Why shouldn't I?" she smiled at him. "You're next."

"Never have I ever cared to date anyone seriously," Warren said. It was obvious what he was doing, trying to make her jealous. Amanda didn't *get* jealous. She barely wore her heart on her sleeve.

A few minutes into the game, Ben and I still had the most fingers up.

Ben cleared his throat. "Never have I ever cheated on anyone." Warren and Gabe each put a finger down. So did Halle and Amanda.

Halle looked at us, "I mean, I'm putting my finger down, but I don't think relationships before college count as real ones."

"Spoken like a true cheater," Gabe said which caused both Warren and Amanda to laugh.

Ben looked at me. "Your turn."

"Never have I ever," I stared at the coffee table in the middle, as if it would miraculously give me the next thing to say. If I said the right thing, Amanda or Halle would be out of the game which meant this game would finally end.

Gabe exhaled a sharp breath and got up. He walked over to the bar area, came back another bottle in hand, and placed it down on the coffee table.

He looked at me, "please make it a good one." He stared at Halle with a smile, "I want to see you get wasted." Then he sat down.

"You wish," Halle looked at him. "*I* won't be the one losing."

My mind was already drawing a blank.

"New rule," Warren said, "anyone who takes too long has to put a finger down."

"We're not doing that," Ben disagreed.

Gabe looked at me, "any day now."

I had nothing left.

"This isn't hard," Gabe continued, "something you have or haven't done with a guy."

Amanda shifted in her seat. I didn't like the looks on their faces, at all.

"Never have I ever gone to a college party before tonight!" *Whoosh, close call.* I suddenly felt a huge sigh of relief. Except, when I looked back up, they were still staring at me.

"Dating," Gabe closed his eyes and pinched his forehead, "what part of keeping it at sex and dating aren't you getting?" He pointed his finger at me. "You're a funny one."

Amanda looked at me. We both knew I couldn't add any more to this game.

"Can we skip my turn?" I asked everyone. "I can't think of anything else."

"Hell no." Gabe said. "That's against the rules."

Ben sat up, "I don't think it hurts to skip her turn, we're both winning."

"Just think of something," Halle said to me, "anything." I wanted to tell her that the rules of the game made it so I couldn't just say *anything*.

"I'm down for giving Annabelle a pass," Ben said.

"Nah." Gabe looked at me. "What's up with you? You've kept things very PG."

"You've done things with guys right?" he asked.

"You're crossing the line man," Ben said.

"We should move on," Amanda looked at Gabe, "just go next."

"I'm okay giving up my turn," I said.

"Either you take these shots as the loser or you play the game," Gabe said. "It's one or the other."

Ben looked at me. "Have you ever been in a serious relationship?"

I just shook my head no.

"There it is," Ben said, still drying to defend me. "She's never been in a serious relationship." He looked at Gabe. "You're up man."

"She can play for herself," Warren said.

Gabe stared at me. I simply looked away and quickly tried to think of something else.

"Guys," Ben sat up. "Cut her some slack."

"I don't have anything left," I placed my cup down on the coffee table and grabbed my clutch. I looked at Amanda. "Can we go back upstairs? Please."

Gabe moved his body to the edge of the couch. His glare zoning in on me. "We said a lot in this game and you're the only one who has all your fingers up."

"Have you actually been with a guy?" he asked.

Ben looked at him, "lay off."

"We're totally moving on," Amanda said. She looked at Halle, "you go since Gabe wants to skip his turn."

"Can we leave?" I asked her and Halle.

"Let's end this game," Ben agreed and stood up.

Gabe continued to look at me, "it's a yes or no."

"It's clearly a no for her bro," Warren said.

I stood up too.

"Hold on," Gabe said, "you've pretty much shown us in this game that you've never been with a guy, and you've never hooked up with anyone."

"It's kind of obvious you haven't done anything with a guy," he added.

I knew what was coming and so did Amanda. The train I was doing a horrible job of stopping. The truth to what only she and one other person knew.

"Wait a minute," Gabe leaned in, his gaze locked into me again. He looked at everyone then at me. "Are you a virgin?"

That was the first time I saw my best-friend speechless.

* * *

There weren't many moments in life when it happened, but it did happen. Time stopping. I'm sure it did, like the world's clock decided to shut off. I couldn't hear the small noise from the sports channel playing in the background anymore. The walls no longer vibrated the loud bass from the DJ upstairs and the muffled voices from the party ceased to resonate around us. All I could hear was my heartbeat. All I could see were their looks of pity.

Ben spoke up first. "I know tons of virgins."

Gabe shook his head. "Who's a virgin these days?"

"Plenty of people," Ben insisted. He looked in my direction. "You want to get out of here?"

"You know what?" Halle grabbed one of the cups. "I'll take the shots and we can play another game."

"Of course you are," Warren laughed, "you were about to lose the game before your friend ruined it."

Everything I was feeling came crashing down. I looked at Gabe and Warren, "I'm a virgin not an alien and I didn't ruin your stupid game." I looked at Amanda. "Can we go back upstairs or get out of here?"

Warren put his arm around Amanda. "Tell me you're not a virgin," he said to her.

"Of course I'm not." She looked at me with pleading eyes not to leave.

"Let's play another game," Halle said. "Just one more."

"Can we please leave?" I asked them. Ben was already walking up the steps, so I followed behind him. When I got to the bottom of the stairwell, I turned around. Amanda and Halle were still seated on the couch with Warren and Gabe.

"Amanda, please, let's leave."

"I'm staying here," she looked back at me. "I'm good."

She repeated herself. "Go, I'm good."

Two

"WAIT UP!" Ben called from behind me when I stepped into the kitchen. I'd managed to pass him even though he was the one to take the lead upstairs.

"Gabe's a lot to take in, but Warren's harmless. He's just – " he paused, "very opinionated." He kept following behind me. "No one cares about this stuff."

He caught his breath. "Seriously, no one does." He pushed past the crowd to catch up with me in the living room. "Wow, you're walking fast."

I stopped to look at him before opening the front door. "Your friends aren't the nicest."

"Yours aren't so great either."

I opened the front door and walked out. The line to get in had tripled in size. Bowing my head, I walked past the bouncer. If I kept walking at this pace, I could get back to Wolf Hall in ten minutes instead of the thirty it took us to walk downtown.

I could hear Ben's footsteps behind me. "Just let it roll off you. Why do you care about what they think so much?"

This guy was determined not to leave me alone. I stopped and looked at him. "They were mocking me and you're defending them."

"With all due respect," he stared at me, "you're making a bigger deal out of this." It not only annoyed me that he was defending them, but that he felt the need to follow me to tell me that. I walked faster.

"Can you stop?" he asked, "for one second?"

He placed his hands in his pockets when I turned around to look at him.

"All I'm saying is that you shouldn't let them get to you. They don't know any better and it was a stupid game. Now it's over so don't let it ruin your night."

"Seriously," I got a good look at him, "why do you hang out with them?"

"I may not be in a frat, but I could ask you the same thing. Parties don't strike me as your thing, you're also nothing like those girls."

I looked down. "That's not the same."

"Sure," he shrugged. "It was just a game, a stupid game, but just a game. Don't let it mess up your night."

"It just hurts that's all," I said, instantly feeling horrible for him leaving the party to chase after me.

"Let it go," his eyes locked into mine, "on behalf of everyone in there, I'm sorry you're feeling this way."

He shifted back and forth. "Do you need me to walk you back?"

I knew he was asking to be nice. "No, my dorm's not too far from here."

"Sleep it off?" he asked.

I looked at him, "sleep it off."

About five minutes out, I no longer felt his stare against my back, but I couldn't follow his advice to sleep it off. A wave of sadness overtook me when I walked into dorm 507. Just across from me, down the hall, Amanda shared her dorm with Halle. Somehow, I always managed to get Amanda's friends *not* to like me.

I'd known perfect. I had *perfected* perfect. So naturally, I assumed that being on campus would be easy for me. Like every other time, I could keep pretending I had it all together despite everything else going on.

I walked past the wooden desk stretched alongside the wall on the right side of my dorm, slid out my chair tucked under, and cut myself another slice of the leftover cake. The room was small and crowded with the twin beds taking up half the space on the left side. The beige walls and dirty white ceiling made it seem a lot smaller than it was, and if it wasn't for the flowery decor I placed around the area, as well as the oversize window near my bed, it would look like a block of concrete.

I grabbed my laptop to pass the time. After a couple minutes of scrolling the web, I went on MGU Reader. The website wasn't live yet. It couldn't be since school hadn't started, but that didn't stop the popular dating gossip site on campus to still have a lot of engagement. I stared at the top banner on the screen – *draft your story and watch it go live first thing Monday morning!*

My mind raced as I skimmed through the posts from previous years. I hovered my mouse over the grayed-out box with a new caption appearing – *don't be shy, MGU Reader wants to hear your story*. Before I knew it, I was typing. Each keyboard sound felt like a release of every emotion I had suppressed. The words I wrote made me feel like I was discovering a new cure. I was no longer striving to be perfect; I could just be. After a couple more minutes of typing, my phone rang.

"Are you back safely?" Amanda asked me. Her voice was muffled. "I'm still here."

"Yes," I whispered.

"Do you need me to come back?"

The me writing this post would tell her how she was feeling, but I didn't. I went back to perfect.

"No, I'm fine." I said, "please be safe."

"Good!" she said, "I love you!" Then hung up.

I quickly deleted my draft and closed my laptop. I didn't have to post it. Just writing it felt freeing. For one hour, I didn't care about anyone else's opinions. For that hour, I wasn't the girl anyone pitied.

* * *

Amanda and I apologized to each other in several ways based on how little or much we'd offended each other. For small apologies, we took small steps like bringing each other our favorite comfort foods or doing something the other loved to do. We'd read a book together or binge-watch cheerleading competitions. The summer before our junior year, Amanda left home to spend the weekend alone. She didn't tell anyone except me, so I lied to everyone on her behalf. When she came back, she handed me a bag with all my favorite goodies and an apology card. We decided then that, for the big apology, we'd do all the steps at once.

"Forgive me?" Amanda asked while handing me two plastic boxes filled with mini cupcakes. We were seated at GRUB, The Greenspring Resources University Building, our favorite hangout spot on campus.

She pulled out a book from her purse and placed it on the table. "It's one of your favorite authors, I couldn't resist." I stared at the newly released copy I'd been eyeing while Amanda handed me an envelope.

"I'm sorry, Annabear."

I understood now why my mom said to accept the apologies that came. When people stared at you like that, it was almost cruel not to.

I opened the envelope, "I'm not mad."

"Seriously? I'm so sorry!" she said while I read her apology card, "I promise I'll make it up to you...you know he didn't mean to be rude, they were just goofing around trying to impress us."

I placed the envelope on the table. "Really, I'm not mad."

She let out a long-suffering sigh. "I swear, I grilled them after you left, me and Halle both did."

"Please forgive me?" she asked again.

"Amanda," I stared at her, "I'm not upset."

She leaned back on the chair. "I was so worried you would be."

"I'm not upset, I accept your apology," I repeated. "I'm just glad you're safe."

"I shouldn't have been so awkward," I added. "I overreacted."

"No." She handed me one of the cupcakes before grabbing herself one. "This is all on me."

"Can we move on?" I asked before taking a bite of my cupcake. "This is so good."

A smile spread on her lips. "I'm officially forgiven? You're really not upset about it?" I shook my head and grabbed another cupcake. Amanda immediately got out of her chair to give me a hug.

"Halle and I had the worst walk of shame this morning," she sat back down, "she's sorry too by the way."

At the mention of her name, I saw a shadow peeking from the tall beam on our left. "Halle, I see you, you can come out," I called out to her.

Halle walked over to us. "I'm sorry too." She hugged me then sat down, "thanks for understanding."

"Apology accepted from both of you."

"We ran into my mom this morning," Halle changed the subject, then took a bite from Amanda's cupcake. She winced. "This is ridiculously sweet."

Although she was very close to her mom who had invited us for dinner right after we moved into our dorms, Halle was carefree and different from her. Halle's mom also happened to be faculty at our shared liberal arts college.

"Lucky me," she said, "she wasn't thrilled. It's bad enough I'm majoring in art history, my mom called me after to ask why she ran into me looking like I'm up to no good."

"You were up to no good," Amanda said.

"*We* were up to no good."

Halle kept going, "I had to come up with an excuse on the

spot. Mom wanted to know why we were dressed like *that*." Halle was interrupted by a sudden scream, followed by another. From where we were, we could see a group of girls excited to see each other again.

"Aren't you glad we're already moved in?" Amanda asked us.

"Yep," Halle said, "still up for that picnic?"

"I'm down," Amanda agreed. They both looked at me.

"Sure."

* * *

"Warren wants to hang out more," Amanda said when we walked outside of the grocery store near GRUB.

"He told me this morning," she looked at me, "what do you think now that you've met him?" she paused. "Before the game."

"I think you can do better," I answered honestly. "Much better."

"You always think that."

"That's because it's true."

She moved her grocery bag from her right hand to her left and locked elbows with me. "This is me talking, I always have the upper hand when it comes to guys."

It was right, she was a pro at dating, if you could call it that. She spent our entire high-school letting guys know that it wasn't *them* before breaking their hearts. Keeping guys away from their property was a constant battle for the Coopers and it didn't matter how many times Mr. Cooper stood out front and threatened them, the boys always came back. There were phone bans, curfews set, and driving privileges revoked. Amanda somehow always figured out a way to sneak out at night and meet her friends and who she called her *boy toy*. I admired how evasive she acted towards love. I admired how much she didn't care or showed she cared.

"How about, I organize another hangout with Warren so you can get to know him, for real this time?"

I looked at her. "You said you wanted something different in college."

"I did, but he's the biggest fish on campus. It'll be fun hanging out with him. Annabelle, I can't date him if you two don't get along."

Our golden rule. She created this rule with the best of intentions, but I never liked the guys she dated even though I couldn't actually say anything. The one time I did date, it had crashed and burned before it could get somewhere.

"We'll hang out with them again soon if you're in?"

"I'm not sure," I answered, "I'll think about it."

"Don't think, just go," she said when we turned into the main street adjacent to the back alley of the grocery store.

A guy bumped into us. "That sounds like horrible advice."

"You don't even know what we're talking about," Amanda said before looking up and realizing who we had bumped into. She unlocked elbows.

"How would you know it's bad advice?" she asked him.

"Anything that motivates..." he nodded his head towards me, "darling here to make a rash decision would be considered bad advice."

"Am I wrong?" he asked with the confidence of someone who couldn't be bothered to pretend he didn't know he was attractive. His high top hairstyle looked like it was styled by the best in the world. His jaw could cut through the tension outside and when he flashed us a smile, a large dimple appeared on his right cheek. It also didn't help that his British accent could melt the heart of any girl. He was tall, dark, and excruciatingly handsome. We had bumped into none other than Kevin Knicks.

He stared at us. "Am I?"

Amanda softened her voice, "arguable."

"Kevin, leave them alone."

My body froze. Jordan Cooper and another guy I hadn't met caught up to Kevin. A lump formed in my throat when I saw the girls they were with.

Kevin looked at Jordan, "I was telling your sister she gives awful advice."

"Don't give him another reason to hate me." Amanda looked at the guy next to Kevin. "Hi, I'm his sister, Amanda."

"Unfortunately," she added.

She turned to me. "This is Annabelle."

"Seth." Their friend curtly said to both of us.

"Whatever, meet us there." One of the girls next to them walked off with her friend.

"Nice tattoos," Amanda said to Seth. "Your sleeve's cool."

"Thanks."

When I looked away from Seth and Amanda, I caught Jordan staring at me.

"Nice to see you again," Kevin said to me.

Jordan looked at Kevin, "let's go."

Kevin looked at his phone, "what's the rush?"

"We'll be late for practice," Jordan said matter-of-factly.

Seth looked at Jordan before quickly glancing at me and Kevin.

Kevin chuckled. "It's 5 o'clock on Friday mate, coach can wait."

Amanda looked at Jordan. "Afraid your friends will like us more?"

"Get over yourself." Jordan said and walked past me. Another drop in my stomach.

"Suit yourself," he said to Kevin before walking off with Seth.

"See you around," Kevin walked backwards behind them, "Annabelle."

As soon as they were no longer in our sight, Amanda turned to me, "I knew it! Kevin's totally into you."

I tried to dismiss the angst I felt towards seeing Jordan again.

* * *

"People watching by myself defeats the whole purpose." Halle called out from the lawn in front of our dorm. "I only asked you to get a few things, were you buying the whole store?"

"Must I remind you that this picnic was *your* idea, yet you wouldn't get the food for the actual picnic part?" Amanda asked her.

"Thank you," Halle said, "I'm starving." She looked through the bags we placed on the blanket. Her legs were extended along the edge of the large beach towel. Amanda sat on the other end. I sat between them.

"So," Halle looked at us, "what took you guys so long?"

"Kevin Knicks is what took us so long," Amanda placed the rest of the groceries on the towel, "he's into Annabelle."

"No, he isn't," I quickly said.

"Yes, he is," Amanda insisted. She looked at Halle, "I told her that when we first met him."

"He's into you," Amanda was firm about it. "I saw it first."

Halle crossed her legs. "What's the juice?" Her infamous expression for asking for information or gossip.

"The juice is," Amanda looked at Halle, "Kevin joined us for Thanksgiving Jordan's freshman year since he wasn't going back to England and kept staring at Annabelle. It was totally obvious he was into her."

It's not that I didn't want to believe her compliment, I just knew it wasn't true. Halle looked at me, so I told her why. "Amanda thinks every guy she *thinks* has a thing for me actually has a thing for me."

Halle simply shrugged. "I can see that. You're hot...in a nerdy sort of way...and you don't know it, guys love that sort of thing."

I glanced down at our shopping bag. I could feel her looking at me, not unkindly, just wanting me to contribute to what she'd just said. She was like Amanda, the Coopers, or I guess the Kevin Knicks of this world. Bold, confident, and attractive. I may have been a lot of things, but hot was not one of them.

"I told her that at Thanksgiving that year," Amanda said. She spent a good amount of time after dinner gushing about his dimple and how cute we'd be together.

"Staring doesn't mean someone likes me," I responded.

"Since when? Staring totally means someone's into you. One of these days, you're going to have to put yourself out there and find these things out on your own."

Halle agreed with Amanda. "If Amanda says he wants you, he probably does."

"You're in college now," Amanda said. "These years are supposed to be the best years of our lives. It'll do you some good to stop thinking about everything else and let go this year. Look, I know I'm the last person who should be giving you advice when it comes to school but seriously, I don't want you to waste this semester."

Then she sold me her final punchline. "Our parents met here."

I had to hand it to her. There was usually no point in arguing with Amanda because, one way or another, she'd make the most sense of things and you were convinced to give in.

"What are we waiting for?" Halle asked. "Let's have the best semester any freshman could ever want."

"Meet more people, do things we've never done before," Amanda looked at me, "loosen up."

They were both so excited, the kind that made you feel like the entire world was yours. Even for a moment, I wanted to feel that too. "Fine."

Three

I WOKE up the next morning to grating squeaks coming from the other side of my dorm. Amanda, Halle, and I stayed up until the wee hours of the morning watching movies and talking about our upcoming semester. I thought I was still dreaming until the noise became unbearably loud.

"I'm so sorry!" The girl placed the bedframe back on the floor when I begrudgingly opened my eyes.

"I was trying not to wake you up!" She moved her suitcase from the floor to the empty bed. "Not that there's any way to do that gracefully with these old mattresses."

"It's okay," I quickly shut off my alarm, "I was about to wake up."

"I'm Jaz," she waved, "your roommate." She paused when she noticed I was staring at the gold bracelet on her left wrist.

"It's from California," she played with the charm of a cross on her bracelet then grabbed the charm with the state's flag. "Have you heard of Crescent City?"

I sat up on my bed, "I've been there before, it's beautiful."

"Most people don't know about it, where are you from?"

"Blakely, Massachusetts. It's a small coastal town not far from here. It's about two hours away from campus."

"Blakely," she repeated whimsically, "it sounds picture perfect."

"It is, it's right by the water." I knew how lucky I was to have grown up there every time I went on vacation. Those places never felt like vacation because my hometown had it al. Only one place I had traveled to compared to the charm of Blakely.

"What brought you to MGU?"

"Family," I answered her, hoping she wouldn't pry further.

She unzipped the suitcase on her bed and took out her clothes. "What college are you in?"

Amanda didn't like that I always used flowers to describe people. Halle confirmed during orientation that it wasn't cool. A *turn-off* as they put it. It wasn't my goal to bore others with it, but it was out of the question for me not to assign someone their flower after I met them. Meeting Jaz, I knew right away, she was my Dahlia. She had a quirkiness to her. A liveliness that radiated all around our dorm. Let's just say for a random roommate, she wasn't bad.

I got up and made my bed. "Liberal Arts, I'm an English major, you?"

"Me too! Let's compare our class schedules when you're free?" She pointed at the pile of clothes on her bed. "I'll be sorting these all day."

"I'm meeting my guidance counselor soon." I grabbed my toiletries. "Maybe we can talk after?"

"Yes! Great to meet you, Annabelle."

* * *

Vandersant College of Liberal Arts, I read the words out loud. Walking here, I noticed three buildings with their last name on them. *No wonder Amanda wants to date him.*

"Ms. Wilson?" A short and rounded man stood at the front of the building. "It's nice to see you, I'm Dr. Gatz." He extended his hand for me to shake. "Let's go in."

The inside of the building had bright lighting and enormous glass windows. It was modern and looked out of place compared to the older ones next to it. Dr. Gatz escorted me into his office on the second floor, "I'm glad you finally made time for us to meet this Saturday, we're cutting it too close, we need to finalize your class schedule."

There were papers all over his desk, but he seemed to know where everything was. He grabbed a yellow folder from the pile. "How do you like the building?"

"It's nice," I answered him. "It looks new."

He opened the folder. "It is." He stopped what he was doing. "There's a basement floor below the first that was kept from our original building, our archives are there."

"For students?"

"No, only the English Department's staff and faculty." He went back to scanning the papers he was pulling out of the folder. "I can give you a tour when we're done here if you'd like."

He looked up. "How was orientation week?"

"It went well."

"I bet it was nice being on campus without everyone. I always recommend that freshmen participate in that. It's a zoo out there now."

"Water?" He offered.

"Thank you," I grabbed the water bottle he handed me.

"Wait until the start of classes on Monday, you'll see students on every inch of campus. Sometimes I lock myself in here and pretend I have meetings back-to-back."

"So, Ms. Wilson," Dr. Gatz moved his chair towards the computer screen, "the school's aware that this is your first year on campus, but you also lost a family member this year."

I'd survived being on campus without hearing it. With five simple words, Dr. Gatz brought me back to that moment of shock.

"I'm sorry for your loss."

The cancer came back, it's fatal this time. The doctor told us.

One month left to live. In an instant, our world came crashing down. *He's gone.* I was there, at the hospital, when my mother told me the awful news. That was how people in my hometown Blakely knew me now. Not as Annabelle Wilson, the daughter of the famous journalist, Jean Wilson, who traveled the world with his child. Or daughter of Marie Wilson, the flight attendant who grew up in Blakely and married him. Now, I was Annabelle Wilson, the girl who lost her dad. But MGU wasn't Blakely. It was a new territory with new people who didn't know my story. I did a good job during orientation to avoid discussing my home life when students would bond and talk about their families. I played my part well. If I remained strong and hidden, people would simply leave me alone.

I glanced down at the checkered floor beneath me before looking back at him, "yes, this spring."

He placed an old school newspaper in front of me. A picture of my dad and a few other journalists was on the front cover with an article they'd written. "He's on our notable alumni list, I like to keep track of everyone."

"I wouldn't be surprised if that's why you chose your major." Dr. Gatz smiled. "Your dad was a great journalist." I swallowed back my tears.

Dr. Gatz took a sip of his coffee and placed the mug back on his desk. "The school recognizes that big life changes can be stressful for our students. My job is to assist you as best as I can, I can work with you on a reasonable schedule that won't overwhelm you.

"We typically require students to take fifteen credits or more to be considered full-time, but we make exceptions for students going through life-altering events.

"What do you say? We make your schedule four classes instead of the required five? You get your bearings and do a regular schedule next semester? I'm more than happy to help, Ms. Wilson."

After some silence, he kept going. "We also have mental health resources for you to consider. You told the school you don't need them, but I want you to know they're available if you ever do. I could probably use them myself, maybe I won't be balding from stress so rapidly."

I looked around his office. A large family picture of his wife and four kids hung on the wall. "Thank you, Dr. Gatz," I cleared my throat. "Thank you for trying to help, but I think I can handle the full schedule."

He didn't look happy with my answer. "You're one of our top students joining our program this year. Your high-school grades were stellar, so we know what you're capable of, but these resources are for you. I've seen students in your same situation fall through the cracks."

I could tell he was uncomfortable. This was his first time having this conversation with me, but my hundredth giving the same answer.

"Really, I'm fine."

* * *

I needed the fresh air after my meeting with Dr. Gatz. He was only doing this job and I guess I had to eventually face being in the same college my dad was in. By the time I arrived at the creamery, a small line had already formed so I returned my mom's call to pass the time.

"Hi sweetie, how did your counselor meeting go this morning?"

"It went okay, he's nice."

"I'm happy things are picking up."

"My roommate moved in this morning, she's in my second class."

"That's great news!"

I sensed her relief. When dad was first diagnosed, right before my sixteenth birthday, I made a decision. I would continue to be their perfect daughter. Being the perfect daughter had one main requirement, I couldn't disappoint my parents. Most people would mind this type of pressure or wish they weren't an only child because of it, but I didn't. The long hospital visits and chemo took a toll on my dad, so it only made sense that I didn't add more stress. Dad taught me to love books so it was decided, I would major in English and follow in his footsteps at MGU. Mom loved gardening so I helped her every summer. We were a small and happy family.

We were invincible when he beat cancer my junior year for the first time and again at the beginning of my senior year. Our winning streak stopped when the cancer came back for round three at the end of my senior year. We didn't beat it that time.

"I'm sure this is hard, but your father wanted this for you. You both talked about this all the time."

It was one of those days when everything hurt. "I know, mom."

"Sweetie," she hesitated. "There's something else I wanted to run by you."

"Yes, mom?"

"I didn't get a chance to when we were moving you in," a small pause, "grandma's been asking us to move to Florida."

Another pause. "You know...all my family's down there now... I think it'll do us some good."

I wondered if she discussed it with Amanda's mom first. "Does Lucy know?"

"She does, she doesn't want us leaving, but you're on campus now. The next four years will be you coming in and out of this home...it would be nice to spend time with family down there. With your dad gone, I worry about us being too isolated up here."

My grandma moved down south after my grandpa passed away and mom's siblings followed shortly after. We didn't talk about dad's family except for when I needed to know how lucky we were to have ours.

"I have to go," she said after one of her alarms rang in the background. Between running off to go to doctor appointments or giving dad his scheduled meals and medicine, we got used to always being on time. "Think about it, okay?"

I loved Blakely. Mom loved Blakely. We'd still choose Blakely as our hometown in a heartbeat even if we both weren't born there. I knew this was something she thought over for weeks, maybe even since the funeral in April.

"Okay," I said, but she had already hung up. I grabbed the creamery door the girl in front of me was holding.

"Annabelle?"

As soon as he said my name, the goosebumps made their beeline straight to my heart. I recognized that voice too well.

"Where's your sidekick?" Jordan asked me when I turned around.

"She's hanging out with her roommate."

He looked at the group he was with. "You guys go in, I'll be there in a sec." We moved to the side to let other students go in.

"You're settled in?" he asked.

I stood there, trying to think of an excuse, or any reason I could give him to not get ice cream. But I couldn't so we stayed silent until we walked inside and all the way up to the cash register.

"What flavor do you want?" Jordan asked me. "You'll love their peanut-butter caramel."

"Mint chocolate please," I told the cashier.

"Mint chocolate for both of us," Jordan repeated, "double the scoops."

I couldn't take cash out of my clutch in time before Jordan handed the cashier a bill.

"You don't need to pay for me," I mumbled. "Thank you."

"Anytime." He looked at the table his friends were seating at after we grabbed our cones. "I would ask you to join us, but I have a feeling you'll say no." I nodded and walked towards the exit.

"On second thought, the weather's nice." He followed me outside. "They won't miss me too much."

I felt him watching me for a moment before he asked, "How are you holding up?"

"Good." I took another bite of my ice cream. We kept walking in silence.

"Did you get any of the postcards I sent you this summer?" he asked out of nowhere. "I figured you'd like them."

I stopped for a second, my skin heating with frustration.

"I did, thank you." Then I kept walking.

"I'm happy I ran into you," Jordan said. "We finally have some alone time." I didn't think it was fair of him to say that since he rarely came back to Blakely.

"You're never home anymore," I blurted out.

He grinned, "you care?"

I looked away. "Not at all, it's just, Lucy hates that you don't come home."

"Yeah, well, home's not exactly the best place for me right now."

"Is everything okay?"

He quickly looked at me. "And you *don't* care?"

"I'm just asking."

"No," he said after a moment. "Dad and I haven't seen eye to eye in years as you know."

I tried to say something back, but I was choked with grief. Jordan moved closer to me then...took a bite of my ice cream.

"Hey!" I tried to grab his cone.

"You're taking forever to eat yours," he laughed, "that's a first for you."

"You're not funny."

He blinked his long lashes at me, "made you laugh." I watched him take another bite of his ice cream. His hair was slicked back like usual, but he grew an inch or two since I last saw him. He'd also developed a tan, probably from the European tour he came back from with his friends.

He grabbed the loose part of my orange hair ribbon and slowly twisted it around his index finger. "You wear these well."

I was reminded of everything at that moment. The electric bolts. The late-night conversations. The army of butterflies. The first kiss.

"What you asked earlier...Seth's older brother is chill so I crash at their place when I'm not in Blakely."

"You used to love spending your summers in Blakely," I said to no one in particular.

He looked like he wasn't expecting me to say that. "I loved those summers because it meant spending time with you."

I didn't know how it was possible to be flattered and upset with someone at the same time, so I started walking again. He walked beside me, and we continued to eat our cones in silence. I noticed every movement he made. How he ran his hand through his hair every time he was about to speak then stopped himself. How he snuck glances at me when he thought I couldn't tell.

"Did you"

"Can we"

"One sec," Jordan threw his napkin in the nearby trash when he was done with his cone, "you go first."

"Did you enjoy the tour you went on?"

"Yeah, it was nice to get away. Listen, Annabelle," he stood there, "can we find some time to talk? There's so much I want to say to you."

I simply stared at him and thought of that summer when he told me he loved me. *What exactly is a Middlemist Red Camellia?* He asked me when I told him his flower. *It means you're rare. No one knows this side of you except me.* He was unlike anyone in his family, and I was the only one who got to see the real him. Past the charisma and the pretense.

I looked away, "I don't think now's the time Jordan." A student in a hurry accidentally knocked the remaining ice cream out of my hand.

"I'm so sorry!" He looked mortified while attempting to grab my scoop and cone from the ground.

I stopped him. "You don't have to do that!"

"I can buy you another one!"

"It's okay, it was an accident," I said. It felt like horrible luck or perfect timing. Either way, I was so relieved, I wanted to buy him something myself. The student lingered for a bit, quickly looked between me and Jordan, before leaving us alone.

Jordan handed me his extra napkin, "I can get you another cone."

I checked the time on my phone. "Thank you, but I need to get going."

We stared at each other for a moment.

"You have something," he pointed at my chin, "here." His eyes fell to my neck.

"Annabelle," he grabbed my arm and gently slid his hand down to hold mine. "I'm sorry about everything that happened between us. The way I left things, I think about that all the time, it wasn't fair to you."

I thought at that moment, there were *some* apologies you could give yourself a pass for not accepting. The apologies that came too late – well after you stopped anticipating them.

"No need to be." I mustered the confidence of Amanda and Halle combined. "We're done anyways."

I pulled my hand away. We both knew I wasn't talking about the ice cream.

Four

BEFORE ORIENTATION, when she came into my life, I hadn't made a new friend in over five years. At least not one that wasn't already Amanda's friend.

"These ones are so pretty!" Jaz said to me when we sat down in the large dome auditorium on the first day of classes. She stared at the ribbons shaping my puffs. "Green and white for MGU?"

"I wanted to wear school colors today," I told her.

"It's a nice touch."

A man that looked to be in his late fifties walked into class as the last remaining students trickled in. He didn't waste any time. "I'm Professor Daniel Lee." He wrote his name on the whiteboard then turned around, "I want to welcome you all to my class, Comparative Literature 48, CompLit48 to be short."

"Meet my teaching assistant," he nodded at the guy who walked in behind him and closed the door. "Ben's going to help me grade all your class work this semester."

Ben, now standing next to him, looked around the auditorium before grabbing the papers the professor handed him.

Jaz stared at me. "Are you okay?"

"Hmm hmm," I resisted the urge to sink further down in my

seat. My eyes stayed on Ben as he handed the first row of students their papers.

"While Ben passes around your packets, I want you to know that I take this class very seriously and so should my English majors. You'll find ways to earn extra credit for my class if you read through the packet. Each Friday, you'll have a pop quiz unless it falls during exam week. Make sure to come to class because I count attendance towards your grade."

Oddly enough, a loud ringtone interrupted his speech. *Sounds just like mine.* The class looked around frantically for the ringtone that dared interrupt his speech. Judging by Professor Lee's cold stare, he wasn't having any of it. It continued to ring loudly before I finally realized that it *was* my alarm ringing.

"Hurry." Jaz said.

"I thought I turned them off."

I searched through my messenger bag, then reached into the indoor pocket to pull my phone out. Right when I turned off the alarm, I noticed Jordan's name in my notifications.

This would have been, in another world, the perfect time to excuse myself and never show my face again. I quickly looked at my professor, "I'm so sorry!"

Professor Lee spoke to the class but kept his stare on me. "You'll find a series of guidelines in your packets, I suggest all of you read it by the end of the week."

Ben walked up to my row and handed me the packets. He was unmoved, like this was the first time he was seeing me. I grabbed them from him and passed the rest. When he moved up to the next row, I sunk even further down in my seat.

There was only one thing to do after my embarrassing moment in CompLit48. Thankfully, I didn't have to wait for Jaz when the bell rang.

"Hey you!" Someone yelled out of the classroom across from mine. The voice sounded oddly familiar and slowed down my power walking.

"Hold up!" They persisted. I stopped and looked at the time

on my phone. *Twelve minutes left to make it to my next class.* I glanced up to see Kevin Knicks.

"Hey," he looked around, "you have a class here?" I nodded. *Eleven minutes left.* I couldn't have another embarrassing moment. Otherwise, I wouldn't have to just run out of class. I'd have to leave the whole of Massachusetts.

His eyes were fixated on me. "What major are you in? Let me guess..."

"English!" *Ten minutes left.*

"You're in my college then." His dimple caved in. "I'm Political Science." He looked past me. "Where's your next class?"

I took a step away from him. "I'm sorry, but I have to go, or I'll be late!" I didn't wait for him to say anything back before sprinting off.

* * *

"It's only day one and I'm bored with mine," Amanda slid the empty chair next to her so I could sit with her and Halle at GRUB. "How were your classes?"

I placed my tray down. "My alarm went off and Ben from the party's my TA."

Amanda raised a brow. "The guy at Warren's?"

"Same class?" Halle asked.

I hadn't told them about the conversation I had with Ben after the party, because I wanted to forget that night altogether. I opened my bottled juice. "Yes, the guy from the party."

Amanda rolled her eyes. "Can this campus get any smaller?"

"Apparently," Halle said.

"It might work to your advantage," Amanda said after a moment.

I looked at her, "how?"

"Having him as your TA. You've already met him, and he knows Warren."

Halle shook her head. "I highly doubt it, he looked like he had a stick up his you know what the whole time at that party." She nodded in my direction. "No offense, but kind of like you did."

I simply looked at her, "none taken."

"Speaking of the party!" Halle remembered something. "Did you guys get on MGU Reader today?"

I took a bite of my panini. "I haven't gotten around to it."

"I did earlier," Amanda said. Halle made a face at Amanda and tilted her head towards me.

"*Ohh*..." Amanda said, "how could I forget! Annabelle, you're going to love the top post."

"That site's such a riot," Halle said to me, "you need to get on it pronto."

I put my panini down on my plate, "why?"

Amanda looked eager to tell me. "There's this poster on there who wrote about being a virgin, I thought of you. You should read the comments, it's going to make you feel better about, you know," she looked around us and whispered, "the whole virginity thing."

"Look at your face," Halle laughed. "I can't take you seriously right now. That's probably *why* they wrote it."

They were talking about someone else, this was nothing but a coincidence.

Halle laughed again. "She said something about virginity not being contagious."

"So funny!" Amanda agreed.

Amanda brought her body closer to mine, and whispered again so the table near us couldn't hear. "Guess there's a *lot* more of you on campus." She ate her fry, "huh. Who knew."

I didn't notice I was holding my breath until I couldn't shake the massive headache I was feeling. I stood up, "I'm going to get a head start on my next class." A sudden feeling of dread sunk in.

"Now? You sure?" Amanda asked. "I can walk with you, I'm heading that way after this."

"No! I mean, keep eating, I just have a lot to do today and I'm thinking of changing outfits since it's so hot out." I pulled my collar away from my neck. "I didn't realize it would be this hot out today."

Halle shook her head, "I already miss freshman orientation." She looked at Amanda. "My professor gave us thirty pages worth of reading for tomorrow, for art."

"I have about twenty," Amanda said. "It's like they want us to suffer."

"Tell me about it," Halle responded, "my first project's due this weekend."

They didn't suspect anything was wrong when I walked out of the dining hall. *This day can't get worse; they must be mistaken.* My post didn't go live. I made sure to hit the delete button and not the live one! *But the two buttons were right next to each other.* I shook away the incriminating thought and dashed to my dorm. It couldn't possibly have been my post.

As luck would have it, I was wrong. My post was at the top of the page. The highest viewed one of the day so far and out of all the posts that had flooded the site that morning once MGU Reader went live, mine was highlighted as trending.

I'd only been on campus for a short time, and I'd already run out of my first college party, embarrassed myself in class, and now, almost outed myself as a virgin to the entire campus. All of this made it more clear, I couldn't recognize the girl staring at me in the mirror. I was scared of her, because she knew. Miss Perfect was crumbling. I closed my laptop in panic.

After a few minutes, I opened my laptop again. I leaned closer to the screen, reading all the comments. Most of them were congratulating me, *anonymous me*, on my virginity. A few mocked me, *anonymous me*, for how stupid and ridiculous they thought the post was. I scrolled down again to the comment section, scanning the new one that appeared.

Why exactly are we in a hurry to lose it?

My mind wandered back to the guy I thought I'd lose it to.

Seeing Jordan's name in my notifications had left a nervous tug in my stomach all morning. Once I was back on leveled ground, I looked at my phone again.

> Jordan: Morning

> Jordan: Goodluck on your first day

> Jordan: I hope we can find time to talk

* * *

Dear MGU Reader:
My fellow classmates
Ladies and gentlemen

I dedicate this post to the entire human species.
I have one question for you, you ready?
Is it so terrible to be celibate? Dare I say…a virgin?

Still there? Good. Glad you didn't faint like some do when they hear the terrible news. I promise it's not contagious.

Why am I still a virgin, you ask?
It's really not complicated. I'm just waiting for 'real' love, 'true' love, 'can't stop thinking about you' love, 'I commit to you and only you' love, 'am I asking for too much and you say no' love. Okay, that part's complicated. Let's start again.

I'm waiting for 'I love you and I choose you' love. Truth is, I thought I found it years ago. Psych, I got my heart broken instead. So you tell me, why is love so hard to find and keep?
I guess until I do, I'll start my cat collection.

Kisses
…Or should I say hugs…

The Virgin

* * *

Even after four days, sixteen hours, and thirty minutes of my post being released, I still couldn't wrap my head around the fact that my post had gone live. People wanted to hear from me, *anonymous me*, but still. They *wanted* to hear from me. I don't know why it excited me, but I liked that it did. Dad always said writing and journalism were exhilarating.

"What's got you so chirpy?" Jaz's sudden entrance into our dorm interrupted my dancing. I turned off the song playing from my laptop.

"Nothing! Just choosing ribbons to wear for the event tonight."

"Do you still want me to do your hair?" she asked.

I nodded. Jaz offered after class on Friday to style my hair for our college's welcome reception that evening. Being roommates was working well for us. It also helped that she was extremely friendly.

"I can do your hair now instead of waiting?"

"Sure," I agreed. "I'll just grab my dress after this."

She pointed to her desk chair. "Come and sit in my lovely booth."

I handed her my ribbon collection before sitting down. "I'm thinking of using this one to match my dress."

She placed a towel around my chest. "Why do you wear them so much?"

"My ribbons?" I looked at her in the mirror while she parted my hair. "It started in my mom's family on her mom's side. We all wear them in our own ways, I wear mine in my hair and my mom puts hers around her wrists."

She plugged in her curler. "Everyone else?"

"Let's see...my grandma's wrist too, my aunt places hers around her purse handles."

She checked the temperature on the curler. "That's cool. How formal do you think the reception will be?"

"Pretty formal I guess, they said to dress that way in the email."

"I wonder how many students will show up," Jaz said. "Have you met other people in our college?"

"No," I looked away. "Besides you and Halle, not really. Maybe tonight."

"You can wear one of my dresses if you're still deciding," I told her. I had to pay her back somehow for doing my hair.

"No, thanks." Jaz said, "I'll make up my mind soon enough."

My eyes wandered over to her side of the desk. It was neatly organized with her books stacked in the corner of her study area. I watched her as she parted my hair into smaller pieces.

She glanced over at my ribbons. "Hand me the first one please."

"Campus is exactly like I expected it to be," she grabbed another one, "it's like everyone already knows each other."

"Most of the students do, but I'm sure Greenspring is nothing compared to California."

"You have a friend here which helps." She curled the next chunk of hair. "Is it me or does everyone talk about the same thing all the time like that MGU Reader site?"

I forgot what I wanted to say next.

"It's an interesting site." She extended her left hand for me to hand her another ribbon. "The girls on campus won't stop talking about that new post from The Virgin."

"I think it's brave of her to post that," she loosened up the curl she scrunched up in her hand, "we should honor and respect our bodies." She sectioned off another part of my hair to curl. "There's a club on campus that's discussing it this semester. You can join me if you'd like."

She placed her curler on her desk, opened her drawer, then handed me a flier, "this one."

I held the neon pink pamphlet with a bright green sign in my hand. *Daughters in Waiting: a place for Christian students to discuss all things friendship, dating, and life on campus.*

"It's part of the Students for Christianity club, SFC for short." She noticed the look of confusion on my face. "It's open to anyone who wants to join."

"Thank you, Jaz," I handed her my last ribbon, "but I'm not religious."

"That's okay, not everyone is in the group, you should consider it." she curled my final strand then placed the flier back in her drawer, "almost done."

"Voila!" She said a few moments later.

I sat there stunned. Jaz wasn't just good at doing this, she was exceptional. She'd managed to weave my ribbons into large curls, making them look like additional and colorful strands of hair.

"Wow, thank you!"

"My pleasure," she removed the towel from around me, "now, *I* have to get ready."

* * *

"Come again!" The student working at the dry cleaners called out.

My phone was sandwiched between my right ear and shoulder while my right hand held my dress bag. I reverted my attention back to the call with my mom once I opened the door to walk outside.

"Send me pictures sweetie," mom said. I heard our home's doorbell ringing in the distance. "Lucy's here, we have dinner plans tonight."

I felt a pang of jealousy. "Tell her I say hi."

"Did Amanda speak to you yet?" she asked. "We're thinking of taking you girls on a spa retreat."

I stopped. "What's the occasion?"

"We miss you girls, that's all."

I couldn't remember the last time we'd spent just us two. If it wasn't for our house filled with the routine guests who checked up on us, we spent a lot of our time with Amanda and Lucy for our mother-daughter dates, mother-daughter movie nights, even moving to campus had been just Amanda, Lucy, and mom. *Your dad being gone,* mom said, *we're thinking we just take our girls to campus.* I initially thought it was weird that Amanda's little brother, Jacob, or even her dad, didn't care to accompany us. I didn't think much of it after.

"When?" I asked her.

"Before you come home for Thanksgiving break, talk to Amanda, sweetie. Let us know what weekend works."

"Okay, I have to go mom, I'll talk to Amanda." I said when I noticed Ben walking in my direction. "Say hi to Lucy for me." I quickly hung up.

"Hey," he looked at my dry-cleaning bag. "I'm picking up my suit from there." His hair was ruffled like he'd stepped out in a hurry, and he wore glasses this time. Large black ones that framed his face well.

"You're coming to the reception?" he asked me.

"Yes, you?"

"TA duties, I'm required." He stared at me suspiciously for a moment.

"I thought about the party last Saturday," he said. Of all the things I thought he would say, this was not one of them.

"Don't let it get to you or the incident in class this week."

Or this. He must have noticed Jaz and I not sitting in the front rows after the first day.

"You strike me as someone who ruminates over things," he added. *Or, this.*

I faked a smile. "It's no biggie." *No biggie?*

Ben just looked at me. "Precisely, it happens to the best of us."

I felt the sudden urge to tell him how I felt. "I have a feeling I won't live that down."

He sighed. "One thing doesn't abide by majority rule and that's a person's conscience."

"Atticus," I was happily surprised, "you've read it?"

"It's a classic," he said. Just by the smile he'd just cracked, I knew books must be his favorite topic too.

"Let's try this again," he extended his hand for me to shake. "I'm Benjamin Falbright, the fourth if you include the other men before me. I go by Ben for short and I'm only a sophomore majoring in English so don't let the TA role intimidate you."

Was he always so *direct*? *Honest*?

I shook his hand, "I'm Annabelle Wilson, a freshman, also majoring in English."

"Nice to meet you, Annabelle." He placed his hands in his pockets and looked past me. "My suit's ready."

"I'll be seeing you tonight?" he asked.

I nodded and watched him walk by. I could hear the door to the dry cleaner's opening and shutting, leaving his trail of cologne. *Mandarin? Coffee?* I couldn't quite make out the sweet scent that lingered.

Five

"WHY ISN'T this on their recruitment ads??"

Jaz asked me but mostly herself. We stood there, taking in the panoramic and breathtaking view of campus staring in our faces. After we stood in silence for a while, we stepped out of the elevator. We followed our way past the balloons, lining up our path to the reception hall on the ninth floor.

I felt strange, nervous in a way I hadn't in a while. I scanned the crowd but couldn't make out anyone else I knew since Halle chose not to come. I looked down at my dress.

"Loving your outfit by the way," Jaz said.

I fixed my posture. "Thank you, you look great too."

She was wearing a black jumpsuit that suited her well. Next to my long purple halter dress, we looked put together.

Jaz looked around. "There's an empty table over there."

We walked to the tall circular table covered with a white cloth near the entrance.

She looked around again, "Do you recognize anyone from class?"

"Not really." I could already hear Amanda. *Make more of an effort.*

Jaz stopped paying attention to me and stared at something

across from us. I followed her gaze to the largest display of dessert I'd ever seen.

"It's definitely calling our names," she said, "come on, let's go serve ourselves."

She kept walking so I followed behind her until Professor Lee stopped me dead in my tracks. He stood there, blocking my way.

"Nice to see you came."

"Hi professor." I looked at Jaz who was already close to the dessert table. "I like seeing my students show up to these events," he said.

I looked down. "Thank you."

He pointed at a table near the entrance. "See the raffle tickets over there? Grab a ticket and hand it to my TA during office hours this weekend."

He raised his eyebrows then crossed his arms. "If you read my syllabus packet...you'll know that these events serve as extra-credit for my course."

"I did," I looked away, "thank you, I will."

He stood there for a second. "Enjoy the reception."

I understood what Professor Lee was doing, I really did. I hadn't yet turned in my first week's assignment, but I had every intention to after tonight.

"I told you he wasn't so bad," Jaz said once I caught up to her. "Give it time."

She handed me a plate, "I got a head start."

After a few minutes, Jaz and I had sampled practically every cookie in front of us.

I was trying to grab my next dessert when Jaz noticed him.

"Six o'clock but don't make it obvious," she said.

I attempted to scarf down the sugar cookie already in my mouth. When I turned around, I was facing Kevin Knicks for the third time.

"Fancy seeing you here," he said. Jaz excused herself.

He grabbed a mini lemon tart from the display. "These are delicious, they always have them."

"Try one with me?" He handed me one then ate his. His eyes glistened as if he'd eaten the most delicious dessert he's ever had.

"They're good," I said.

"I can tell you've had better," he smiled.

"No," I giggled. "They are good."

"I was absolutely knackered, but I see I made the right decision to come," his eyes ran down my dress, "you look nice."

"Thank you," I tried avoiding his gaze.

"Like my suit?" Kevin asked. I reverted my attention back to him. He was dressed in a blue suit that fit him well. I didn't think any suit *wouldn't* fit him well.

"I'm glad I ran into you after class on Monday," he smiled, "it was like pulling teeth trying to get Jordan to tell me about you."

My chest tightened. I grabbed another cookie and placed it on my plate.

He looked at me. "No history between you two, right?"

My heart froze. I ran my finger along the rim of my plate. *Did Jordan tell him something?*

"I thought I noticed a spark when I visited Blakely," he said. I went into a frantic cough. My eyes watered while I tried to remain steady by gripping the dessert table. He grabbed a water bottle and handed it to me. After I found my composure, I glanced at the girls who were watching us. Instead of their previous looks of disdain, they now had grins.

"Sorry about that," I said to Kevin once I could catch my breath.

"It's cool," he looked at my plate, "you should slow down on those." *It's not the dessert I'm choking up on.*

One of the girls staring walked up to us. I knew it was my turn to leave and hers to stay so I quickly excused myself.

After a couple more minutes of mingling with some faculty, I was already exhausted with the social interactions. Since dad died, anytime I felt like taking a leap, daring to hang out with new people, I couldn't. Wolf Hall seemed like the best place to be, even if it was just blocks of concrete.

I looked around the room to find Jaz, but she was busy somewhere. I quickly made my way through and stepped out. That's when I noticed Ben who was talking to a faculty member near the elevators. I ducked my head and took the stairs.

* * *

"Hold on," Kevin jotted towards me outside of our college building, "you bounced on me in there, you didn't like the reception?"

"I'm watching a movie with friends tonight."

"I see." He grabbed his phone from his pocket. "Is it alright if I get your number?" *There's no way this is a good idea.* I looked away from him. Two factors were working against me at this moment. Kevin was Jordan's best-friend *and* I didn't date. Not since that summer anyway and that barely counted.

"I've been meaning to ask you for your number, if you're worried about being my mate's sister's friend..."

I stopped him, "it's not that."

"Then you're cool with it?"

For a second, I thought of what Amanda would say. *Don't think, just go.* Or even Halle. *If Amanda says he wants you, he probably does.* I grabbed Kevin's phone and typed my number in it. He called me right away.

"Just checking." He spun the phone in his hand. "I'll text you." He walked away not knowing he was only the second guy I'd ever given my number to.

"This is a *look*!" Amanda said, once I joined her outside her dorm. "Jaz did this?"

"I know, I can't believe it. You'll never guess what just happened!"

Halle stepped out of their room, "nice work."

"The coolest thing just happened," I told them, "I changed fast so I could come tell you." It dawned on me. "Why are we standing outside? Shouldn't we go in for our movie night?"

They looked at each other. I peeked through the cracked door. "Oh."

"It's last minute but they invited us to this party tonight, we can't pass it up." Amanda gave me her Cooper smile. "Come with us."

I tried to hide my disappointment. "We already made plans."

"Let's change them," Halle said to me.

"What's going on?" Gabe asked. Halle walked back in.

I looked at Amanda, "I was so excited for this movie, I also have to fill you in on the reception."

"I know, I'm so sorry, but it's Friday night."

"Yooo Amanda," Warren called her. She grabbed my hand to walk into the dorm with her.

I stood there for a second, a little annoyed at having to face Warren and Gabe again. They were both seated on Halle's bed and staring.

"You coming out with us?" Warren asked me.

"We may be out past your bedtime," Gabe joked.

Amanda looked at them, "knock it off." Gabe laughed and passed a cup to Warren.

"How was the event?" Halle asked me while spraying her perfume. "Did you see my mom?"

"Yes, we didn't talk long. She wanted to know why you didn't come."

Halle handed the perfume to Amanda and didn't say anything back.

I looked at Amanda, "We're not doing movie night?" Gabe laughed again.

"Can we reschedule it?" Amanda asked. She put on her lipstick while I remained standing by the door.

"Please join us?" Amanda asked me. "The party's invite only."

"You already have your hair and makeup done," Halle added.

Gabe snickered. "I think I know your friend more than you do."

I'm not letting you get under my skin. I knew this was, pretty much, the only way I could rectify what happened at the party.

"I'm beat." I forced the brightest smile out of me. "It's been a long night with the reception, don't let me ruin your plans. Have fun for me? We can always have movie night some other time."

I hugged Amanda and Halle before walking out.

Back in my dorm, Jaz hadn't yet returned from the reception. I grabbed my class notes and books but couldn't find it in me to open them. Dad was always the one person I enjoyed talking about books with. It was always fun for us to read and discover new authors together.

Instead of reading, I found myself going back on MGU Reader. The new comments were now asking me to write another post. So, I did, and this time, I watched it go live.

* * *

Dear MGU Reader:
My fellow classmates
Ladies and gentlemen

I see you're curious to know what it's like to be a campus virgin…
You brave souls…The replies from your inquiring minds have been oh so brutal. These are fair questions and I'm just the person to answer them. Lucky for you, I'm also in the mood.

You ready?

Being a virgin sucks. Like really sucks. Not in a 'I hate it' sucks. More in a 'when the heck will it happen' sucks. It's not that I don't want to ever have sex. I eventually do with the person I love. So, the waiting sucks.

Being a virgin feels like waiting for the perfect relationship that never comes.

Being a virgin feels like seeing all your friends, one by one, lose their virginity and you're still the good old virgin.

Being a virgin feels like building something up in your head that no one else sees the significance of. Except some of you under my last post. So, cheers to us virgins! We need it.

Kisses
...Or should I say hugs...
The Virgin

* * *

"Change of plans," Amanda said into the phone. "I'm not sure we can make it anymore."

I stopped walking. "I already took the bus, I'm here."

"Okay," she hesitated, "give me an hour..."

I swallowed over the lump, then took a breath. "It's fine, call me when you're on your way."

The first two weeks of school had flown by, and Amanda was spending all her free time with Halle and their crew. Even though the fair was *their* idea, yet again, I wasn't surprised they'd changed their minds.

I placed my phone back in my clutch and stood at the entrance to take it all in. It felt like sensory overload as I looked at all the rides. Different music played around me including a live band not too far from the entrance. A mix of old songs, some echoed impromptu karaoke, and the familiar sound of the carousel hung in the air. The game booths were practically calling my name, but I made mental notes of the first things I wanted to try. *Cotton candy first. Ferris wheel second.* Then, *funnel cakes.*

I walked over to the Ferris wheel line minutes later with my purchased ticket already in hand.

An older man at the end of the line looked at me. "You're here alone?"

"Umm, not really, I'm waiting on my friends."

He nodded as if he already knew my white lie, "come." He walked me over to another older man by the railing, guarding the entrance to get on the Ferris wheel.

"Let her in," he turned to me, "use your ticket for another ride, this one's on me." He tapped my shoulder and walked away.

"What's a pretty young lady like you doing by yourself?" His friend asked me. I wasn't sure how to respond. He looked at the line and yelled out. "Anyone care to take this young lady on a ride?" I was mortified when he asked and even more so when he got a response.

"I will!"

Nervously, I glanced up. Kevin was walking past the line to get to me.

I turned to the older man. "Seriously, I can wait in line, I don't mind."

"Nonsense," the man smiled, "let this kind gentleman take you." He opened the gate for us to walk through then asked the next people in line for their tickets.

I sat next to Kevin, my nerves shot. To our distance, I could see Jordan and the rest of his friends standing away from the line. His eyes were fixated on us.

I stared straight ahead when we were moving. From our view now, it was all open fields outside of the fair area.

"Annabelle," Kevin smiled at me, "why aren't you responding to my texts?"

He texted me a few times, asking me how I was, and if I was interested in meeting up. Frankly, he was way too handsome and way too close to Jordan to even consider it. I thought it best to ignore him altogether.

I cleared my throat. "I've been busy."

He immediately laughed and looked at me. "That's usually my line." He shook his head, "nice."

The wheel stopped moving.

"You know a good way I've made mates around here?"

I looked at him. His deep brown eyes almost glowed next to all the lights.

I stared down. "No, I'm not sure."

"Bought concert tickets for their favorite artists."

I thought he was serious at first then realized he was holding back a grin.

"It's partially true," he laughed, "the student body here is completely self-absorbed. Come on...hit me...who's your absolute favorite musician?"

I thought about it. "Jamie Etienne."

"I've heard of her, loved the new record."

"She doesn't have a recent one."

He smiled. "See how easy that was? Conversation is easy." I looked away, face beaming.

"There it is, you should smile more," he said.

I glanced at the crowd when the wheel moved again, catching a sudden glimpse of Jordan, still staring at us.

"Who's yours?" I asked him.

"You ever heard of ACHE?"

I shook my head.

"He's an alternative rapper. They play his music all over the UK, I'm a bit obsessed."

I laughed a little at that answer. "I'll have to hear him then," I said, surprising both of us.

"If I text you his work, will you respond?"

I swallowed nervously. *What did I have to lose?* I hadn't smiled much in a while, it felt right to say yes.

I glanced at him, "definitely."

"You should hang out with us," Kevin said when we stepped off the ride.

I could see Jordan, his friend Seth, and some guys I didn't recognize walking towards us. I turn to Kevin, "I had fun, but I don't want to intrude." I pointed at the food section. "I wanted to try some other stuff anyway."

He was about to say something else but suddenly stopped to

look behind me. Before I could turn around, a pair of cold hands grabbed me, and I let out the biggest scream of my entire life.

"You should have seen your face!" Amanda couldn't contain herself, "I've been calling you!" I checked my phone and noticed I had two missed calls from her.

Jordan and his friends stopped next to us.

"Hey," he said to me. He looked at his sister, his eyes flaring momentarily. "How did you guys get here?"

"I took the bus," I said.

"What's it to you?" Amanda mumbled. "Jane dropped me off."

"Jane?" I grabbed her purse from the ground. "Where's Halle?"

Jordan looked back and forth between us. *Who* are they?"

"You've got to be freaking kidding me." He gave Amanda a look that could kill. "When are you ever going to grow up?"

She held me for balance. My stomach flipped while I held her steady.

"We should go back to Wolf," I said to her. I wasn't prepared for world war three between the two of them. It didn't matter where we were, they never got along anymore.

Jordan looked at his friends, "I have to get her back to campus."

"You're our DD man," one of them said.

Kevin looked at Jordan. "You need us to help?"

Jordan shook his head. "I'll come back to get you."

He stared at me. "My car's in the lot."

Six

JORDAN SHIFTED HIS WEIGHT. We were stopped at a red light, having already spent the first fifteen minutes of the ride in silence. The night was pitch black and his headlights paved out the road in front of us. I looked at Amanda, who was asleep in the backseat. We had avoided world war three, but I was now aware that the conversation was now up to us.

"You could have told me you needed a ride to the fair," he said as if this was still normal. "I would have given you one."

"I used to give you rides," he added.

The knot in my stomach grew. The first time the three of us were in this jeep was right after he got it as a birthday gift. He gave us rides everywhere. He drove us around so much, it felt like we had our own private chauffeur. Somehow between that and his first semester at MGU, things changed.

"It feels like ages ago," I responded.

He turned to look at me, "not for me."

My stomach, which was already doing a poor job of holding in the cotton candy I ate before the Ferris wheel, was now turning in on itself.

"Did Amanda ditch you?" he asked.

I paused for a second, trying to figure out if I should respond.

"Typical." he said bitterly and pressed his foot on the gas. He changed between radio stations, looking for one to fill our gaps of silences, finding nothing but static noises.

I finally allowed myself to look at him, remembering there was a time when they didn't hate each other. "Why do you keep thinking the worst of her? You're too hard on her."

"You're way too easy on her." He glanced at me. "You're going through a lot, the last thing you should be doing is worrying about my sister."

It sounded honorable, but I knew deep down it wasn't. We weren't in touch and it was our moms who told him about my dad passing. He came back to Blakely the day of the funeral and left that same night. Before that, he hadn't been home since fall his freshman year.

I felt him tense up. "Kevin asked me for your number, I told him he'd have to ask you himself," he said. "I wouldn't get in the way of that if that's what you wanted."

I sat looking straight ahead, my entire body stiff. We were both quiet for a while.

Anyone who loves you will guard your heart, always, my dad told me after he found me crying in my bedroom. He didn't know it was about Jordan, but he knew it was about a boy. He stayed there, comforting me. *If they don't, you come to me.*

I trailed my thumbs against the palms of my hands while Jordan switched the stations again, desperate to fill out the silence. There was once a time we didn't run out of things to say.

* * *

Making it back to Wolf Hall without saying another word to each other was tough. Making it back into the dorm building with a sleepy Amanda and *not* wanting to be noticed by the resident supervisor or RA was tougher. Boys weren't allowed in our dorms, and we weren't allowed in theirs.

Jordan quickly rushed me into the elevator and pressed the

button to the fifth floor. As I watched him carry Amanda into the elevator, I thought of how much he'd change.

"What are you thinking?" he asked me with a hint of disappointment.

"Nothing."

The elevator stopped. "Anyone around?"

I looked outside. "Nope, we're in the clear."

He carried Amanda into her dorm. Somehow, she was still sound asleep.

I couldn't help but chuckle. "She can sleep through anything."

He stared at her for a moment, "just like the lake house. Our parents were livid when the neighbors called about a noise complaint."

Straight away, he switched his posture and gave the best Lucy impression I'd ever seen. "Your dad and I are at an important event for the business, and you promised us you could handle staying there just you kids. You're the oldest, Jordan. We're expecting you to be the responsible one."

I shook my head, "I can't believe they thought we were having a party."

"We're just having a blast laughing, is that a crime?" Jordan repeated what he'd told his parents. That was the first night we'd stayed up all night, just us two, because everyone else had fallen asleep. That was the first night I told him my wish.

I had the sudden urge to end the conversation before I was reminded of yet another thing that had changed between us.

"We should go," I placed Amanda's purse on her nightstand and walked out with him. As I shut her door, Jordan watched me attentively.

"It's so no one can come in," I placed Amanda's keys in my purse.

"Smart," he said. I expected him to walk back to the elevator. I figured the next time I'd see him would be during some other random encounter on campus. But he didn't turn around, he followed me to my door.

I avoided his gaze. "Thank you for giving us a ride." He just lingered there, staring at me.

Every hair on my body prickled up when he asked. "Do you mind if I come in?"

It was barely a whisper, "sure."

I twisted the handle with clammy hands, very aware of his presence. I pressed my hand against the door and slowly counted to five before fully opening it.

"Color me shocked." he said as soon as we walked in. "You've never been the messy kind."

My bed had piles of clothes on top of it and my desk was covered with snacks. At least the fluffy green rug, flowery decor, and Jaz's clean side made the dorm look somewhat decent.

"Just give me a second to get this sorted," I quickly said. He stood where he was and looked around. I grabbed all the clothes on my bed and shoved them in my closet. Before turning back around, I could feel his body heat drawing near.

"Grab a seat over there if you'd like," I pointed to my chair and rushed past him to sit on the opposite side of the dorm. Thankfully Jaz wasn't there so I could sit at her desk.

He shook his head, but eventually went to sit down.

"Annabelle, is now a good time to talk?"

I simply shrugged.

"I have to admit," he leaned back on my chair, "I was taken aback you ended up coming to college, I was sure you'd take a break or something." His eyes narrowed in on me, "follow through with what you told me."

My stomach churned. He pulled me aside at the funeral, asking if I was *really* fine. Everyone was so focused on mom who couldn't give the eulogy like she planned, so I stepped in. Afterwards, he asked me that question. It didn't matter that we hadn't spoken in forever, I said the first thing that came to mind. *I want to get out of here for a little, find myself, see the world, like my dad.* Our conversation wasn't long, barely five minutes. Before I knew it, Jordan was having an argument with his dad outside the venue then quickly left. Without saying goodbye. Two months later, I received my first postcard.

He placed his hands behind his head. "I think...if anyone can do it, it's you." He was so sure that he still knew me well, so sure that he could just pick up where things left off, that we could talk like old times, like nothing had changed. I wanted to wipe the knowing smile off his face.

"Thank you," I said instead.

"I haven't stopped caring about you, Annabelle, if that's what you're thinking. There's a lot you don't know." His eyes dropped to my neck before he looked back up. "Can we talk now? For real?"

In any relationship, there was always the one who listened more and the one who spoke more. I was the listening one in ours. It never bothered me, as I enjoyed it. He had more stories to share anyway. But things *had* changed – mainly for me – and when I needed him to listen, he wasn't there.

"There's nothing left to say, Jordan."

I listened when he wanted to vent about his dad or the colleges he wanted to go to instead and how much he didn't want to go into his family's investment business. I listened when he gushed on and on about joining MGU's soccer team. I was always listening to him when he wanted to talk, when he needed to talk. I finally noticed he never gave me that same courtesy. Tonight would have felt like old times if he had simply been there when I needed him most.

The words came out before I could stop them.

"We spent the best two weeks of our lives before you left for college. I loved you and thought you loved me too, I thought you wanted a future with me. I expected you to come back that break and tell our families that we were seriously going to do this, but you didn't. You brought Kevin and avoided me every chance you could. You left for college again, called here and there, then finally broke the news. What was it you said? Oh, that's right. *It's not the right time. I'm in college and now, your dad has...*you couldn't even finish your sentence, so I had to do it for you, *cancer*."

As much as it pained me to keep going, I held nothing back.

"You went from my best-friend's brother to my first love to a complete stranger in two years. The worst part? You didn't even have the decency to try to be a friend."

I looked him dead in the eyes. "Did I get that right or is there more to talk about?"

He sat up. "I can't do this." *Typical*.

He picked up my chair and came to sit across from me.

"I honestly thought I was doing the right thing." He grabbed my hands. "Those two weeks meant more to me than you will ever know. I wanted to be there for you, I just didn't know how. When I came back this spring...I thought that was it, I thought I was never getting you back."

He leaned closer, "I thought you moved on."

I let go of his hands. "We hadn't spoken in months when you came back."

He lowered his head to the floor. "The postcards were my last attempt to see if things could ever go back to what they used to be, I got the hint."

I took all the strength I had left to look at him. "What was I supposed to do besides move on?"

His eyes were flooded with regret. "I made a mistake, but it's too late now, isn't it?" For a minute, neither of us said anything.

"What I said in the car...." he leaned forward even more, "it's not my place to tell you who to date, I know I can't stop you... that's why I said I wouldn't get in the way. I want you to be happy."

I looked past him, no longer sad, no longer upset, just met with the realization that I hadn't considered what that word meant for me in a while. Happy used to mean riding in his jeep or going to the lake house. It meant waking up early on Saturday morning and making waffles with mom and dad. It meant spending all day reading or planting. Happy was thinking that being perfect could solve everything. But happiness was a fantasy, elusive as the one I'd created by attempting to be perfect.

I tried for a good minute or so to come up with something else to say to him. We finally had it out, no more guessing what the other thought, no more wondering if things could ever go back to somewhat normal, no more hoping they would.

"You stopped wearing it," Jordan whispered. His words were like sharpened knives scraping my skin. My shoulders tensed, I couldn't manage to look at him.

"You promised you wouldn't," he said with a strained voice and got up before the pain could consume us. He opened the door then stopped.

"Fall in love once, get married, and never get a divorce," he said with his back facing mine, "that's what you said you wanted, and you wanted it with me."

Happy only made you hide behind the reality that life happened, and all the happiness and perfection in the world couldn't stop this one thing from happening, no matter how well you crafted it not to – your heart could still get broken, in and outside of your control.

"I wanted that for us too, even now," he said then walked out.

* * *

I sat on Jaz's chair, frozen, for what felt like forever. When I checked my phone, I saw Amanda's name on my list of missed calls. I grabbed her keys and rushed out of my dorm.

"Amanda? Are you up?"

When I walked in, she was asleep with her phone next to her pillow. Warren's name was on her list of outbound calls including mine. I placed the phone back on her dresser and walked out.

* * *

Dear MGU Reader:
My fellow classmates
Ladies and gentlemen

This one goes out to the gentlemen that read this post. Ladies, let's sit this one out, shall we?

Ahem.

Some of you clearly don't know what it's like to get your heart broken. Like earth-shattering, can't move, can't sleep, broken. Wanna know how I know? It's not hard to tell based on your comments under my posts.

Tell me, what makes you think that us virgins can't be brokenhearted? What makes you think we're emotionless robots who have never caught true feelings?

Since you're confused, let me clear things up for you. It's possible to get your heart broken as a virgin. It doesn't matter if you give your all to someone and they tell you it's not you or save your all for someone and they still tell you it's not you. I think your heart shatters the same. I think your heartbreak can still hurt just as bad – virgin or not. And lately, it hurts.

Kisses
…Or should I say hugs…
The Virgin

Singlegal: u r the best one here
 MGUsophmore : I feel personally attacked
anon554: ^ cry about it
Lea78@: finally someone I can relate to
sarah36: I look forward to your posts

rubby: I have a bright idea! How about you just get laid and stop spamming this fun site with this mess?

Anonymous200: your posts are epic

patriotsfan: I love this, but can you please add in more humor next time?

virgin23: I'm not ashamed of my virginity because of you

Jazm!ne: my friends & I made a celibacy pact last week. thanks for motivating us <3

Marygrace: heartbreaks are the worst

* * *

"Greenspring Spa!"

Amanda repeated herself while applying her lipstick.

"I've never heard of it," her mom said.

"It's actually called Greenspring Spa and Retreat Center, they opened a few years ago," Amanda handed me the phone.

"Halle told me her mom goes there all the time," she yelled from her closet and held up a top for my approval. I shook my head no. We were on a two-way call with our moms, planning the spa retreat they wanted us to go on.

"It's right outside of campus," Amanda said.

"Okay, we'll look into it." Lucy responded. "We can't wait to see you Aces." Since we were little, Lucy called Amanda and me, her Aces. She said being only daughters was always a reason to celebrate.

"We'll have a full weekend planned," mom added.

Amanda quickly changed out of her shorts, "I can't *wait* for this retreat, I already need it," she hopped on one leg while attempting to put her jeans on, "but...why can't we wait until *after* our semester? I'm going to need it more then."

There was a pause, murmurs, then silence. Amanda and I exchanged a look.

I held the phone closer to my mouth. "Are you guys there?"

"Yes sweetie!" Mom said. "It's not ideal, but we can do another one after that if you want, we just want it before Thanksgiving." She wasn't one for last-minute plans, not since the cancer. I was still trying to figure out why this retreat was suddenly urgent.

"umm...*sure*." Amanda zipped her pants, "it's okay, just wondering." She grabbed the phone back. "We gotta go, love you both!"

She threw the phone on her bed and looked at me, "I owe you a big one for getting me home last night."

She took out a pair of socks. "Jordan's totally going to be an ass about this. How was it?"

"The fair?"

"No, silly," she sat on her bed and put her shoes on. "The ride! Let me guess, he went on and on about how terrible of a person I am."

I shrugged. "It wasn't like that."

She stared at me, "really??" She shot me a joyful look. "Would you look at that? I guess I'm off the hook!"

She got up. "How do I look?"

"Like you're going on a date. The red lip might be a tad too much for daytime though."

She checked herself in the mirror. "You're right, I can add it later." She dabbed some off then handed me her bracelet to hook.

"What are you doing again?" I asked her.

"Trivia after dinner, it's at their house." She turned to me. "Are you sure you don't want to come?"

I shook my head no. Professor Lee stopped me after class and said I had to put in more effort. I knew I needed all the extra-credit points I could get so later tonight; I had one priority.

* * *

Ben Falbright IV. I took a deep breath before knocking on his door.

"Come in," he said from inside.

"Annabelle, hey, what brings you here?" He asked when I walked in.

I lifted my raffle tickets. "Can I still get extra credit for the reception and the faculty discussion I went to this week?"

"Reception might be too late; you're supposed to hand those in right after the event." He got up from his desk and grabbed the tickets from me. "No problem, I'll count them both in."

He walked back to his desk. It looked like he could go on forever typing but then he stopped to look at me. "Grab a seat or look around, I'll be done in a sec."

"Okay," I chose to look around.

It was a small and beautiful office with a large print of a map of the world hanging behind him. Smaller photographs of different places circled the larger print. My eyes gravitated to the bookshelves facing each other on opposite ends of his office.

I looked at the one on my right. "Is all this yours?"

Ben looked up. "The books or the office?"

I tilted my head to see the top book on the shelf. "Both."

He placed his glasses on his desk. "Professor Lee taught a bunch of my freshman courses and offered me the TA position. I was lucky, this used to be an old closet no one was using. I asked if I could, and he said yes."

"That's really nice of him. I didn't know sophomores could be TA's."

"It's not common, but he knows how badly I want to teach so he's paving the way for me to do it. I'd be sharing a space upstairs with at least three other students if it wasn't for him."

He got up from his desk and walked to stare at the bookshelf with me. "These are all mine." He placed his hands in his pockets. "You can call it hoarding or passion."

"I'd call it passion." I noticed the Fitzgerald copy I read a couple of times before. "This is one of my dad's favorites." *Was.* I walked to the other bookshelf.

Ben joined me. He reached out to grab a heavy slipcase he carried to his desk. I watched him carefully remove a collection from it. I counted about six books when he handed me the first one.

"Another Fitzgerald," I said when I saw the cover, "is this a vintage collection?"

He nodded. "My family gifted me this set before I came to MGU, he's one of my favorite authors."

I skimmed through the book. "I haven't read a lot of his work, just that copy over there."

"Yeah? How come?" His question was innocent, he was genuinely curious, but it didn't stop me from fighting back a tear.

"Just something my dad and I shared." I continued to look around the bookshelf, landing on another vintage set.

Ben came to stand next to me. "I can lend you any of them if you want."

"Really?" I said, a bit too eagerly. "That's kind of you."

He looked towards his desk. "Good timing on submitting your raffle tickets, I was heading out soon."

He walked to the door to escort me out and I caught a whiff of his cologne. *Musk? Ginger? Definitely Lemon.* An odd combination that smelled great regardless.

"Is there anything else I can help you with?" Ben asked.

"No," I said, too quickly again. "Have a good evening."

Seven

AFTER THOSE TWO WEEKS, the first month of school flew by. Except for this, I wasn't as much of an outcast in Amanda and Halle's budding friendship. They spent almost all their time together, it made sense I joined them too.

"Help me place this on the table," Halle took out a large plastic cover from the reusable bag on the floor. We were in one of GRUB's private rooms, helping Halle with what she called her "secret project". It wasn't much of a secret now as I looked at the paint buckets on the floor and the blank white canvas against the wall. I knew she only told us that to get us to agree to come.

"What exactly are we doing?" Amanda asked while spreading the tarp to cover the floor.

Halle looked at her. "Is the suspense killing you my dear?"

"Halle!" Amanda said. "This is a lot, even for me."

"Go with the flow and trust me on this," Halle grabbed her homework paper. "It says here that I have to paint an immersive art piece and get help from at least one other student, and it has to be something meaningful to me and the other person."

Amanda looked at the paint jars on the floor. "This is a terrible idea."

"This is the creative space of GRUB," Halle said, "it's what we do around here." She looked at the door next to her. "Bathroom's right here, we have all the supplies we need, and I've sorted it all out, we're good! Are you going to help me? Pretty please?"

Amanda walked over to grab the canvas and laid it down on top of the table. Halle opened one of the paint jars.

"I reserved the room for two days," Halle said. Amanda and I immediately looked at her.

"For the paint to dry," Halle added.

Amanda scoffed. "We couldn't do this anywhere else because?"

"Has to be on campus," Halle put her hands up. "Don't be mad at me, be mad at my professor."

She released an exasperated laugh. "Will you two just trust me?"

Normally by now, I'd thought of every excuse as to why we couldn't go through with this. *It's messy*, I would say. *What if we get in trouble?* But I pushed all of it away this time. I walked to the table and stood next to Amanda. "So, what do you need us to do?"

She looked pleased. "Do what I'm doing."

We watched as Halle poured the paint into smaller containers and placed it at the edge of the table, near us. She dipped one of her rollers in the blue paint and spread it on the canvas.

"My color's blue," she said. "Red is yours, Amanda, and green, Annabelle's." Amanda and I each grabbed a roller.

I wasn't much of a painter or an artist like Halle, but I had to admit, her project was fun. I didn't feel any growing concerns and allowed myself to get lost in it.

"You know what Halle, you're pretty good at this," Amanda said midway through.

"I know," Halle said. "I told you to trust me." When my eyes adjusted to the painting that was beautifully coming together, I felt her staring at me.

"I like seeing this side of you, we should do this more often," she said when I looked up.

Halle was a force of nature and getting acclimated to her *with* Amanda, all the time, was a lot. I was deeply relieved that we were finally getting along.

"Me too," I said.

"Has he asked you out yet?" Halle asked me.

"Who?"

Amanda looked at me, "who else?"

I fixed my eyes on the painting, "not yet."

Kevin and I were texting frequently now. Mostly about music or his practices. He'd also started briefly walking with me after class. Halle and Amanda said one of these days, he would ask me out. I was hoping one of these days would come soon.

"Annabelle," Amanda stopped her painting. "You have to say yes when he does, don't second guess this."

"He made a move so he's into you," Halle agreed. "Just don't get too invested and it's a piece of cake." She said it like she was declaring her middle name or the current time ticking on the clock in front of us. To girls like them, dating was a piece of cake. *What if he doesn't ask me?*

"If you're lucky," Halle kept going, "you might finally do the deed this year."

Amanda let out a loud gasp followed by a breathy laugh. "You little troublemaker you!" She circled the table to get to Halle, holding her paint roller. Halle tried to run away from her and slipped on the tarp.

"Amanda, don't you dare!" Halle said, but she didn't seem to mind that much when Amanda caught up to her and spread a dab of paint on her face then splashed her shirt. Halle quickly got up and reached into the green paint bucket with her hands.

Amanda's eyes suddenly widened. "You wouldn't dare."

Halle matched her previous glee. "Watch me."

She grabbed Amanda and spread the paint all over her. They proceeded to run to the paint buckets and spent the next few minutes spreading paint all over each other. All of a sudden, they turned to me, smiling at the two of them from behind the table.

"No." I took a step back. "You can't, please don't." I tried to escape but they were too quick. They pinned me with their hands on the tarp and spread paint all over my face.

"You guys are the worst!" I said between bursts of laughter, "I was going to go to the library after this!"

"Not anymore," Amanda said and dabbed me some more.

"Look at us," Halle said in the middle of the three of us, laid down on the tarp. She looped her arms around us. "We look ridiculous."

Amanda laughed, "I don't know, I think red's my color." She turned to Halle. "Did you decide what you're naming this project?"

"I'm calling it," Halle lifted her fingers and spread them, "female bonding."

Amanda looked at us then started hysterically laughing again. Halle followed right after.

"GRUB is totally charging you a damage fee," Amanda said.

Halle shrugged, "totally."

Seconds later, the three of us were clutching our stomachs.

*** * ***

The first thing Kevin did when he saw me walk out of CompLit48 was talk to me.

"Hey," he said. "How was your weekend?"

"I hung out with Amanda and Halle, how was practice?"

"We're ready for our next match." He walked me towards the exit doors of the building. "I thought about you." He was quiet for a minute. "I've been meaning to ask you something."

My whole body buzzed. There were rare moments in life when you could predict the future. One, when the doctor walked out of the emergency room and wouldn't look at you. Two, when the boy who'd been texting you nonstop finally asked you out.

With a grin, he lifted his hand to push my ribbon to the side. His eyes drilled holes into mine. "Can I take you out on a date this weekend? We have a match on Friday, but I'm free Saturday."

I knew he couldn't feel my heart bouncing around in my chest.

"Yes."

"Nice." His dimple appeared, "formal or casual?"

I didn't have much time to think if I didn't want to be late to my next class.

"Umm, casual."

"It's a date then, see you Saturday."

"Kevin asked me out and I said yes!" I barged into Amanda and Halle's dorm as soon as classes ended.

"That's the big news??" Amanda quickly got up from her desk.

Halle was lying on her bed, reading a magazine. She lifted her eyes over the front page. "We told you it was only a matter of time, congrats!"

Amanda hugged me, "I'm so happy for you."

"Finally, your first date," Amanda had the biggest smile on her face, "Attagirl!"

This is for the best. I could try this again, with Kevin.

Halle joined in as if she was the conductor of a train. "Choo! Choo!"

* * *

"Oh no, no, no," Amanda sat me back down on Jaz's chair. "Don't chicken out now. How would you know you've met the right guy without first dating him?"

Halle searched through my jewelry, "she's right."

I spent all week contemplating my decision to go on a date with Kevin, but I couldn't anymore. He was picking me up in an hour and the girls were helping me get ready.

"What about these?" Halle showed me another pair of earrings. I nodded at her, just barely.

Jaz stared at me. "Stop worrying." I grabbed my pink ribbon for my hair.

"You're going to look hot in these," Amanda placed two outfits on my bed. She looked at Halle. "I've always wondered who Annabelle would go on a date with, she's so picky."

"You sure got lucky for someone who's picky," Halle said to me.

"Annabelle and I like to do this thing we call datecap after my dates," Amanda told everyone. "She helps me get ready and when I come back, I give her all the details."

She smiled at me, "now it's your turn."

I walked over to my bed when I was done placing my ribbon around my afro.

"You really can't go wrong with either of these choices," Amanda said so I selected the black jeans and pink halter top laid out.

Halle handed me a pair of dangling crystal earrings when I was done changing, "try these."

I put them on and looked in the mirror. "They're beautiful."

When I was done getting ready, Amanda handed me her black wedges before I walked out to use the restroom. This was my second trip in under twenty minutes alone.

I stood there in the restroom, trying to think of a way of escape and save the embarrassment of being rejected again. Technically, this wasn't my first date. It was the one everyone else could know about. Jordan and I spent two weeks sneaking out of our houses, driving to different places in his jeep, and spending countless hours together, talking about nothing and everything. And then it was over.

I stood in the bathroom until a sense of boldness washed over me. I rinsed my hands and walked out.

The first thing I noticed when I came back to my dorm was Jaz's smile then Amanda gliding her body away so I could get a good look at the chocolate cake on my desk dripped with caramel frosting. When I noticed it, Halle immediately pointed to the message written on it. *No longer a date virgin!*

"You're too funny." Tears swelled in my eyes. "Thank you, you didn't have to."

"We know," Amanda said, "it's a do-over."

Halle cut each of us a slice and handed us our plates. "We're making up for your birthday."

"You're honestly the best."

"We know that too," Amanda joked.

"Don't forget what we told you," she said, "he may be one of the hottest guys that's ever graced planet earth, but he's the luckiest guy for getting to date you so tonight, be cool and relax."

"It's really not that big of a deal unless you make it one," Halle said before taking another bite.

A second later, my phone vibrated.

Kevin: I'm here

I looked up at them, "he's downstairs." I quickly glossed my lips.

"Don't make him wait," Amanda pushed me out of the door with Halle and Jaz walking behind us. I knew she was afraid I'd change my mind again at that second.

"We can't go down there with her," Halle said. I stepped into the elevator, the three of them watching me.

I took a deep breath. "It's just a date, right?"

"Yep, and you'll tell us all about it later," Amanda said and pressed the going down button.

"You've got this!" Amanda, Jaz, or maybe Halle yelled once the elevator shut.

Suddenly, it was pitch black. I was back in that room. It first happened when my dad got sick. The long chemo hours were tough on me and mom. Having to wait for my dad, desperately hoping it was the last one we'd have to go through, wrecked us each time. I couldn't concentrate so reading didn't help. So, I came up with one scenario then another and another. Soon enough, I was playing out different scenarios to life events that had already happened which made waiting bearable. When the doctor came out that day and walked past me, I knew it was only a matter of time before mom came out too and gave me the news. It had worked twice before but this time, I could no longer envision his healing.

I stood in the elevator, my mind swirling with dozens of pictures of my date, the one I finally wouldn't have to sneak around for. But it wasn't Jordan who stood outside waiting for me, who was leaning on the railing in front of my dorm building with a single red rose, who was dressed in a dress shirt and black pants despite this being a casual date. It wasn't Jordan who asked me out.

Kevin simply stood there. "You look beautiful."

My stomach flipped, "thank you."

"You too," I said. "Sorry, I meant handsome."

He handed me the rose. "This is for you."

"Thank you again."

I didn't think it was possible to float and stand at the same time.

We stared at each other for a second too long.

"How does an outdoor movie at Vandersant Field sound?" Kevin asked while walking us to his car.

"It sounds great, what movie's playing? I'm up for anything."

"It's an older one," he responded. "I haven't seen it yet, but I hear it's good."

Kevin was already walking past me to get to the passenger door when the blood drained from my face. *This can't be.* Not today, not today of all days.

I stopped. "Umm...why are you driving Jordan's jeep?"

* * *

Kevin slowly gestured for me to get in the car. "I hope you don't mind, my friends and I drive each other's cars all the time."

I realized I couldn't go on this date if I didn't get in.

I looked at him and stepped in. "Sorry, I didn't mean to startle you."

Kevin waited for me to sit down before walking to the driver's side.

"He's in Manhattan this weekend," he turned on the engine. "I drove him to the bus stop."

"Umm," I started but that's as far as I got. It was hard to think of something after the wind got knocked out of me.

"I get it, loyalty," Kevin shook his head, "best-friend's brother's mate is tricky, it's unfortunate they don't get along."

He looked at me. "It's even a mouthful just saying it, but we're not dating them so who cares?"

"You're right." I took a deep breath and held my composure. "I'm happy to be going on this date with you."

"Same," he said. "Amanda may have a problem with this, but Jordan couldn't care less, he told me he has no issues with it so we're good." My stomach dropped.

He looked at me. "Did you get a chance to listen to the new playlist I sent?"

I had one choice left to make at this moment. *Relax.* I could still hear Amanda.

I turned to him. "The first song was amazing, I keep playing it in my head."

"I told you they were epic! You just had to give them a chance."

"Is the air alright?" Kevin asked while adjusting the vents. I nodded. He shifted in his seat. "I think I told you this, but our next match is here next week, I'd like for you to come."

"If you want," he added.

"I do."

We both looked away.

"How long have you played soccer?" I looked at him again.

"Did you always want to play for MGU or for an American school?"

"I was your typical lad who played almost every sport growing up. Coach scouted a few of us and MGU offered me a scholarship I couldn't pass up."

He glanced at me. "You know you're the only girl who's had a blank face after I've said that?"

"Oh, I'm sorry! I didn't mean..."

"No problem." He laughed quietly. "I like that about you."

He cleared his throat. "What about you? Why MGU?"

I pressed my head against the headrest. "My parents went here."

It was the answer I gave to everyone at orientation and a few people over the summer. Most people wanted to go on or ask more. And they did. Shortly after, they got the hint.

Kevin was quiet for a moment then turned to me. "I liked meeting your dad that year, great guy."

I closed my eyes, anticipating what he would ask next. *What do you miss about him?* No, it's our first date, it would be *how did he die? If you don't mind me asking.*

"What do you miss about him?" *Jordan must have told him.*

"A lot, too much really."

The thought of Kevin having met my dad before we officially dated hurt. Just like the thought of my dad never seeing me date also did. I suddenly wanted to know what he would have thought of this.

He gripped the steering wheel. "My dad means the world to me." He stopped himself. "I can't imagine."

He lowered the volume. "I'm sorry for your loss, Annabelle. My family's pretty close like yours is."

Was, I wanted to say to him. He met my family when we were close. With me and mom lately, we were everything but.

I looked at him. "What else are they like?"

"They're great people." His dimple caved in. "I look up to my dad a lot, that's why I chose politics."

"He's a judge, right?"

"Yep, I'm thinking of going into policy though," Kevin switched lanes. "Mum's a nurse."

"Both sides of my family originally immigrated to the UK from Cameroon. We're tight, you meet one of us, you've pretty much met all of us. I'm the oldest as you know, I look out for my brothers a lot."

Kevin surprised me in the best of ways. He spent the rest of our ride talking about his family and siblings and supposedly the fact that he was the strongest and funniest. But if I asked them, they'd probably say it was debatable. I was the listening one again, but I didn't care. That was the thing about Kevin. He wasn't just attractive and funny, I was finding out, he was thoughtful. He was also the type to laugh through life. I found myself wanting to laugh alongside him.

"It's empty over there," I pointed to the free parking spot when we drove into the outdoor movie area.

"Nice catch," Kevin said. "I'm not shocked it's packed, it's beautiful out." He took one of the only remaining spots facing the projector screen. "What would you like to eat?"

"Whatever you want."

"Nooo, don't give me that." His smile didn't budge. "Still have that sweet tooth?"

I couldn't hide my growing smile. "I always do, but I'm up for any food. Seriously, you pick."

"They don't have lemon tarts over here but I'm sure I can find something worthwhile." He placed the car in park. "Wait here while I go grab us stuff."

I watched Kevin walk away between the parked cars and quickly took out my phone to call Amanda.

"He took us to an outdoor movie night," I said when she picked up.

"Let's see...he wants to be cozy, that's totally a good sign!" She yelled over the music. "Make sure to be chill and enjoy your hot date. I'm with the boys and Halle, text us when you're back."

"I will," I said, "and Amanda?"

"Yeah?"

"I am," I smiled, "having a good time."

She paused. There was a moment there. Amanda didn't just have those moments when she didn't say anything. In an instant, it was gone.

"Love you, Annabear."

"Love you too, Mandabear."

A couple minutes later, Kevin walked back to the jeep. He'd managed to carry two sodas between his neck and chin and enough food in his hands for an entire family. I stepped out of the car.

"You should have called me, I would have helped you."

"No problem," he moved closer to me, "grab these for me."

I took the sodas from him. "Is all this for us?"

"Just in case you don't like some stuff," he grinned, "wait here." He walked to the trunk and opened it. I heard some shuffling, a low grunt, and finally, "you can come now."

"I got carried away," he said when I walked over to him, "hope you like it."

My hand flew to my chest when I noticed what he'd done.

It no longer looked like a trunk or Jordan's jeep for that matter. It was like staring at our own private but small restaurant. A large blanket covered the space. He'd managed to put lights all around it and had our food laid out in the middle on a small table. On it, my rose was in a small vase and under it, a portable stereo. One that looked like it made musicians sound extra gifted.

"Don't like the film? Say the word." He pulled up two albums. "We don't watch it and listen to these epic beats instead."

I took a deep breath and got a good look at him. I wanted to remember this moment, the moment I moved forward.

"Do we have to choose?" I asked him.

"No," his dimple caved in, "anything for you."

Eight

"Here I am, trying not to make it obvious and laugh at the same time, and here coach comes," Kevin reached over to grab the popcorn, same time as me.

"You go," I pulled my fingers back, my heart racing. We weren't just enjoying our first date, neither of us had paid any attention to the movie.

"Where was I?"

"Your coach walked in when you were trying to erase..."

"Right!" Kevin said. "He figured out what was going on and that's pretty much it."

"You got away with that one too?"

He grinned. "I got off easy."

"Shoot," he nodded his head towards the screen, "credits are rolling."

I turned away from him, I didn't want this date to end.

He glanced at me. "Still up for a concert?"

I simply looked at him and raised an eyebrow.

He grabbed one of the albums he brought, the same one he included in the first playlist he sent me and placed it in the stereo.

"You heard him on your phone and computer," he said, "but I bet you, you haven't heard ACHE like this yet."

Between the people walking around to get back in their cars, the movie staff walking by to grab the trash, and the other vehicles driving off, listening to this album could cause a scene.

I looked around us, "here?"

Kevin smiled, "here, they won't kick us out anytime soon." He pressed play.

The first song started, and he leaned back.

"Close your eyes," he said.

I didn't at first. I hesitated while watching the cars around us leaving. Then I leaned back as well. Suddenly, it was pitch black again.

When I first played those scenarios in my head, it was the greatest thing when they'd come true. Like the first two times when dad got cured, I truly felt magical. So, when Jordan left that night after the funeral, I played another one. I closed my eyes, and I was back in his jeep, listening to music. I was the happiest I'd been in a long time. When I opened my eyes again – listening to this album with Kevin – I realized that I didn't have to wait around for Jordan to feel this way again. Kevin was right next to me.

* * *

By the end of our date, Amanda had already left me a bunch of texts letting me know she was *dying* for our datecap. And sure enough, I was dying to share it with her.

All the books I read over the years could never prepare me for this moment. When chemistry pierced through heartbreak and birthed butterflies, again.

"I had a great time tonight," Kevin said to me outside of Wolf.

I met his gaze, "I did too."

He shifted from one foot to the next. "We should do this again."

"Less casual," he said, "a proper date."

He leaned down. *Brace yourself.*

He planted a kiss on my forehead.

His eyes rested on me. "See you Monday."

Exhale.

* * *

Amanda didn't wait for me to get back into the building to text her. She didn't wait for me to get to her dorm or even our fifth floor. She was already downstairs, right in the lobby.

"Oh my!" She immediately grabbed me. "Did you see the way he looked at you? He's totally asking you out again."

I grinned from ear to ear. "He did."

"Ahh! What did I tell you? Staring totally means he's into you."

After a few more seconds of filling her in on the date, I looked behind her, "where's Halle?"

"She's on her way back," Amanda said.

Minutes later, Halle walked into the lobby. "What's the juice? Start from the beginning!"

"Annabelle scored a second date," Amanda said.

"With Kevin Knicks of all people," Halle said, impressed. "Nicely done."

"It went really well," I told her, "he wants to take me out again."

"Did he kiss you?" Halle asked. Her question made me pause. *Should he have kissed me?*

"No, but he was very respectful and kissed my forehead instead."

"Huh." Halle said. "It could mean one of two things. He's either fond of you or sees you as a friend."

"Did he want to kiss you?" she asked. "On the lips, there's a difference."

"There is, but I saw them." Amanda said. "He totally does."

"I think so, I don't know," I said, my heart calming again. "I'd like to...if he does."

Amanda jumped forward and gave me a hug, Halle did the same.

The three of us jumped up and down, right there in the lobby.

Amanda stopped jumping. Then suddenly, she grabbed me. "My Ace!" she yelled.

* * *

Dear MGU Reader:
My fellow classmates
Ladies and gentlemen

They say fall's a great time at Greenspring. I think they're right, it's already off to a good start. Hint hint, I'm not talking about the weather.

Dating is fun. So much fun, I've just gone on one date, two dates, three dates, four dates? Who's counting?

Kisses
…Or should I say hugs…
The Virgin

anon#@: Tell us more!
Candylloooove: Does he know you're a virgin?
Virgin23: Are you meeting them on the apps?
Anoonymmouss: he'll find out she is soon enough
Fashionablynotlate: Girl, ur in college. Have fun <3
imnothere: I guess I need to be celibate to meet the good guys on campus #fml
mgu44378: Please consider staying pure
Gamerboy11: I'd want to know if the girl i was dating was a virgin
Lucittabee: If she stays a virgin, that means she can only date a certain type of guy.

<u>Daisylyra:</u> why? ^

<u>virgin senior:</u> are all these dates with the same person?

* * *

It began, unexpectedly. My first real dating experience. For the next three weeks, Kevin took my mind away from everything. From school and all the ruminating thoughts about my dad. Even Jordan.

But there was one thing, he still hadn't kissed me. I was starting to worry that Halle was correct. He was a star athlete afterall and maybe he *did* only see me as a friend.

"I mean," Amanda poured herself a drink in her dorm, "he's still taking you out, he invited you to another game tonight."

"Match," Halle corrected her.

"Match," Amanda said, "with your friends and gave us tickets."

"That counts for something," she added.

"Just ignore the groupies," Halle said.

I glanced at her from Amanda's bed, "thanks?"

"Annabelle, I've always told you." Amanda walked over to hand Halle a drink before looking at me. "Basic chemistry with the right guy is this; Guy asks you out, guy takes you out, guy kisses you, guy makes out with you, guy hooks up with you, then boom! He's in love and you're in love."

She walked over to stand in front of me. "You're just waiting on the boom, but it'll come." She cupped my cheeks with her hands. "I'm sure of it."

Halle raised her drink, "We're all just waiting on the boom."

I chuckled. "What would I do this semester without you two?"

Amanda re-filled their cups.

I looked at my phone. "We're going to be late."

"That was quickly lived," Amanda took a sip of her drink

then applied her lipstick. "It's because I love you that I'm doing this."

I winced. *Don't remind me.* They both really didn't care to go to these matches with me, especially Amanda who had no desire to see her brother play. Since Kevin and I started dating, I had avoided running into Jordan. I was fortunate that after the last match we went to, Kevin met me and the girls at GRUB, before going back to hang out with his team.

"I need you there for moral support," I looked at Amanda with begging eyes, "until he kisses me?"

Halle laughed and handed me her drink. "This should calm your nerves."

Amanda looked at her. "I've been trying for years, won't work."

I stared at both of them. "Please, hurry up! I want us to have good seats."

* * *

We arrived at the packed stadium when the players were already on the field. Fortunately, we were able to sit in the middle. I looked behind us. For a stadium that could hold close to the entire student body, every seat was practically filled.

"Look," Amanda accidentally bumped into my shoulder. She pointed at the scoreboard. "They're in the lead."

"He said they were undefeated," I said to her. I looked over the turf and saw Kevin. One of the players passed him the ball and he ran his way across the field, attempting to score the next goal but missing.

Halle leaned over Amanda to look at me. "He's good."

"I can make out those tattoos from here," Amanda said after a while. She was staring at Jordan and Kevin's friend, Seth, who wasn't in the game, but sitting on the bench.

"Your brother has the ball now," Halle said. Jordan was always good at the sport.

"Cooper! Cooper! Cooper!" Some people chanted behind us. Amanda rolled her eyes. "*This* is why I don't like to come."

"It could be worse." Halle snorted a laugh. "It could be someone else's last name they're chanting."

My eyes were glued on Kevin. I watched him glide across the field again. He was so determined to score a goal and was just waiting for the right opportunity. An opposing team member mistakenly passed him the ball and he headbutted it down to his knees, straight to his foot. He ran the ball to the half point mark and stopped. Then, as if he'd done it a thousand times before, he kicked it directly into the goal.

"Wow," Halle said.

I stood up immediately, "go Kevin!" I knew he couldn't hear me, but I was too excited not to cheer him on.

"See..." Amanda said when I sat back down. "You're just waiting on the boom."

I looked back on the field. Jordan was standing still, staring straight at me with a frown on his face. That's when Kevin noticed me and waved. Both Amanda and Halle looked at me.

"Boom incoming," Amanda whispered to me just as the announcer rang for half-time.

"You sure you don't want to stay?" I asked Amanda and Halle, who were already standing up to leave.

"Absolutely, positively, no." Amanda said, "can't let this buzz wear off." She looked around the stadium in disgust, "here."

I looked down and saw that Kevin texted me.

Kevin: wait there after the game

Kevin: I have something to show you

"Let us know who wins," Halle said.

"Okay, love you, be safe," I said to them before they walked away.

* * *

It was strange, I had to admit, to be close to both guys and only be fixated on Kevin. Once again, he surprised me.

"What did you think?" Kevin met me in the bleachers – after the crowd had dwindled and the few people left were trickling out.

"Good job tonight, Kevin," a guy walking past us said to him.

"Thanks mate," Kevin said and looked back at me.

"You guys were amazing," I said to him, "even better than last time."

He inched closer. "That's probably because you were there."

"I was there last time."

"You'll just have to keep coming then."

There was a heavy silence.

I cleared my throat. "You wanted to show me something?"

"Sure did," he looked towards the field. "Come with me."

When Kevin reached out to grab my hand, my whole body heated up. I could feel the warmth of his body cutting through the air and enveloping me. He started walking me across the bleachers, past the empty locker rooms, to the other side of the stadium, straight to the middle of the now empty field. That's when he stopped.

He took a deep breath. "Wait for it."

He looked up then walked in a circle around me, "five, four, three, two." At one, all the lights in the stadium and field shut off.

My stomach fluttered and my heart skipped a beat or three. One by one, the lights turned on again. It took me a second to realize they looked to be dancing or following a melody. I let out a long exhale, eventually making out the sound.

"It's my favorite artist," I whispered to him.

Kevin walked closer to me. "I owe a few guys on the team for doing this for me."

He leaned forward to touch my green ribbon. "You wore this for our game?"

"Yes, since it was a home game," my voice trailed off.

He secured his arm around my waist, not once moving his eyes away from mine.

"I've been wanting to do this for a while," he said, without so much as a blink. "You're unlike anyone I've ever met before."

He continued, "I didn't want to cheapen it."

I let his words sink in, noticing there was another rare moment. Amanda was right, yet again. It was a moment that up until this night, I wasn't exactly sure of. A third time you could predict the future. When the guy you'd been dating was dying to kiss you.

My voice was too quiet, not even sounding like my own. "Cheapen what?"

"This."

He leaned down and lifted me up, wrapping my legs around his waist. He placed one hand behind the small of my back and another behind my neck. Then he kissed me.

Suddenly again, it was pitch black. But it wasn't me creating another scenario, it was me enjoying this moment. I was still trying to find my balance when he put me down.

His deep eyes stayed on me. He extended his hand for me to grab and this time, he moved me along with the music.

I stared at him. "Who knew Kevin Knicks was such a romantic?"

"Let's see," he said. "Dad, mum, my three younger brothers." His dimple caved in. "Now, you."

His eyes narrowed at my lips. "It was nice to kiss you."

He leaned down and kissed me again.

* * *

"What are your plans next weekend?" Kevin asked me outside of my CompLit48 class.

"Not much, Amanda and Halle have frat events they're going to so I'm mostly free. I also have some exams coming up that I need to study for."

He walked me towards the exit. "Need my help?"

"No," I sighed. "I'm fine, thank you for offering."

"There's a restaurant I want to take you to, would next Friday work? Team's away this weekend and next Saturday."

I nodded, already eager to see him again.

"Next Friday works," I said. *Saturday, what could be this Saturday?*

My reading essay. "Crap!"

"What?" He asked me.

"I have to head back to class, I forgot to grab something."

"Good for Friday then?"

"Okay!"

My stomach went a million and one direction when he leaned back down to kiss me. I turned around and rushed back into the dome auditorium. Professor Lee was in a conversation with Ben. They both stopped to stare at me.

"Annabelle Wilson," Professor Lee said, "forgot something?" He handed me the sheet of paper.

I looked away. "Yes, thank you." *Great.*

"Next one's due this weekend," he stared at me, "don't hand it late."

I quickly glanced at Ben before dashing out.

Nine

"WHAT DO YOU THINK?" Kevin asked me in front of an Italian restaurant off campus that overlooked a vineyard. Thankfully, we hadn't driven there in the jeep but one of his other teammate's cars.

"It's really nice, thank you for bringing me here."

"I've been here a few times," he said. I noticed the girls walking out of the restaurant, staring at us.

He looked at me. "You're chilly?"

No matter the number of dates we'd gone on, I couldn't get used to the looks we got together.

"Annabelle?"

"Huh?"

"Are you chilly?"

"Oh," I rubbed my arms, "no, I'm fine." He took off his vest anyway and placed it around my shoulders. His left dimple caved in, "anything for you."

We all had them. Those words or phrases we refused to part from. When we got comfortable with someone, we said it to them. For Kevin, this was his. *Anything for you*. He said it to me all the time.

He led me inside the restaurant. Straight away, the hostess smiled at him.

"Welcome to Isabella's!" She greeted us, "table for two?"

"We have a reservation under Knicks," Kevin said.

"Knicks," she looked over the list on her stand. "Ah, right this way." She walked us to our table and waited for Kevin to pull out my chair then for him to sit down.

"The waitress will be with you shortly." She was about to turn then stopped herself. "You two make a beautiful couple."

"Thank you," Kevin looked at me then back at her, "I think so too." *Couple?!* I wished I could call Amanda and Halle telepathically.

"How were your exams?" Kevin asked casually, as if he hadn't just removed the air from the room. He unfolded his napkin and continued to stare at me.

I looked to our right, a few more tables staring.

"So...." he raised a brow, "how did they go?"

"I don't know," I let out a sigh. "Okay...I guess. I have my CompLit48 exam next week." I wasn't doing a good job of keeping up with my classes, everything distracted me these days.

"I'm dreading midterms," I admitted.

"One hundred, it sucks you have other exams so close to it," he said.

We stared at each other for a moment. There hadn't been a date we went on when we weren't enjoying each other's company. Kevin made it all feel effortless. Which was why when Jordan called me again last week, twice, I never answered.

I gazed at him. "How do you balance polisci and soccer?"

He shrugged. "Professors are pretty easy on us, the perks of being an athlete, I guess."

"A proper playlist gets me in the mood to study," he added.

He tilted his head slightly and grabbed my hand across the table, "I bought those books you kept raving about, I like the first one so far."

I smiled. "I knew you wouldn't be able to put them down once you started reading the series."

The waitress appeared with our menus.

"Do you know what you want?" he asked me.

I shook my head. "I'm not sure."

"Mind if I order for both of us then?"

"Not at all."

"You'll love it," he said to me.

He looked at the waitress. "Calamari for appetizers, your veal plate, and carbonara." When he was done, he placed my menu on top of his and handed it to her.

"You said you've been here before?" I asked.

Amanda told me I had to work up the courage to ask him how many girls he had dated and been with or at the very least how many he was currently dating. Halle said that despite him totally being into me, guys always had more than one option, and a college athlete, triple. I had to be five steps ahead, just in case.

"You're cute when you do that," he said.

"Do what?"

"When you get pensive, you get this tiny line on your forehead, it's cute."

I looked at the table. It was starting to be impossible for my stomach to handle anything when I was around him. He said and did everything right.

His shoulders shook. "You're doing it again." His laugh was distinctive, infectious. Every time I heard it, it made me laugh too.

I let out a giggle, "I don't mean to."

He grabbed a piece of bread from the basket the waitress placed on our table and dipped it in the bowl of olive oil next to it. I did the same.

"Annabelle," he fixed his eyes on me, "if you're wondering whether or not you're the first girl I've taken here, the answer's no."

I am a little jealous.

"I've dated a lot," he said, "the options have kind of always been there."

I wasn't sure what to say to that. He watched me dip another piece of bread before eating it.

He stared at me. "You're not an option." A flicker of hope washed over his eyes. "I wanted to ask you something, and I'm hoping you say yes to it."

He looked away for a brief second then straightened himself, knocking the wind out of me for the second time at dinner.

"Will you be my girlfriend?"

I sat there for a moment, because it was happening again. It's not like I ever planned it – when the flower for the person came to me. Kevin didn't have to say or do anything more for me to know exactly which flower he was.

"Earth to Annabelle?" He let out a nervous laugh. "I thought you'd say yes."

I couldn't believe he was second-guessing my answer.

"Yes," I reached out to grab his hand, "of course I'll be your girlfriend."

* * *

"Have you told your mum about us?" Kevin asked me when we rushed into Wolf to get to my dorm after dinner. I quickly pressed for the elevator.

"That we've been dating?" I asked him when we stepped in. I was embarrassed to tell him I hadn't. I knew she'd want me to focus on school.

"Not yet," I finally said and looked at him, "I haven't gotten the chance to."

My heart pounded loudly each floor the elevator passed through. *Please don't stop.*

Incidentally, the elevator stopped, and I heard footsteps. *Please don't let this be my resident supervisor.* Jaz walked in instead,

I froze. I could hear myself breathing, which meant she probably could too and so could Kevin.

"Hi," she said flatly to both of us then turned her back to face the door.

We weren't seeing each other much lately but still, this was very unlike Jaz. To my surprise, she walked out on the fourth floor, not saying another word.

I cleared my throat once she left. "Sorry about that."

Kevin shrugged. "Your mum's met me before, what's not to like?"

The elevator stopped on my floor and I held him back and looked out before telling him it was okay to go. We rushed to my door, and I immediately opened it.

"I talk to my mum about everything, including the girls I date." he said. It surprised me that he told her about us, even if they were close. He stopped to look around. "Cute dorm."

I tried to hide my uneasiness. Only one other guy had been in here.

I looked away from Kevin, "sorry for the mess."

"It's not so bad." He took a seat on my bed. "I don't miss this though. Annabelle, my soccer house is ten times better than this."

I ignored his comment and sat down at my desk facing him, his proximity made the room seem even tighter than it already was.

His gaze dropped briefly to my mouth. "One of the lads back home says hell froze over if I'm serious about someone."

What? I thought, that can't be true. A guy like him must have fallen in love already, no less than three times.

"Really? It's that surprising to them?"

"Oh yeah." He shot me a sympathetic look. "You have no idea."

He patted my mattress. "Why don't you sit here?"

My throat was dry when I tried to say something back. I was nervous. As if to emphasize this, my stomach rolled again. I got up and sat down next to him. He gently took off my glasses and placed them on the shelf hanging on top of my bed.

"You've worn a different ribbon every date we've gone on," he said softly. My mind was saying yes, but my lips couldn't move. I was really close to his face, so close, I could make out the small brown fleck in his right eye.

He scooted closer. "You know what's epic?"

I could barely hear my own words, "what's that?"

"I thought you were so unique when I first met you," he said. "You didn't give me the time of day. It's like you were lost in your own world, I find that appealing about you." He scooted even closer. "When you came to MGU, and I found out you were single, I figured, might as well, I got nothing to lose."

If I stopped to process what he said, this moment would escape us so I moved closer, closing the space left between us.

Kevin lifted my chin, "I don't think you realize how special you are."

Our thighs were touching. One more movement and our lips would too.

"I like that," he said.

He placed his left hand behind my back and leaned my face towards his. I felt my own heartbeat escape me. In exchange, he gave me his. His lips were soft, and I could taste our dinner from earlier. But I didn't mind. By this point, it was the safest I'd felt giving my heart away since the lake house.

He pulled back, "I have another record to play for you." He laid down on my bed, then pulled me next to him and took his phone out of his pocket.

"You're a good kisser," he whispered in my ear before pressing play.

My goosebumps seemed to follow the music. They traveled from my toes, stopping at my chest, before rushing to my heart. I finally felt emotions I desperately wanted to feel again. He pulled his face towards mine and kissed me again.

I was halfway lost in our kiss when Jaz walked in.

"I'm so sorry," I pulled away from Kevin, "but you should go."

He kissed me again before getting up. He grabbed his phone, "see you later, girlfriend."

"Girlfriend?" Jaz asked when he was out of our dorm.

I just laid in bed repeating, *"girlfriend."* I liked the ring to that.

She just stared at me. "Does he know about..."

I sat up. "No, I haven't told him yet."

Up until recently, Jaz didn't know I was a virgin and was really happy to find out when Amanda mentioned it during one of our datecaps in my dorm. I liked Jaz, I did. But she had these moments when she was really invasive and constantly asked me to join her club.

She let out a sigh. "Look, we may have our differences, but you really don't need to rush this."

She was about to keep going when our door swung open, and Amanda beelined straight to me.

"I saw your text!" Amanda flopped on my bed, "I'm totally going to be late to this pregame, but you need to spill! He asked you to be his girlfriend??"

"He did!"

"I have so many date ideas we can go on with him and Warren! How did he ask you? Was it everything you've dreamt of?" she stopped. "He's too hot not for it to be, you've waited forever for this!"

I proceeded to fill her in on everything that happened. I was too busy sharing all the details to notice Jaz had walked out on us.

* * *

Dear MGU Reader:

My fellow classmates

Ladies and gentlemen

What's a kiss that doesn't stop? You guessed it, a good make-out session. I'm beginning to really like those lately. It's hard enough to walk with my head on straight these days, it doesn't help that he won't stop taking my breath away too.

Kisses
…Or should I say hugs…
The Virgin

Jackiesoph: Does he know you're a virgin??
Desiee: I'm sure she hasn't said anything.
anon#@: she should tell him
Candylloooove: don't do what they're saying, or you'll scare him away. Give it a few more dates.
Anoonymmouss: you should trust your instincts.
#virgin59+: I don't think she should be deceitful but that's just me.
KawaiiGirl: U should tell him soon
Imnothere: go with the flow
SammyWorks: wait at least two months before telling him
emily44378: 3-4 months then tell him
Jazm!ne:: says who?
virgin23: I tell guys that I'm a virgin right away
mgu2099: she should tell him when they're official
Rubby: Most guys in college only want to hookup. He's going to be pissed when you tell him.

* * *

Kevin: still at the library?

Annabelle: Yes :(

Kevin: I'm sure you'll do good

Kevin: see you tomorrow :)

Annabelle: Thank you :)

I placed my phone down on the library table, sighing quietly. I spent most of the weekend studying for my CompLit48 exam on Monday and I was still squeezing in six hours this Sunday. The fact that I couldn't memorize some stuff wasn't good. I looked over my study materials, once more, devoting close to two more hours before calling it a night. I grabbed my notes from the library desk and organized my bag to head back to my dorm.

When I turned the corner to walk out, I bumped into Jaz.

"Annabelle, hi!"

"Hi!"

"Are you leaving?" she asked me.

She looked next to me at a wide opened door. An entrance sign right in front of it – Daughters in Waiting.

I nodded, "yes."

"You look like you wanted to go in," she said.

I brought my strap further up on my shoulder. "Not at all." I could tell she thought I wanted to go in and chickened out. "I'm actually heading out."

"Oh." she said, but it sounded just like, *I don't believe you.*

She looked back and forth between me and the sign, "I'm going if you want to join?"

I felt my voice drop to my stomach. "I can't."

"No pressure, you can join us and see if you like it, it's only one hour." she said as two girls went into the room. "It'll go by really fast."

I felt bad for declining, but I couldn't go in with her.

She looked at me. "Were you thinking of going in?"

"No," I said. It finally hit me. Even though Jaz was friendly, she couldn't take my answer for what it was. It wasn't enough I couldn't go in with her, she had to know exactly why.

"I already have plans after this," I looked away, "I'm meeting up with Amanda tonight."

Jaz simply stared at me. "Say hi to her for me."

"I will!" I rushed past her to the staircase and texted Amanda right away.

> Annabelle: What are you up to?

Amanda: Warren's

> Annabelle: Can I come?

Amanda: ...

Amanda: seriously??

Amanda: I mean, totally! Of course!

"You came here," Halle said when I walked up to her and Amanda in front of Warren and Gabe's house. It was more of a question than a statement, but I just shrugged.

She struggled to focus on me, "I thought Amanda was joking when she said you were coming."

"It's only us and a few people right now," Amanda said with rosy cheeks.

I looked down, "I can only be here for a little bit if that's okay."

"There's that but," Halle said. "I haven't known you that long, but I know this, you hate parties."

"All we're doing tonight is getting wasted, I'm done with my exams," she added.

"Halle!" Amanda looked at her. "This isn't an actual party so stop trying to talk her out of this. Can you give us a sec miss know it all?"

Amanda waited until she was back in the house before leaning on my shoulder, "sorry, she can be a lot..."

She came inches to my face. "You do hate parties."

She let out an accidental burp then lowered her voice. "Why are you here?"

I shook my head, turning back to mush. "I ran into Jaz."

"Not again," she rolled her eyes.

I couldn't shake the overwhelming sadness hitting me. "What if it's the universe trying to tell me something?"

"Listen Annabelle, that club is not something to be a part of so stop considering it."

"I know." I said, knowing she was right.

When mom told me the news, Amanda was the first person I wanted to call. I just couldn't find the courage to say it out loud, to anyone. I sat there, unable to move. I watched the nurse walk over to my mom and grab her. Mom's wailing had to have been heard across our entire hometown. Amanda met me there in the waiting room, not even ten minutes later.

Our eyes met each other. We stood for a few minutes outside of the house, not having to say another word. We both knew, I missed him terribly.

"Don't be alone," she grabbed my hand, "come in with me."

Ten

⨑

"MY, MY, MY," Gabe stared at me like he was seeing two of me instead of one. "If it isn't you."

All Warren did was smirk next to him.

Amanda looked at both of them, giving them looks that told them not to say anything.

"Hi," I waved at everyone, stepped over one of the bottles on the floor, and sat down next to Amanda on the stand-alone sofa. It didn't look like they were doing much besides drinking and maybe playing another game. Somehow, the basement looked a lot smaller this time.

"You're the girl dating Kevin Knicks right?" One of the girls seated on the large sectional couch asked me. She was shorter than all of us and had jet-black hair and pale skin with almond-shaped eyes.

I nodded, "yes."

"I'm Jane," she said. "Nice meeting you."

"You too," I whispered.

Amanda looked at her friend, "she's his girlfriend."

Warren raised his eyebrows.

He looked at Amanda. "You still coming to the football game?

You can't beat VIP and free booze." From the side of my eye, I could see Gabe getting up.

Amanda looked at me, "Warren invited us to his family's VIP suite for the rival's game in a few weeks."

Warren looked at me. "You can tag along."

I looked away, "thank you."

Gabe walked over to the bar. "What is it your parents do again?" he asked. I felt Amanda's body tightening next to me. I didn't think he was asking me until I looked up and he was walking back to us with a tray in hand.

"My mom's a stay-at-home mom," I told him and said no to the shot he was extending towards me.

"She used to be a flight attendant," Amanda said and grabbed hers.

He looked at me. "What does your dad do?"

I sat locked in place. He handed Jane one.

It snuck up randomly, the grief. I took a deep breath and prepared myself for the looks of pity that would come right after I answered him.

"What does your dad do?" Gabe repeated himself. Suddenly, it was pitch black again and I wasn't sad. I was a normal student, attending normal college parties, and enjoying myself.

I opened my eyes and looked at Gabe. "Can I have one?"

Warren and Halle stopped their conversation to look at me. Gabe smiled wide when I grabbed two instead of one. Amanda just looked at me very quietly.

I came here for the wrong reasons, but that didn't matter anymore. Nothing mattered now. All I wanted was for the grief to go away, even if for a second.

* * *

"Dad!" I ran to him, "You have to read this one, it's so good! It's my new favorite!"

He looked up from his newspaper, "which one sweetie?"

I handed it to him and he read the title out loud. "Wonderful Adventures for the Eight Year Old."

He smiled at me. "If it's your new favorite sweetie then it's my new favorite too. So, where does my little girl want to go on our next big adventure?"

"Everywhere!"

He repeated after me, "everywhere?"

"And else!"

"Everywhere and else?" He let out the biggest belly laugh, "Everywhere and else, here we come!" He put his newspaper down and stood up to grab me, spinning me around the kitchen.

Mom walked back in, laughing at us. "Come on you two, help me with the waffles."

* * *

I didn't feel dizzy. Not when I first woke up from my dream. It wasn't until I tried to stand up that the sharp pain hit my head. And I noticed the grief was still there. It hadn't gone anywhere. I also noticed all the glasses on the table in front of me.

I quickly got up. *Ouch.*

"Amanda?" I called out her name.

It didn't take me long to figure out that it was only Jane and two other people in the basement with me. They were both sleeping.

I walked over to the closed door by the TV. "Amanda?"

I walked towards the stairwell and called out her name again.

"Stop yelling," someone slurred from the couch, "she's hooking up with Warren."

"What about Halle?" I asked them.

"How would I know?"

I picked up my phone and called them. I walked upstairs after the fifth attempt to reach them. No one was in the living room, or kitchen, or even outside when I walked out. So, I stood there and called him.

"Hey," Kevin said drowsily, "don't tell me you're still at the library."

I hesitated. "No."

He paused. "You sound different."

"I don't mean to bother you...I just...I don't want to be alone right now."

"Are you in your dorm?" he asked.

"No, I'm not."

"What's going on? It's 2 o'clock." I heard ruffling. "Don't do anything, don't go anywhere, just stay right there, alright?"

"Send me your pin," he added, "Annabelle?"

"Yes?"

"Stay where you are."

Less than twenty minutes later, Kevin found me, seated outside of the boys' house, waiting for him. He barely parked the jeep before rushing out. "Are you alright?"

I stood up, "yes," and kissed him. He pulled back.

"Were you drinking?" He looked at the house. "Why are you sitting out front?"

"I met up with the girls after the library," I tried to kiss him again, but he pulled back again.

He simply stared at me. "What's gotten into you?"

I pulled my hands away. "I'm just happy to see you, that's all."

"Let's get you out of here," he said.

I stopped. "I don't want to go back to my dorm."

He placed both hands on the back of his head and let out a sigh. "You don't want to go back to your dorm and never want to come to my house. Where am I supposed to take you right now?"

It was a little moment. Nothing big, but it meant the world that he was here.

I looked at him. "Everywhere and else."

"Everywhere and else?" He stood there, studying me, then eventually. "Alright, anything for you."

He didn't say anything when he walked me to the car and opened the door. He didn't say a word when he got in the driver's seat. We sat there in the jeep. It was quiet until he looked at me.

"Have you ever been everywhere and else in under an hour?"

I looked at him. "Is that possible?"

His dimple appeared. He grabbed his phone, turned on his Bluetooth, and pressed play.

I watched him pull the car in motion. He started slow then increased the speed. He drove fast through campus, around the different buildings, with his playlist blasting. The grief left and the ride went like a bleep. Except for this one moment when he gazed at me again. He locked one hand with mine, kept his other hand on the steering wheel, while I lowered the car window and placed my free hand out. It was pitch black again, but this time, the scenario didn't change. It was still Kevin holding my hand. When I opened my eyes, he was circling the parking lot once more at full speed and I could see *Wolf Hall* right next to me.

There was a time I brought these flowers home and they wouldn't bloom. Mom told me it wasn't their season yet. She said once they did, I wouldn't have to worry about them lasting. She said I could even bring them indoors if I wanted to. They weren't hard to plant like I thought, they worked inside or out, I just had to wait.

Like flowers, there were people we met who could surprise us. People who were nothing like we expected them to be.

Kevin parked the car and looked at me.

"You need to get some sleep, you have an exam tomorrow."

Right then, that's when I knew without a doubt. He was my Orchid.

* * *

"Annabelle." Jaz gently pushed me awake.

I woke up, startled, feeling an unbearable migraine.

"We have to go take our exam," she was fully dressed and ready to go.

I looked around our dorm. "How did I get back here?"

"I left the door open for you guys," she said.

It came back to me, he carried me. *Get some sleep*, he said, kissed my forehead, then left.

"It's a good thing he brought you back," she said and handed me a water bottle, "get up or we're going to be late."

"Please go without me."

"No." She wasn't budging. "Get up."

I grabbed my toiletries, rushed to wash my face and brush my teeth.

Jaz was deathly silent during our walk to class. I felt even more guilty when we arrived five minutes after the exam had started.

"Grab a seat." Professor Lee avoided looking at us. "Ben will hand you the exam."

I avoided looking at Ben when we took our seats in the front row. As soon as we were done, I texted Kevin that I was going back to my dorm to get some rest.

No matter how many of my alarms went off that afternoon, I didn't wake up until that early evening. When I lifted my eyelids, Jaz was seated at her desk.

"You should hydrate, it'll help," she got up and handed me a water bottle. "I brought you food, it's in the fridge."

She grabbed her purse, "I'll see you later." She walked out before I had the chance to thank her.

When Jaz left, it was just silence. The most horrible kind that stretched forever. I eased out of bed and checked my phone.

> Amanda: saw you called, I'm upstairs with Warren

> Halle: all good??

> Amanda: Hangovers are totally the worst, don't feel bad about it if you get one

> Halle: welcome to college

> Annabelle: False alarm, Kevin drove me back

. . .

Amanda: Warren says we were fun last night.

Amanda: Bring Kevin next time!

Kevin: Are you up?

I was about to text Kevin back when I received another call. My heart froze. I immediately sat at my desk.

"Hey." That's all Jordan said at first.

"It's not my place," he said, "but I heard Kevin on the phone with you last night."

His voice was low. "Are you doing okay?"

"I'm fine." I replied. "I just had a lot to drink last night."

I felt his voice in my gut. "You don't drink."

I went to sit at the foot of my bed and looked out my window, wondering how he could still have this effect on me.

"It was just a party," I said.

"If you say so."

He was thinking hard about what I said, or he was upset. Either way, he sounded disappointed. "If you want to talk, I'm here." He hung up.

* * *

"It's great you could meet me here on such short notice, Ms. Wilson." Dr. Gatz said to me when I walked into his office. "I'm sure you have much better things to do on a Friday afternoon, have a seat."

He handed me a small stack of papers from his desk.

I grabbed them from him and sat down. I was busy packing up my weekend bag for the spa retreat when Dr. Gatz emailed me to urgently meet him in his office.

"I received your grades from your professors," he looked at me. "Are you aware you're failing your classes?"

I looked down at the papers.

"Your results came back for your midterms and your overall scores. Ms. Wilson, you have three Cs and two Ds."

I considered what this meant. I sat there still, knowing there was nothing left to say. I completely dropped the ball.

"It's not ideal, but the Cs are still passing. You can't have the Ds." He rubbed his head. "You're required to score a B- or above in your core classes and right now, you're failing both of them. I want you to be honest with us and tell us if you need help, tutoring, counseling, anything."

He handed me another paper. My fingers shook while I stared at it in my hand.

"You failed your CompLit48 midterm, it's the only midterm you received an F in. I'm afraid you won't be able to get a passing grade."

"These are the foundations for future classes in our department, I'm concerned for you because we've missed the withdrawal deadline."

I sat quietly, feeling defeated, waiting for the dreaded news to follow.

"I want you to succeed here."

"Ms. Wilson," he said. I looked at him.

"I've requested for the school to give you one more try before taking what I feel should be the last approach. I've asked each of your professors to send me weekly updates on your class grades. You'll also need to do as much extra credit as you can. You know how flexible our department is with that. Go to events, join a club, volunteer, do whatever it takes to get these scores up.

"I'm also requesting for you to get mandatory tutoring at our tutoring center on a weekly basis. If after all of that, you don't get your grades up by the end of next month or pass your final exams with acceptable scores, I'll have to agree with the school on their suggestion to place you on academic hold and request mandatory bereavement leave.

"Which means you'll restart again as a freshman next fall, understood?"

"Thank you for giving me another chance, Dr. Gatz." I said, my voice unsteady.

"Try your best, Ms. Wilson. I know you can."

* * *

"My Aces!" Lucy reached over and grabbed Amanda and I into a tight hug. "I've missed you so much."

We'd just spent the past forty minutes driving to the spa retreat and I was grateful that Amanda had fallen asleep in the car and mom had been busy checking her emails, because I had no idea how to process the meeting I'd just had with Dr. Gatz. In a way, this relaxing weekend was coming at the perfect time. Even if it was unusual for us.

"Mom, please don't be overly emotional right now." Amanda stared at Lucy. "It's only mid-October and we just left home."

"I'm allowed to cry when my only girls go to college."

"We're already in college," Amanda said. "We went through this during summer, please not again."

"My point exactly!" Lucy rolled her eyes and hugged us again. "You'll know what I mean when you have your own daughter."

Amanda and her mom were so much alike, it was like looking at a spitting image of the future and the past, both in looks and personality. They butted heads a lot, but I always thought it was because they were so similar.

I snuck another glance at mom, still in the car, on a new phone call.

"Who's mom on the phone with?" I asked Lucy. If anyone knew, it would be her.

"She just has a few things to take care of."

I was about to ask her more when mom got out of the car.

"I've missed you," I gave her another hug.

"Me too, sweetie."

"So?" Amanda looked at them. "What's the plan?"

Mom took out her phone. "It's only dinner tonight. Tomorrow, we have breakfast first thing in the morning, group massages, then our facials starting at noon."

"We're here until Sunday right?" Amanda asked.

Like clockwork, mom checked her phone. "Sunday's Meni Pedi then we drive you girls back."

"Nice!" Amanda said. She turned to Lucy and proceeded to fill her in on a few things. My mother simply nodded, excused herself, and dashed away to make another phone call while we waited in the lot.

During dad's treatments, mom became like a superhuman for taking care of him. She had it all planned out for him. All his scheduled meals, medication times, and relaxation times. Even our conversations had to be planned in case dad got too tired to talk about it at another time. Everything we did as a family became part of a routine, one we all followed along with seamlessly. I knew my part to play. I supported her as best as I could with mending the chaos that was unraveling around us. When dad died, the routines didn't stop. They only worsened.

"Who were you on the phone with?" I asked her when she walked back to us.

She quickly grabbed my bag with one hand. "Let's get checked in."

I'd spent the entire week wondering what to expect from mom this weekend. She'd called me three, maybe four times, since I came to MGU. I stayed back and watched the three of them walk in first. I had a dreaded feeling that this wasn't just because they missed us. This had to be, as I'd come to get used to, another planned conversation in our scheduled routine.

Eleven

MY EYES WERE INSTANTLY DRAWN to the place when we first checked in. It was small, charming, and had the cozy appeal of a secluded cabin in the woods. It also helped that there weren't many people.

"Nice pick girls," Lucy said when we approached them in the only dining area available. "How do you like your room?"

Amanda shrugged. "It's not bad."

Lucy and mom made sure ours was connected to theirs.

I sat down next to Amanda.

"How did your midterms go?" Mom asked us. My jaw tightened.

Amanda answered first. "I totally aced mine." She looked at Lucy and said in the most sarcastic of voices. "I'm learning all I can about *HR*."

"You, my daughter," Lucy shook her head at her, "are too sassy for your own good." Despite how quickly they butted heads, their relationship never changed.

"I know the drill," Amanda drank her diet coke. "Have fun, graduate, then join our family's business. Don't worry mom, I won't waver from it." Lucy simply rolled her eyes.

Mom's eyes were fixated on me. "What about you sweetie?"

I glanced across at her. I could tell she already knew something.

"Fine, I guess."

"Enough with this exam talk!" Lucy said. "Give us your college updates, I would have been chatting my mother's ears off by now at your age."

"That's because you always have something to say, mom," Amanda said.

"Pot, I'd like for you to meet kettle," Lucy said. Mom and I chuckled.

"Whatever." Amanda rebutted. "You met dad like your first week of school, I'm sure you had a lot to talk about."

"There's more to college than boys." Mom chimed in. "How are your classes?" I could feel her eyes on me as she asked, "any clubs you've joined? New friends?"

"Mare," Lucy paused. *Mare and Luce. Thick as thieves.* Only they could call each other by their nicknames. "I told you Amanda's pledging right? In my sorority!"

I looked at Amanda. I knew she was considering it, but she hadn't confirmed it to me.

"Good for you," mom said to Amanda. "Luce knows some great people you should get in-touch with, I'm sure their kids are at the school too." She looked at me. "What about you Annabelle? You still haven't mentioned any clubs or groups that you've joined?"

"I'm not in any yet."

She tried to hide her look of disappointment. "That's one of the best parts of being at MGU, there's a world of options here."

Lucy smiled at me. "How are things with Kevin?"

My stomach fluttered at the thought of him. "They're going pretty well."

Mom shook her head at Lucy, "I couldn't believe it when she told me she was dating him last week."

Amanda looked at me and whispered, "last week? Cold." She'd been nudging me to finally work up the courage to tell mom I was seriously dating. Despite having already met Kevin, I knew there was no way mom would approve of this.

Lucy looked at me, "I told your mother not to worry. Kevin's a good guy and he's close with Jordan."

"She has other things she should be focused on," mom responded quietly.

"Kevin's a great boyfriend." Amanda came to my defense. "He's totally consistent." As if she knew just what to say to them to take the pressure off, she added. "Totally night and day from the guys I date."

"I'd love to see him again then!" Lucy looked at Amanda. "What's going on with the guy you're dating?"

Amanda let out a deep sigh. "We're not dating mom, we're talking."

"What does that even mean?" Lucy asked. Amanda and I giggled.

Amanda looked at her mom. "It means we're seeing where things go."

"Be careful not to do that for too long." Lucy told her. "Guys always know what they want."

Amanda rolled her eyes, "time's changed."

"Enjoy your semester but focus on your studies first," mom said.

"Amanda has a good new group of friends," I came to her defense. "Warren's nice, I like him." Amanda gave me a look, one that was pleased I was saying anything nice about him.

Lucy stared at Amanda. "I'd like to meet him eventually."

"Well, you've already met Kevin so that counts for something."

"I haven't met Warren yet, smartypants." Lucy said. She looked at mom. "We met our husbands on campus. Wouldn't it be nice if they did too?" We stayed silent for a moment too long.

It wasn't unlike Lucy to be optimistic about us meeting our significant others at MGU. Lucy was a part of the biggest sorority and met Amanda's dad during a sorority-frat party. As for mom, she accidentally ran into dad on campus and the two became inseparable. Lucy even told me that when dad met mom, she was the one to get him to loosen up. They were carefree together, fun, adventurous. They married right after college and three years later, they had me. That's when mom gave up her flight-attendant career to take care of me. They didn't want to have more kids. They said they wanted to pour out all their love to one other person and each other.

Mom ate her breakfast. "None of that dating stuff should be on your mind right now, certainly not you, Annabelle."

* * *

I dipped my toes in the water and looked at Amanda. "It's perfect weather."

Our moms were beat after dinner, so we decided to go outside to the private pool and hang out there before calling it a night.

"When are you pledging?" I asked her.

"Next semester," she said. "Mom totally jumped the gun announcing that, but Halle's doing it too, Warren says one of his friends doesn't mind being our big if we want."

"Big?"

"Big sister. She'll be like Halle and I's mentor while we pledge."

I looked down at my swinging legs. "Lucy's probably thrilled."

"I just wish she'd stop putting so much pressure on me, it's exhausting." She turned to me. "You're lucky Marie never hounds you about any of that. Mine's relentless."

"She's preoccupied with other things," I said softly.

Amanda kicked her legs in the water. "What about you? Are you ever joining a club?"

"I kind of have to now," I said. "For extra-credit."

"Why?"

"I'm failing school."

"You? There's no way!" She took her legs out of the water and turned to face me, "failing?"

"Only my core classes. That's why Dr. Gatz wanted to meet with me."

"That doesn't even make any sense," she said. "What else do you do besides stay in your dorm and hang out with us?"

"I hang out with Kevin," I said.

She shook her head, "that doesn't count."

"Of course it does."

"Annabear, I love you, but Halle and I spend a lot more time with Gabe and Warren combined in a week than you do with Kevin."

"That's not true," I looked away. She placed her feet back in the water and looked ahead.

"I haven't been studying. I haven't wanted to study, I'm all over the place this semester." I kicked my feet back and forth. "I've been pretending like everything's fine for a while now and it's starting to catch up to me.

"I can't stop thinking about my dad and how he spent his college years, he was really involved here. You heard my mom earlier; she sounded so disappointed in me.

"It's like everything keeps escaping me. What if joining Jaz's club isn't the worst thing in the world?"

"Not this again," she looked at me, "are you just trying to get Jaz to stop nagging you? Is that what this is?"

"She doesn't nag me." I said, a little hurt.

"There are a hundred other groups you could join. *Fun* groups, groups that are going to be better for you and make you feel good about yourself."

"I know, but SFC was his favorite." I paused. "Lately, I've just felt so distant from him, I never thought it'd happen." A lump formed in my throat. "Not so soon."

We didn't say anything for a while before she scooted closer and placed her arm around my shoulders. "I miss him too, we all do."

We watched the trees being swayed back and forth by the wind as we dangled our feet in the water.

"Can I ask you something?" Amanda asked suddenly. I shook my head yes.

"Didn't your dad's family disown him because of religion?"

"His family didn't approve of mom."

"Because she wasn't religious."

"I don't know the full story."

"What else is there to know, Annabelle? Your dad grew up religious and your mom doesn't believe in a higher power, so they shut her out. He chose her over them, what's so bad about that?"

"I'm not saying it's bad," I looked down at my hands, "I'm just saying there's a whole side of my dad I never got to know and now he's gone."

"I don't think anyone expects you to have the same experiences as your dad on campus." she said, "I totally don't."

"I hate to think of everything he kept from me because he didn't think I cared."

Her face was hot. "Don't do this because you're hoping for something that won't happen, there's no such thing as a higher power."

I braced myself for her punchline.

"Annabelle, I'm telling you," she fixed her eyes on me, dead serious. "Jaz's club is social suicide. Join the sorority with me and Halle. You're already dating one of the hottest guys in school, people are starting to recognize you."

She was right.

"This semester turned out so different than I expected...but enough about me! How are things with Warren and your classes?"

"I'm just having fun right now. It's not like any of this school stuff will matter once I graduate."

"Does that ever bother you?"

"Like it's always bothered Jordan? No, you know that. I've never had big career plans, I don't mind working for my dad.

"But do you know what Warren asked me the other day? He had the audacity to ask me to be friends with benefits with him as if a million guys wouldn't line up to date me, I shut that down so quick."

In the pause that followed, I felt her energy change.

"You deserve better, Mandabear." I could tell she was wondering if she did. Amanda had never wondered if she deserved a guy.

"How could you even question that?"

She ignored my question. "Even if it's just for fun, Warren's the richest guy in school. His family owns this whole town. I can't just blow him off, mom and dad will be happy about this and maybe mom will finally get off my case."

"What was it you told me when I went out with Kevin for the first time?" I asked, mimicking her. "He's the luckiest guy for dating you."

"I think..." I splashed her and jumped in the water, "you should follow your own advice, Amanda Cooper."

She smiled at me. "You always see the best in me."

"We see the best in each other," I said. She shook her head and jumped in.

We both eased our backs against the water, staying afloat.

"Are you falling in love with him?" Amanda asked me after a moment.

The thought of Kevin immediately made me smile. "I think so, maybe, a little."

"Tell me when you do," she whispered.

"Annabear?" She stared at me. "How long do you think you'll stay a virgin?"

"I don't know, it's not like I'm counting down the days or anything."

"Do you think you'll tell him soon?"

"I'm trying to work up the courage to tell him." I could tell she had something else on her mind. Her silence was deafening.

"What is it? Tell me."

I could feel her eyes on me when she asked, "You're not The Virgin on MGU Reader, are you?"

My body gave in, and I momentarily sank in the water. *Amanda knows.* I thought of every excuse I could give her while floating back up. My legs barely kept me afloat.

She was shaking her head like it was nothing. "There's no way it's you. You don't do that kind of stuff."

"It seems so stupid now." She swam around me, not looking at me, mostly talking to herself. "I thought for a second she was like I don't know...the confident, *badass*, version of you or something...it was so ridiculous of me to think that," she laughed, "like seriously, she's nothing like you."

You must tell her now. I had no reason to keep this from her. Amanda was the one person who wouldn't judge me, the only person I knew wouldn't care. All I had to do was tell her how I felt that night at the party, how alone and sad I was. Tell her it was a mistake. I just had to tell her everything and go back to campus on a clean slate before everything blew up in my face. My grades were already suffering.

"Amanda," I said when she finally looked at me, "there's something I want to tell you."

"Honestly," she continued talking to me, but mostly to herself again. "I find that poster so weird and judgmental. She thinks she's special because she's a virgin and she should get a pat on the back or something. Look at you, you're a virgin and no one knows except me, and a few other people and you couldn't care less.

"I can't believe her posts are so popular. What's so special about boasting over the fact that you're a virgin? It's totally dumb!"

Her words left me stunned.

When I could finally find my voice again, I asked her. "You think she does it to boast?"

"Only a person craving attention would go on an anonymous platform telling people about their virginity. Like, at least give us something fun to talk about."

"Ladies!" One of the spa workers interrupted us. "Pool's closing in five."

Amanda swam out of the water. "Let's get out of here."

Twelve

"OKAY," mom said. "We're done with breakfast." She looked through her phone. "First thing first is our massages then our facials."

Amanda poured herself coffee from the pitcher on our breakfast table. "I slept like a baby last night, my skin's going to be flawless after this."

I'm glad one of us did. I tossed and turned all night, replaying her words in my mind. If one thing was clear, she could never find out I was The Virgin, which meant another thing, I had to stop posting.

"What movies do you want to watch afterwards?" Lucy asked us.

"My pick's a romance," Amanda said.

"I'm up for anything," I said.

"Jacob sent me a pic last night." Amanda drank her coffee. "Dad let him have friends over while you were out of town?"

I immediately looked up. "Since when? I thought that only happened after our freshman year of high school?"

Amanda looked at me, "exactly." She looked at Lucy. "Last time I checked, my younger brother's in sixth grade."

Lucy looked uncomfortable. I noticed mom was now hyper-focused on her empty plate.

Amanda chuckled to herself. "Knowing dad, he's probably having them eat and do whatever they want while he goes off to play golf with his buddies."

"But when it was me," Amanda went on. "I never heard the end of it, and I had to beg to have friends over."

"That didn't stop you from having them over, did it?" Lucy asked.

"Yeah, but it's still not fair." Amanda smirked. "I'm just saying, I would be grounded for weeks if I had friends over and you weren't home, even if it was dad's idea."

Lucy looked at Amanda, "enough." Amanda and I exchanged a look. It wasn't like Lucy not to take a joke or banter back and forth with Amanda.

"Fine," Amanda said sarcastically. "Sorry I asked, don't bite my head off."

"Finish your cup, Ace," Lucy simply said to her.

Mom looked at us with a forced smile. "We don't want to be late."

* * *

I grabbed a can of soda out of the vending machine before walking back into the spa room. The group massages were silent and my first round of facials with just me and mom wasn't any better. Halfway through, she'd walked out to take a phone call.

"Where did you go?" she asked.

"I needed a drink," I said, looking around. "Where are the estheticians?"

"I told them to give us a moment."

I knew this was it. What mom scheduled for us to talk about. The reason for this weekend altogether. Lucy probably came for moral support.

"Your guidance counselor called me."

I slowly walked over to my massage pad and sat down.

"You're failing your classes, sweetie? Since when do you fail your classes?"

"We worked out a plan for me to get my grades back up." I avoided looking at her. I couldn't stand to see her disappointed in me. "I have it under control, mom."

"Do you?" She raised her eyebrows. "Is dating Kevin you having it under control?"

That stung. "He's actually been helping me."

"You have an F," she lowered her voice, "you're better than this."

For a second, we just sat there, more aware that dad was gone.

"I'm fine. I'll figure something out."

Another few seconds passed.

"There's something else I wanted to talk to you about, Annabelle," mom's voice was low, filled with immense sadness. Unrecognizable, even through all the changes.

Then it hit me. This retreat wasn't scheduled after my meeting with Dr. Gatz, it was scheduled before.

"I'm going to sell the house sweetie."

I picked up a piece of thread hanging off the mat and flicked it to the floor. "You said I could think this over."

"I know, but I spoke with grandma some more," she hesitated, then looked at me. "It's the best for us."

"For us or for you mom?" I asked miserably.

"For us."

"Does Lucy know?"

"What does this have to do with what I just told you?"

I couldn't let her finish. "Why don't you come to me anymore?"

"I come to you."

"Not like before, not since dad got sick. All you do is go to Lucy." I watched her, frozen, not knowing what to say next.

"I miss him too, mom. *I* need you," I said.

"Oh sweetie," she immediately got up and walked over to my mat and grabbed my hands. "This move is for us. You may not see it now, but you will one day. That's why I'm going to sell the house sooner than expected."

She reached over, wiped my tears, and went right back to her planning. "The realtor thinks I can get a good sell on it...you and I can have a fresh start in Florida...by Christmas if we're lucky. When you graduate from MGU, you'll get to go wherever you want. You won't have to come back to Blakely and be reminded of everything that we went through with your dad there."

She sounded so final, having already crafted me in her plan. But I was still stuck on what she'd first said.

"A realtor?" I could barely let the words out. "What about thinking this over and discussing it once I came home?"

"I'm home all day sweetie," she said. "Lucy and I agreed on this, we'll spend Thanksgiving day with the Coopers, and organize the house."

I rose to my feet.

"Are you hearing yourself mom? You brought me to this retreat to tell me you want to spend our first Thanksgiving without dad organizing our house for sale? Is that supposed to make me feel better?"

"I'm your mother and I'm concerned about you," she said. "You may not see or get it now, but this is the best for both of us. I promise you one day you'll thank me for it."

"I seriously doubt it."

"Annabelle Lucille Wilson!"

I could probably count on one hand how often mom called me by my full name.

"How could you possibly expect me to be okay with this?" I paused. "Unless you don't care?"

"Of course I care! You're the person I care most about in the entire world."

"I highly doubt it."

"How could you even say that?"

I flung my arms in the air. "Geez, I don't know mom. Maybe it's the fact that since we got here, you haven't spent an hour away from your phone or that only Lucy cared to ask me about Kevin or the fact that I told you, I begged you not to let me come to school and you didn't care, because it didn't fit your laid out plan for me."

I stopped, tears streaming down my face. "Or the fact that you don't seem to have any idea how painful it is for me to be here without dad to call or talk to!"

She walked over to me and held me. "Sweetie, I love you more than anything and so did your father, but you have your whole life ahead of you."

"Selling the house is for the both of us, we have to move on." Her voice broke. "Plus, your dad would have never been okay with you skipping a year of school."

I pulled away. "Before or after you took him away from his family?"

She stood there, unmoved. There was an uncanny stillness between us. I knew I couldn't take back those words.

"Sweetie, you'll get your grades up." She crossed her arms. "And when you come home, we'll move forward on selling the house."

* * *

Lucy opened the door connecting our hotel rooms that next morning. Amanda and I both looked up at the same time.

"We can give you your space, Aces, but please remember how much we love you." As Lucy said this, mom walked through the door. I looked away. Amanda and I had canceled all activities for the rest of the day with our moms.

"Jordan's agreed to give you a ride back to campus," Lucy said to us. Amanda grabbed her pillow and screamed into it.

"You wanted your space so we're giving it to you," Lucy said. She looked at me again. "Know that we love you regardless."

As much as I hated the thought of seeing him, I didn't even care. The last thing I wanted to do was talk to mom.

"Whatever," I got out of bed. "I'll go get ready."

Minutes later, we were saying our goodbyes.

Mom placed her hand on my cheek. "I love you."

"I can't do this right now." I stepped into the backseat to a waiting Jordan and Amanda in the front.

"Text us when you're safely back on campus," Lucy said. "See you at Thanksgiving."

When we had driven further away from the spa, Amanda turned to Jordan.

"The heck is going on with mom and dad?"

"Watch your tone."

"No, what's going on with them?"

"Do you ever realize that the world doesn't revolve around you or is that impossible for you?"

"Actually it does, Jordan, so just answer the question."

He shook his head. "You're so freaking selfish, all you think about is yourself."

"Who else am I supposed to think about? You?" She reclined her seat. "Sorry about the fair if that's what you're looking for."

He looked at her amazed. "You think I still give a crap about the fair? It's your life, suit yourself. Drink it away if you want."

"Ruin it for all I care," he added.

"Totally!"

"Will you two just stop?" I asked them. "Just stop fighting!"

They both didn't say anything. Jordan shifted in his seat. He caught my stare in the mirror then looked away.

Amanda cleared her throat and looked back at me. "You'll have time to make up your grades, Annabelle, and we can still talk your mom out of selling the house."

"Thanks, I really hope so."

We stayed quiet for the rest of the ride. When we arrived back on campus, Jordan barely let us get out of his jeep before driving off.

"The way I can't stand him," Amanda said when we were back in her dorm.

"I'm going to call it a day and stay in," I said to her, feeling defeated.

"You sure?" she asked then gave me a hug. "Come to Warren's if you get lonely."

"Thank you, love you." I grabbed my stuff and walked to my dorm.

The retreat had gone about as horribly as it could have gone. I should have known by the urgency of it that it was only planned to give bad news. I should have seen it coming, but I hated that I could see it now. That rare moment. The one that snuck up on you unlike the others. That awful fourth moment when you could predict the future.

"Hello?"

"Why are you calling me?" I asked him when he didn't answer.

"Hey," he said. "Amanda mentioned something about your classes in the car. I wanted to check, are you doing okay in them?"

"That's not why you called."

It was inevitable. Only a matter of time when the scenarios had to stop. When you had to stand on your own two feet and follow your own path.

"That's not why you called, Jordan." I took a deep breath. "You called because you don't want me to forget you. One minute you're checking up on me and the next you act like I don't exist. You act like you don't care then you act like you do. You tell me you love me then you change your mind. I'm tired of your whiplash. I'm tired of you watching me leave then trying to reel me back in. I'm so sick and tired of our families making this year worse than it already is."

"Annabelle, what –"

That moment when you just knew. It was only a matter of

time when the world closing in on you started to change you forever.

"Please stop contacting me, Jordan. *Please,* let me go."

The last shriveled threads of perfect, finally ripped.

"Oh, in case you forgot, I'm dating your best-friend."

Part 2

Thirteen

THE MORNING DAD PASSED AWAY, mom and I rushed to the hospital with him. I sat in the waiting room, flipping through a bunch of how-to guides. *How To Heal When Your Loved One Dies, How to Move on After a Death, How to Not Be Depressed When You Lose a Loved One.* And my personal favorite, *How to Remember Them.* I was surprised when I didn't feel sad like the guides said I would, the sadness came much later. What I first felt was fear. The fear of knowing that one parent was gone and now, another could be too. I watched the nurses frantically move around me, occasionally stopping to hand me something, then briskly running away again. It was written all over their faces, they dreaded having to tell me.

I found out that when people were happy to see you and had good news to share, it showed in their posture. It was the way they turned towards you, never in a hurry to leave. It was the way they fixed their eyes on you, never looking elsewhere. My first time going to the *Daughters in Waiting* group with Jaz, it seemed, everyone was happy to see me.

"Hi!" A girl around my height walked up to me. She had long twists and a birthmark on her neck. "I'm almost positive you're in my college."

"Liberal Arts?" I asked her, not recognizing who she was.

"That's it! You're in one of our classes," she said after I told her my schedule.

"Don't mind my sister," another girl approached us, "she's always excited to see new faces here."

She had an uncanny resemblance to the first girl except she was slightly taller and didn't have the birthmark.

"I'm Roxy Ngono, this is my sister, Rachel." She hugged me like her sister did.

"How did you hear about us?" Rachel asked.

I looked at Jaz who was already inside of the library room we were having the meeting in. "My roommate told me."

I looked between the two of them, "I'm sorry, but are you?"

"Twins?" Roxy finished my question.

"We are," they said in unison.

Rachel smiled. "We get that all the time."

"If you're also wondering," Roxy went on, "the last name's West African."

"That's cool," I responded.

"We're sophomores in your college," Rachel said. "This is our second year in this group, what year are you?"

"I'm a freshman, nice to meet you."

"Annabelle!?!" My resident supervisor, Kacie, approached us. "I didn't know you were thinking of joining this group?" She gave me my third hug of the day. Kacie was always busy, and I rarely saw her outside of our mandatory dorm meetings.

She leaned in close to my ear and whispered. "Did you see the flier for our group in your orientation bag?" She looked at the twins. "I always have to sneak those in since the school won't allow me to include them."

She smiled at me. "It works, we get the occasional new faces. Come on, we start in two minutes."

"She's awesome," Rachel said to me as we walked in. "She's always on fire for God."

I was prepared for neon pink or something close to the flier advertising their group that Jaz had shown me. Instead, the room had large and unassuming white walls. I looked at the four rectangular white conference tables that created what looked to be a circle so that everyone in the room could see each other. I couldn't count more than twenty of us there.

"We can grab those seats," Roxy pointed to the three chairs next to Jaz, so I followed them. I sat between Jaz and the twins.

Kacie spoke up first. "Welcome to another week of our bible study slash hangout slash debate session." Everyone started to clap.

I shifted in my seat.

"There are some new faces this week so I'm going to give a quick introduction and we'll get started. I'm Kacie Miller, senior and president of the Students for Christianity club on campus, SFC for short. I created our Daughters in Waiting group within SFC my freshman year, because I wanted girls like me to have a safe place to talk about dating on campus or our overall college journeys."

Kacie spoke a mile a minute like she couldn't afford to lose what she wanted to say.

"It grew from dating to every topic imaginable but dating primarily. We discuss dating, love, and relationships on the even weeks, and we choose random topics on the odd ones. This is our safe space, and we have zero tolerance for disrespect, everyone here's free to express themselves as long as they do it out of love. The only requirement I have is that we all enter these discussions with an open heart.

"I'm your girl if you need more information regarding SFC or any other Christian group on campus! We have a new student joining us today, Annabelle, would you mind introducing yourself?"

I felt my stomach clench.

"Hi, I'm Annabelle, I'm a freshman." I looked at Jaz next to me. "I was looking for a new club to join so umm, I thought I would try this one."

Kacie smiled, "We're happy to have you here." She looked around the room. "Annabelle's on one of the floors I supervise." A few heads nodded and smiled at me. Some welcomed me into the group.

"Alright, let's get started!" Kacie said.

"You can share mine," Rachel slid her bible closer to me.

I sat there unsure then quickly said, "thank you."

"We're going to continue with the book of Ruth this week," Kacie said. "The theme is...drumroll please..."

I looked at the girls beating on their seats and chairs to make the drumroll sounds, wondering how anyone could possibly be this excited right now. But then I remembered her only requirement for joining the group.

"Friendship!" Kacie said.

"Who wants to pray for us before we start?" Kacie asked the group and a student on my right offered to. I watched them bow their heads.

I knew Amanda was probably right, it was unlikely I'd come to know my dad better through this group or SFC. Still though, it didn't hurt to try. This was the one adventure I could go on with him that no one else had a say in but me.

One by one, I watched them read out of their books and heard them discuss what they'd just read. It felt like a whole new world, completely different than what I had ever experienced.

"What else do you think about their friendship?" Kacie asked, bringing my attention back to the topic.

Someone to my left responded first. "What stands out to me is their devotion to God, their mutual love for him kept them together."

"I love how close Ruth was to Naomi," Rachel said. She looked at Roxy. "I'm so grateful I have a twin I would do anything for."

"They both contributed to their friendship instead of just taking from it," another girl said.

The girl next to her looked at her, "Ruth literally sacrificed her future to be with Naomi when Naomi needed her the most and God blessed them both in the end. That's so poetic."

"Is it even a sacrifice though? She got her Boaz," another girl said. They all laughed at that one.

Jaz whispered to me. "Boaz is supposed to be like a modern day billionaire."

"Oh." I simply said.

Kacie looked at everyone. "How do you guys think we should apply what we see in their friendship with the ones we're forming here?"

I wasn't exactly sure what to make of her question, but I thought of mom's friendship with Lucy or even my own with Amanda. *I can't imagine anything tearing us apart.*

Roxy spoke up. "When we go through hard times, we're meant to lean on each other and actually help each other."

"Did anyone consider that maybe we should branch out more with our friends?" A girl across from me asked. "Ruth and Naomi were not alike at all...I think I should try harder with the friends I make here, all my friends look like me."

"That's a great point," Kacie said and continued the conversation.

"Sooooo," Jaz stopped me as soon as we walked out of the library. "How did you like it?"

I wasn't sure how to tell her it wasn't terrible, but it's not like I enjoyed it either.

"I don't know," I said, "everyone's really nice."

"That's a start." She started walking again. "Will you come back? Sunday evening isn't the most ideal time to meet, but it works with everyone's schedule."

"I see." I could already hear Amanda. *Totally social suicide.*

I simply shrugged. "I don't have another club right now, Sunday works."

She smiled. "Good."

* * *

"Hey you," Kevin grabbed me outside of CompLit48. I held him a little longer.

"I've missed you," I said. His whole face lit up.

I tightened my arms around him, "I'm sorry I haven't been in the best of moods." He was at an away game the past weekend, and I couldn't see him before he left.

"That's alright." He grabbed my messenger bag and walked me towards the exit. "I'm thinking, lunch or dinner to cheer you up a bit?"

He flashed his breathtaking smile. "Scratch that, let's make it where they only serve dessert."

So far, our relationship was electric, and Kevin did nothing but continue to surprise me. This was what I always wanted, someone who wasn't subtle with showing he cared, who didn't want to hide that he cared.

I leaned forward and kissed him. "I'm thinking, it's only a good idea if it cheers you up too. Do you have a suggestion?"

"There's a frozen yogurt place downtown we can check out," he said. "I haven't been yet."

He grabbed me again and planted another kiss on my lips.

I reluctantly pulled away and looked towards the door. "If we don't walk out now, I'm going to be late for my next class."

"We don't want that," he smiled and kissed me again. When we pulled away from each other, Ben was rapidly approaching us.

"Sup?" Kevin asked Ben when he stopped in front of us.

"Hey man," Ben said to Kevin. He looked at me. "Do you mind if I speak to you?"

"Sure," I said to Ben. I looked at Kevin, "see you later?" Kevin leaned down and kissed me again.

"Call you later," he said before walking out.

Ben stared at me. "You're required to do tutoring for Comp."
I know.

"Come to my office hours anytime today, I have something to run by you."

"Sure, can I stop by after my classes end? Around six-thirty?"

"Works for me," he said.

* * *

"Hey!" I sat down next to Amanda and Halle at GRUB while they ate their dinner. "I can't stay long, I told my TA I'd come to his office hours now."

"What for?" Halle asked me.

"He wants to talk about tutoring."

"Totally don't envy you, but they would be stupid to fail you," Amanda said.

"It's not them, it's me." I stopped my alarm before it had the chance to ring. "I'm just happy they're giving me another chance."

She stared at me. "You still haven't told us how that club meeting went."

I grabbed a potato chip from her plate, "some other time." I stood back up, "wish me luck?"

Amanda was now profusely typing away on her phone.

"Who is it?" Halle asked her.

She looked up. "I'm texting my mom. I asked her again what's going on with her and my dad and she dodged my question."

Hearing this, I had no idea what to say. Mom and I hadn't spoken since the spa besides a text she sent to tell me she loved me.

Amanda looked at Halle. "My parents and Jordan do that all the time. They hide things from me and think I'm too stupid to find out."

"They don't think that of you," I replied.

Halle narrowed her eyes. "Parents always do that."

"I should go, Ben's waiting on me," I squeezed Amanda's shoulder and walked away from them.

* * *

"Make yourself comfortable," Ben said.

He was wearing his glasses again. "I just have to finish this quickly..."

He looked up from his desk when I sat down. "I'm finishing up some work."

He hit a key on his keyboard. "Done."

I now had his full undivided attention. I looked down at my hands.

"Professor Lee placed you in his *'danger to be placed on academic hold'* list," he paused. "Yep, that's a thing."

He got up. "It's the list no student should be on, much less you." He walked over to one of the bookshelves against the wall and sat on the floor. "Join me."

I thought he was joking at first, but when Ben moved his eyes from me to the floor, I realized he wasn't. I slowly stood up and sat down across from him. My back leaning on the opposite bookshelf.

"Now that we're on the same page, how does someone who loves to read as much as I do," he inched up a brow, "which I didn't think possible, be failing a reading class? One of the classes required for your major?"

I just stared at him. "Is this a trick question?"

"No. I'm genuinely curious."

"I have a lot on my mind, I haven't been studying as much."

"I don't believe that."

I looked at him. "What?"

"I don't believe your excuse."

"It's true," I said, flustered.

"We both know it's not," he said, "not the full version anyways."

I struggled to think of what to say next.

"I don't believe you because you're someone who cares a lot." He said, "I know you care, because you spent days thinking about that stupid game. There's no way you cared that much and don't care about your grades."

He was watching me, really wanting to know. "I offered to tutor you."

"You did?" *Why?*

"Yes," he stared at me. "I'm almost positive if you go to those group tutoring sessions, it won't work out well. You technically only have one month to fix your grades before break. One-on-one tutoring is perfect."

"Don't they have that at the tutoring center?" I asked. I looked into it last week to see my options.

"They do, but it won't be anyone from the actual class, much less me."

I wasn't sure what to say to this.

"Why are you doing this?" I asked him after a moment.

"I'm your TA," he said. *Of course. It was his role.* I suddenly felt bad for not checking with him sooner.

He tilted his head. "When I found out you were on the list, I requested to tutor you. Students on the list never make it out of the list and I believe I can get you out of it."

"My reputation's on the line," he added.

"That's...nice of you." I said, still confused. "Thank you."

"No need to thank me. It's too late to get an A but with my help, you'll pass this class with a B-."

Even with him saying it, there was a part of me that didn't believe I could pass the class. One of the reasons I had yet to register for tutoring. I also had to figure out a way to break the news to mom, somehow.

"What if I don't?" I asked him.

"I know you will," he said.

"If I'm wrong and you don't pass," he looked around the office. "You can have any one of my vintage slipcases." He looked at me. "I never share those."

I glanced at the shelf behind him. "I can't take any of this."

"Then pass."

We stared at each other. I was waiting for a gotcha moment, but I knew he wasn't a jokester. He was serious.

"Deal?" He asked.

I thought of Amanda's advice. *Don't think, just go.* Oh well, I guess here goes nothing.

"Deal."

"Meet me here at this hour every Monday and Wednesday until your final exams. I'm positive you'll pass all your classes, not just CompLit48."

"You didn't say any of my other classes before!"

"I'm saying all of your classes now, are you in?"

I felt him stare at me as I contemplated everything he'd just said. There was only a month and a half left of the semester. What did I have to lose? I needed all the help I could get.

I let out a sigh. "I'm in."

Fourteen

"HE WASN'T THRILLED," I told Amanda while we poured toppings on our frozen yogurts. Kevin and I's date switched to a double-date when Amanda quickly reminded me that she had yet to approve of Kevin, officially. It was our golden rule after all.

"Why would he be?" she asked me. I looked back at the guys sitting down, who had just gotten their toppings. *I don't do dates*, Warren said to her. Yet, he was here.

"He doesn't think it's necessary and offered to tutor me himself."

"I would take that offer in a heartbeat."

I poured more chocolate syrup. "He's not in any of my classes. I need to put my head down and pass." I handed her the syrup. "It looks like I actually might now."

"He's just supporting you," she said, "but guys are territorial, he doesn't like the idea of another guy spending time with his girlfriend."

"It's tutoring."

"It's never just tutoring."

I shook my head. "Ben isn't like that."

She looked at me, "and you know that, how?"

"I don't know, I just do," I looked back at the guys. "I like Kevin, he has nothing to worry about."

"He has my vote for best boyfriend you've ever had," Amanda joked. "No, but seriously, I like him. He's a junior and he hangs out with us and he really likes you."

"I really like him too."

She stopped, mid-dipping her sprinkles. "Does this mean what I think it means?"

"Not yet...not soon...I don't think..." I inched closer to her, reached her ears, before whispering, "I'm just waiting on the boom."

Her voice was a low shriek. "When you're ready, I better be the first person you call."

"Like always."

"Yo, you girls coming back to the table or what?" Warren asked.

"Relax," Amanda said to him when we walked over.

Warren looked at her, "I was telling him about the VIP seats for the rivals game coming up." MGU took its football games very seriously. Greenspring was about to double in size, welcoming twice the student population.

Kevin placed his arm around my chair and looked at me, "I told him I can't make it."

"Soccer team's doing their thing later that night," he looked at Amanda. "The invite's to all of you."

I took a bite of my yogurt. I thought a lot about it, but I was still trying to come up with a good excuse not to go. It didn't help that this was the first and only party they were hosting.

"Over my dead body," Amanda said flatly.

He stared at her. "Are you ever cool with Jordan?"

"No and I'm fine with that," Amanda looked at me, "you're still coming to the VIP suite though, right?"

Warren nodded at me. "This girl hates parties, the first time..." Amanda kicked him under the table.

Warren looked at Kevin, who was busy taking a bite of my yogurt. "She ran out so fast after that game when..."

Amanda kicked Warren again.

"Kevin!" Amanda said.

He looked up at her, "yes?"

"I'll come," she said. "Annabelle would love to have me there."

She gave him her Cooper smile, "and Halle." She looked at Warren, "you and Gabe too." Warren just shook his head and checked his phone, oblivious to the damage he could have caused. The last thing I wanted was Kevin to find out I was a virgin like this.

Kevin placed his arm around me then took another scoop of my yogurt. "This is really good."

* * *

"Welcome back!" Kacie greeted us when Jaz and I walked into the Daughters in Waiting meeting. We grabbed our seats next to the twins.

"Are you doing Worship Night with us?" Roxy asked.

Rachel leaned over her sister to speak to me. "We do it to kick-off rival's weekend."

"I haven't heard of it," I said. Unlike last time, a couple more students were in the room with us.

"It's this coming Thursday," Rachel said. "We meet up on Old Green Lawn overlooking campus and flash our candlelights."

Her sister chimed in. "We worship for an hour and bless the campus before the weekend starts."

"It starts at 11 PM and goes until midnight," Rachel said.

I recognized this well, being best-friends with Amanda. They were in clear persuasion mode.

"The due date to sign-up is tonight if you want to join us," Roxy said. "Kacie likes to keep a count of who's coming to know how many candlelights to provide."

"Thank you," I looked at the three of them. "I'll think about it."

"You should come," Rachel smiled at me. "We'd love to hang out with you outside of here."

Kacie finally spoke. A change of direction.

"We're going to pick up from last week in the book of Ruth, but we're back on an even week so our dating topic for today is..."

Like last time, they all beat their seats and tables to create the drumroll.

"Waiting on God for love or taking initiative ourselves!"

"I love this topic already," Jaz said just as Roxy placed her bible next to me.

Minutes later, the girls were in a passionate discussion.

"We're supposed to wait," a freshman spoke up. "We're told men are supposed to lead, I think it's ridiculous to pursue a guy."

I watched back and forth as they shared their opinions, one after the other, without missing a beat.

"We're not supposed to just sit back and do nothing, that's unrealistic. We need to let guys know we're interested, they're not mind readers."

"Faith without deeds is dead, there's no way God wants us to just sit around and wait."

"Doesn't it depend on each of us?" Roxy spoke up. "Ruth had to go out and somewhat pursue Boaz but then Rebecca didn't really have to seek it."

"So Ruth took initiative, but Isaac and Rebecca waited?"

"Something like that," Roxy said.

"I think we should pray to see what God wants us to do," a girl on my right said, "maybe some of us are supposed to take initiative like Ruth and others are meant to wait."

"Guys," another girl looked annoyed, "in all those examples, they still had to take some form of initiative. You can't just wait around for love, that's unrealistic, especially in college."

"I think you can," another girl disagreed.

"It doesn't matter what God asks someone else to do,"

another student spoke up. "He doesn't work the same in our lives. My mom pursued my dad and they've been happily married since. She made it known she was into him, and he asked her out and the rest is history because I'm here."

Kacie looked at me, "Annabelle, what do you think?"

In the past, it would have been easier in this moment to just disappear. To close my eyes and go somewhere else. But they were all watching me. I felt a nervous tug in my stomach.

"I don't know." I looked down. "I'm not..."

"That's okay." Kacie smiled at me. "In your life, what has worked for you? Waiting in general or pursuing?"

"Umm," I started with shaky breaths. "I've always waited." I looked at Kacie. "I don't know if that's necessarily a good or bad thing."

I glanced around the room and took another deep breath. "I just...I've always thought it best to wait on love."

"I like being pursued, it shows that they really want you," another girl said.

"Does it though?" The next girl commented. "Some people pretend like they want something with you when they genuinely don't, waiting doesn't guarantee anything."

"I think courting does."

"Explain what that is for those who don't know in the room," Kacie said.

"It's not exactly biblical," the girl who brought it up looked at me. "But courting is something we do when we want to date someone intentionally towards marriage."

"Thank you for explaining," I said in a low voice.

"I've heard horror stories," another student chimed in. "People are so quick to say, God told me you're my spouse." A few girls started to laugh.

"It works well when it's done well," someone else chimed in. "It sets a good foundation for love and marriage. It helps us wait well, two of my cousins got married after courtship."

Another girl shrugged. "Waiting takes the pressure off. I know if a guy's not trying to court me, he's not really interested, but I always make sure to give signals so he at least knows that I'm interested."

The girl next to her nodded. "It's simple, we take initiative when it makes sense and wait on God to confirm if they're the one."

"Or we give hints and let the guy pursue us and wait on God to confirm that this is a relationship he approves of," a student on my left said.

"We're not helpless here," someone else spoke up. "I'm taking initiative."

I closed my eyes and let out a huge sigh of relief. My heart was finally going back to a normal pace.

* * *

"Go ahead, I'm going to call my mom," I told Jaz when we were back in Wolf. I stood in the lounge, waiting for her to be out of sight.

As soon as the phone rang, mom picked up.

"Hi sweetie," she said. Her voice was a tiny whisper, but it still drowned out everything else in that moment. I could picture her right away. It was 8:05 PM on a Sunday so she was at the kitchen table, done with leftovers, and catching up on the news.

"I wanted to say that I'm sorry," I began, "I'm sorry for what I said at the spa."

I bit back my tears. "I miss you, mom."

"I miss you too," she said. "I wanted to respect you for needing your space." I felt a deep pang in my throat. She was the only parent I had left.

"I'm sorry about everything," I said.

"I'm sorry for how things ended with us at the spa," she let out.

"Mom?"

"Yes?"

I didn't say anything at first. I could hear it in her voice, she wanted me to be okay with her selling the house, but I wasn't. I simply didn't want us to fight.

"I'm here." I said. "I'm always here if you want to talk about dad, about anything. I'm here if you need me." I paused. "I love you."

"I love you too, Annabelle," she said. For a moment, a tiny moment, I could hear her sniffling. "Say hi to Kevin for me."

I held the phone against my ears, taking in her words. I knew that was her way of trying to be there for me as well.

"I will."

After our call, I stayed in the lobby for a little while longer before deciding to go back to my dorm.

"Please hold it!" I called out to the three girls that had just walked into the elevators.

The first girl smiled at me and held the elevator open. I stepped in with them and grabbed my phone to text back Kevin.

> Annabelle: almost back at the dorm

> Kevin: okay, calling in a few

I was so busy looking at my phone that it took me a minute to realize what they were talking about.

"The Virgin's posts were so fun to read," one of the girls said. I pretended to scroll through my phone.

"I wonder where she went," girl 2 said, "I read her comment section all the time now before I go on a date."

"There are so many cool dating gems on there," girl 3 said.

"I sent her posts to one of my friends, she's thinking of creating something like that at her college," girl 2 said.

The elevator stopped on the third floor.

Girl 3 smiled at me, "take care." She walked out with her friends.

Even though my posts were still trending despite me not writing anything in a while, I hadn't heard anyone in public talk about them besides Amanda, Halle, and Jaz. Maybe I was doing the wrong thing by not posting altogether – one more post couldn't hurt.

* * *

Dear MGU Reader:
My fellow classmates
Ladies and gentlemen

Missed me? Don't be shy, tell me if you did.
I've sure missed you. I took a small break, much needed of course, but I'm happy to be back. A quick update shall do.

I'm in a relationship. I know…I know…crazy when you think how my semester started. In case you're wondering, I'm still a virgin. I haven't had *that* conversation yet. Cheers to finally attempting to.

Kisses
…Or should I say hugs…
The Virgin

Annonnnn: YAYYY!! You're back.
FuntimeSunTime: we've missed u
SweeetMaggnolia77: dating sucks for me but I'm not focused on that.
Lacie_Sm: site was boring without u
MGUGal: Glad to hear you're still a virgin,
I was beginning to think you lost it
Henrietta20: welcome back :)
Massachussettsbae: so happy to see you posting again
killerbees54: The semester wouldn't be the same if you didn't come back
ComputerGeek4!: I'm also in a relationship now :)
SameOldSameOld: ^^

M_G_UVirgin: Let us know once you tell him!!

* * *

"There you are," Ben said. He told me after class to meet him in our CompLit48 classroom instead of his office. Aside from another student I passed by in the hall, no one else was there when I made my way into the auditorium.

He got up from the front row and walked over to me.

I looked around. "Are we not studying?"

"We are."

"In here?"

"Yep." He tossed the red stress ball he was holding in one hand. It went up to the ceiling and when it came back down, he caught it with his other hand.

"Do you know what the secret to tutoring is?" he asked. I shook my head no.

"It's building trust and reducing fear," he then threw the ball for me to catch. It was almost like he knew I would catch it, because he walked back to sit in the front row without waiting for me to.

"So, Annabelle, what's your favorite book?"

"I have too many to pick one."

He smiled and lifted his hands for me to throw the ball back at him. "Your turn."

"To do what?"

"Ask me a question."

I held the ball in my hand for a minute too long, deciding if I made the right choice to come here or even agreeing to tutoring with him. But instead of letting myself fall back into a whirlwind in my head, I asked him the next question.

"Why do you want to be a teacher?"

"I've tutored my younger brother and other people for a while now, it made sense for me."

"Do you enjoy it?"

"Not your turn." He threw the ball back at me. "It's mine."

I stood there for a second then went to sit down, two seats away from him.

"Why do you hate small talk?"

"What do you mean by that?" I asked him.

"That's not technically a response," he said, "but since it's your first time and you asked, I'll cut you some slack."

I held my breath.

"I overheard your friend mentioning it at the party after you left."

I sighed. "I make small talk."

"You didn't answer my question," he said.

"Do I have to?"

He was silent for a bit, observing me, then finally said, "no."

For a long while, or what felt like a long while, we were both quiet.

"It's kind of a long answer," I said.

"Try me," he looked directly at me. "I always have time for honesty."

It was as apparent as the night I first met him; he wasn't one to mince his words or even care to.

"Umm, I don't hate small talk...I used to not mind them,"

I took in a breath. "We used to go on a ton of hospital visits before my dad passed away. Most people wanted to get updates on how he was doing so they would start by asking us anything and everything they could think of on the spot. What they really wanted to know was how his hospital visits were going. Eventually when we were talking, they'd just get to the point."

"I started wanting people to just get to the point...not for everything...just that, I guess." I looked at him, "that's also why I hate parties, a little."

He simply looked at me. "My condolences." He lifted his hand, surprising me. He was ready to move on.

I tossed him the ball. "Let's see..."

I tried to think of something. "What do you want to do when you graduate?"

"Teach." *Right.* He tossed the ball to me. "Was MGU your first choice?"

"It was my only choice," I tossed him back the ball. "Do you live on campus?"

"Nope, I live with my parents."

When it was my turn to answer again, Ben asked me a question related to the class. It happened so swiftly; I didn't even notice his question didn't catch me by surprise. We continued on like that. Us asking each other back and forth questions based on what Professor Lee had been teaching.

"Let's end here," Ben said, getting up. I looked at my phone, shocked to see we had gone over the two-hour limit we'd given ourselves.

Fifteen

THE PROCESS WAS easy for the most part. Flower blooming. I knew each step like I knew the back of my hand. First was getting and planting the seed. Second, germination. Third, roots and stem growth. Then, leaf formation. By the time the stage for floral differentiation occurred, I could already guess what the flower would really look like and how healthy it would be based on the soil mom and I planted the seed in. Because of this, it didn't take me long to know the flower for the person.

Yet here I was. Days after meeting them, sitting next to them in one of my classes, and going to Daughters in Waiting, I still didn't know which flowers the twins were.

"Stop," I said to Jaz who was mid-sentence. *I'm going to Worship Night.*

"I'll go, you've totally convinced me."

She smiled. "We need to do your hair fast then." She rushed over to my dresser to pick a few ribbons. "What time are you meeting Kevin?" She asked while looking through the pile. "You want to stay for the full hour, there's a special at the end."

I walked over and chose a couple of green and white ones. "He has dinner with his teammates tonight so I'm meeting him after."

I looked down at my phone. "Speaking of."

"Hey you," Kevin said when I picked up.

"Check out the playlist I sent you and pick a song you like," he said.

I couldn't describe the sudden feeling of glee I felt. "How come?"

"You'll see."

I gushed then remembered what I wanted to speak to him about. "I'm going to do Worship Night with them after all, what time do you want to meet up?"

"What time is it over?" Kevin asked me. I asked Jaz.

"Around midnight if you don't stick around," Jaz said. "The group's going to the diner afterwards."

"I'll be done a little after midnight," I told Kevin.

"Alright, I'll pick you up after," he said. "Text when you're done."

After we were finished getting ready and putting my hair into two buns, Jaz turned to me. "You two are getting really close."

"Me and Kevin?" I asked her. Somehow, I had gotten used to Jaz's feelings of concern that she was never shy to voice. "Don't you think we should be?"

She shrugged. "It kind of looks like you're rushing it," she stared at me, "even if he's a great guy."

The first thing that popped into my mind was what he'd say to me being a virgin. I was dragging telling him, because it was nothing to me to keep waiting, but to an athlete, I'm sure it was everything. I shook the feeling off.

"I've never been pressured into it, I'm fine." I changed the subject. "Are you dating someone?"

She shook her head. "I have no desire to."

"Check out our outfits!" Amanda barged into my dorm with Halle. I looked at them, both dressed in matching blue shorts, black tights, white shirts, and brown boots. Even matching ponytails.

Halle twirled around. "How do we look?"

"Like showstoppers," I said to her. "What's the juice?"

"The juice is, it's official!" Amanda said. "We're going with Warren's friend as our big." She spun around as well. "She invited us to a party tonight."

I looked at them. "You're in the sorority already?"

"Practically," Amanda said. "But not officially until next semester." She walked over to me. "This hairstyle suits you well."

Halle leaned against my closet. "It's unfortunate you're looking this dolled up for a sing-along."

I rolled my eyes. "It's not a sing-along, it's worship night. I'm meeting Kevin after." Jaz shook her head.

"Amanda explained it to me, and I still don't get it," Halle said. I didn't have the heart to tell her, neither did I, but that wasn't going to stop me from going.

Amanda scoffed. "I don't either." She looked at me. "We'll cut you some slack though, it's not like you understand any of this sorority stuff we're doing."

"You, my friend, have a point," Halle said to Amanda.

Amanda walked over and placed her hands on my cheeks. "And you, my friend, still need to tell me about this club."

"Give me time, are you meeting up with the boys afterwards?"

"Yeah, join us if you can." Amanda said. "Warren likes Kevin."

They both walked towards the door.

"Don't do anything I wouldn't do," Amanda said.

"That doesn't leave her with many options," Halle said.

Amanda blew me a kiss, "toodles!"

* * *

I had no idea it'd be this packed when we got there but if it wasn't for Roxy frantically waving her arms at us on Old Green Lawn, we would have surely missed her. She was standing next to some other girls from our group.

"Where's Rachel?"

"She went to grab our candlelights," Roxy said. She pointed to the edge of the lawn, right on the dividing line between campus and downtown. Almost every inch of the lawn was filled with students and the walkways were lit with MGU's colors. Behind us was Old Green, the oldest house on campus which housed the president and his family.

"Is it always like this?" I asked her and Jaz.

"It's only my second year coming," Roxy said. "But it was like this last year too."

I looked across the lawn, "really cool."

"Grab one!" Rachel met up with us moments later. "I'm so happy you came!"

She handed us our candlelights. "We should move up so we can get a good view."

"Of what?"

Roxy pointed to the edge, "of that." I turned around to see the students clearing away from the edge to make room for Kacie and a couple of students, all holding instruments.

Kacie held up a microphone. "Who's ready for our seventieth annual Worship Night?" The crowd erupted in cheer. I held my candlelight close to my chest.

A guy joined Kacie and grabbed the microphone she was holding.

"Thank you, Kacie, I know we're especially thrilled," he said into the mic.

"That's the school's choir leader," Jaz said to me.

He went on. "Tonight, we're going to worship God and make his presence known all throughout MGU!" Everyone cheered again.

I watched them silently, not sure how to respond to any of it.

Jaz looked at me. "Let me know if you get uncomfortable."

I simply nodded and observed them. Maybe it was because mom was on the back of my mind, but I felt so shaken up. I looked down at my phone. 10:55 PM. Right now, she was already asleep. I looked back up, knowing I couldn't leave. Since dad was a member of SFC, he would have been a part of this.

"We're going to get started in five, four," everyone else joined Kacie in counting down. At one, the choir started to play and my whole body went numb. It was funny how you could be surrounded by a crowd of people and still only want one person next to you. *Everywhere and else.* I could see him picking me up and spinning me around the lawn. Just us two on another big adventure.

"Annabelle, look!" Rachel said. When I looked up, I saw the first firework, then the next, and the one after that. Soon enough, I was letting myself get lost in the moment.

"You can turn your lights on now," Kacie said.

Right away, I looked to the bottom of my candlelight to turn the switch on. It happened quickly so when I glanced back up, I didn't recognize him at first because he was smiling. He looked different than all the other times I saw him. *Less serious*, I thought. I immediately looked away before Ben could notice me.

"Who's ready to chant?" Kacie asked us.

"Green, green," the choir leader lead everyone into a chant.

"Green, green," everyone on the lawn yelled collectively, "the mighty green machine!"

In a second, they made our turtle mascot's name sound cooler than he was. They kept chanting and I kept watching. I had to admit, I was intrigued now, watching them light up all of campus from this very lawn.

Rachel looked at me halfway through, "We're glad you came." She placed her arm around me and so did Roxy. It dawned on me, for the first time in years, since that day I heard, *your dad has cancer,* I truly felt at peace. That's when it hit me.

How could I have missed it?

The Ngono twins were my Lavender.

* * *

"How was it babe?" Kevin pulled me into a tight embrace when I walked into the car he drove in to pick me up.

"I cannot put it into words." I kissed him. "You love music." I kissed him again. "You should have been there, you would have loved it!"

He laughed and started the car, "not that kind of music."

"Seriously." I stared at him. "It was incredible."

His dimpled caved in. "Let's go to my house so you can tell me all about it there."

"No." I quickly said. "Mine's closer, why don't we go there?"

"Really?" He looked confused. "None of my mates are there right now. Doesn't it just make sense to go to mine?" I froze.

"Mine's it is. I have the place to myself."

"Can't believe you haven't been here yet since we started dating," Kevin said when we got there.

I kept moving, ignoring the hole in my stomach while he walked us from the parking lot to his house. The same house he shared with his teammates and the same one he shared with Jordan. It took all of me not to faint. All semester I had avoided coming here. I made it a point to only hang out with him at GRUB, or after a match, or the library, or another public space on campus. Besides that last time in my dorm, we hadn't been in a private or intimate space like this, just us. I couldn't avoid it anymore without looking suspicious.

"What was it called again? Worship something?" Kevin looked at me before placing the key in. "I've never seen you this excited." If only he knew coming here after was blowing up my nerves to an unimaginable level.

He stopped. "I can't believe this is your first time here." For a moment, we just stood there. I had no more excuses left.

"Are you sure your roommates aren't here?" I asked him.

"Positive," he smiled. I was attracted to Kevin, stupidly attracted, but I wasn't ready. Not yet. Especially not here.

I held my breath as he opened the door. The first thing I noticed when we entered was how surprisingly clean and organized everything was. Aside from the posters of the bikini models and athletes, the leftover pizza boxes on the wooden kitchen table, or the oil stain on their gray carpet, the house was nice.

"Surprised?"

I shook my head no. He chuckled.

He grabbed my hand, sending shivers all the way down my spine. He looked to our right. "This is the kitchen."

"Nothing fancy, the standard," he said and opened the door to our left. "First bathroom, girls use this." He stopped himself. "I meant guests use this."

He grabbed my hand again, walking past the living room. He opened the first door facing us, "this is Seth's and our other teammate's." He walked me to the door right next to it, "their bathroom."

He walked me to the next door after that and stopped. My heart was beating exceedingly fast. So fast, it no longer sounded humanly possible.

He opened it with one hand, "This one's mine." He paused. "And Jordan's but he's not here so." His voice trailed off. I could feel him staring at me.

I quickly turned around and walked back to the living room.

"What do you normally watch?"

I heard his loud and exasperated sigh behind me. "A bit of everything." He sat down next to me on the couch, "I don't watch much on the box." He stared at me. "It's hard with my schedule," he scooted closer, "but you know that."

"Now...where were we?" He grabbed the back of my head and brought my face to his then kissed me. He traced his fingers along my torso and almost reached my jeans. I immediately turned to face the TV and his next kiss landed on my cheek.

"Yeah, but what do you normally watch when you can watch TV?" I asked him with heavy breaths. I knew he could sense I was nervous and although he quickly masked it, I saw that he was annoyed.

Kevin rubbed his eyes. "I don't know Annabelle...sports and stuff, mostly soccer. Jordan had a match on but left when I told him you were coming."

"What?" I sat up, "you told me your friends were out."

He shrugged. "Jordan wasn't, I texted him on the way here." He looked at me. "It doesn't matter, he didn't mind leaving."

"I do it for him from time to time," he added. My stomach was in knots.

Kevin looked concerned. "Are you alright?" He grabbed my arm. "Do you want water? Something to drink?"

"No...it's just...you said no one was here and that's why we couldn't go to Wolf Hall."

"One of my mates was here," he stared at me, "don't you want us to have alone time?"

"We do," I said.

Kevin shook his head. "Actually, we don't."

"Guys aren't allowed in your dorm, Annabelle. And you always want us to hang out in public. What's so bad about me bringing you here?" He asked me. A couple of seconds passed by without us saying anything. He leaned back on the couch.

"When do you think you'll be ready?"

"Huh?" I quickly looked at him.

He looked at me then sat back up. "When do you think you'll be ready to take things to the next level? Babe, we've been at this for weeks now and all you do is let me kiss you. You don't think I notice that you rarely ever want to be alone in a room with me? I don't want to push you into anything you don't want to do so when do you think you'll be ready?"

I looked away from him. "Does it bother you?"

"No, just wondering," he looked away, "pretty much every girl I date would have been okay with taking things to the next level by now."

"It hurts to hear you say that," I muttered after a moment.

He grabbed my other hand, "I'm not saying it to hurt you, it's the truth."

I tried not to think about all the girls on campus who would love to be in my shoes. Kevin didn't have to date me, he chose to date me, and I was starting to really like him.

"Come here babe," he scooted closer to me than placed his arm around me. He grabbed one of my ribbons and moved it around his finger. "I don't know what you have or haven't done, but you're nothing like girls I've dated."

"That's what I like about you." He quickly kissed me on the forehead. "I don't mind taking it slow."

"I don't know when I'll be ready Kevin...to take things to the next level with you, I hope I am soon or eventually."

He shrugged. "We don't need to rush it now."

He leaned in and whispered, "anything for you."

Sixteen

Dear MGU Reader:
My fellow classmates
Ladies and gentlemen

You were right. You have my full permission to give me your 'I told
you so'. It's not the easiest thing to tell the boy you're dating you're
a virgin. Between you and me, I don't even want to.

Kisses
...Or should I say hugs...
The Virgin

kennedy: I think guys want to know these things right away
$virgingirl$: I would be so afraid to have this conversation
popcorn&champagne: ^ why?? It shouldn't matter if he likes you
baseballlee: what the heck r u waiting on? any girl i date better
never surprise me like that
sarahlock: i'm trying to stay celibate this semester, y'all have any
other tips?
virgin438: ^ don't be alone with him

Laciekim: ^ hold yourself accountable & find support

11Virgin: I heard your first time isn't magical

kathiia: it's not that big of a deal

Anonym2@: why do I have a feeling you're about to lose it?

chi90: stop expecting it to be amazeballs

Candylloooove: It's not rocket science, if you're alone with them you'll be tempted to every time

mgu30: don't pressure yourself. Don't lose it if you're not ready

fiveminusfive: it's childish as hell to 'wait for someone special' just freaking lose it

RedApples: she keeps putting it on a stupid pedestal

* * *

ACCORDING to Amanda and now Halle, it took effort. My hair had to be just right. My makeup, *close to flawless.* And my outfit? *Don't even think about getting it wrong.* Tonight was the football rival's game and three hours from now, I was meeting Kevin at the soccer house to spend time with Kevin and his friends. *Sadly, Jordan too.* I pushed away the thought.

"That one," I grabbed the red top Amanda handed me in her dorm and with my other hand, her coffee. "Please, I desperately need this, I didn't get any sleep last night."

Halle raised a brow, "good or bad?" I simply shrugged.

"Trouble in paradise already?" she asked. Amanda looked at me.

"I'm just tired," I answered.

"Girls, you know what I was thinking?" Amanda asked us.

She grabbed the coffee back, walked to her fridge, and opened a bottle. "We're hanging out with the boys tonight." She poured herself a drink. "When was the last time we had fun, real fun, just us girls?"

She looked at Halle. "Please don't bring up that awful project you had us do at the start of school."

Halle smirked. "I won't then."

Amanda handed Halle a cup. "I think we're due for a girls' night."

"I'm picking up what you're putting down," Halle said.

Amanda looked at me. "You can bring your new friends from the club."

"Really?"

She shook her head. "Ask them if they're interested."

"Okay, I'll ask them," I said and made a mental note to text Jaz and the twins.

Halle leaned closer to the mirror, applied her lipstick, and looked at Amanda. "What do you have in mind?"

Amanda shrugged. "I'm not sure yet."

I was suddenly conscious that I hadn't introduced Amanda to a new friend in years. I couldn't remember the last time I did. I walked over to her college wardrobe and looked through her sweaters, trying to decide what to wear with my black jeans and red top.

"You're anxious?" Amanda asked, my back facing her.

"For what?" Halle said to us. "Oh, parties."

I turned around. "You two are always liked, it's easy for you to fit in. What if no one there likes me?"

Amanda handed me a cup; I shook my head. "No thanks."

She shrugged. "You have nothing to worry about."

Halle looked at me. "Once you warm up to people, they can't help but like you, you're pretty hard to forget. How is it you still don't know that?"

Amanda stood there, watching the both of us. It's not that Halle didn't give compliments, she did, but this one seemed like a total out-of-body experience coming from her.

"Thank you."

"Don't thank me." She kept her eyes on me. "Just know it."

Amanda cleared her throat. "Here's what *I* know." She said as my alarm rang. "It's time to go."

* * *

"Follow me," Halle led us. "Gabe said they're in suite 10."

I looked around, completely amazed.

Amanda smiled. "Ten times better than the soccer field, right?" I simply nodded. It was no less than triple the size of the soccer stadium and filled to the brim.

Halle turned to Amanda when we reached the VIP floor. "Did you get a hold of Warren? I can't reach Gabe."

Amanda looked at her phone. "He says to just come in." We walked over to the velvet ropes, blocking people from passing unless they had a specific ticket. Amanda scanned ours and we walked over.

"Yo, you're here!" Warren said when he saw us. He admired our outfits first before leaning in to kiss Amanda. "You girls look nice."

"You already know the drill," Warren said to us. "Grab whatever you want." He looked at Halle. "Gabe's around here somewhere."

"I'll go find him," Halle said and walked off. Not that she needed to go far, because you could see everything from where we were standing. Their VIP suite was carpeted and air-conditioned. I had the clearest view of the stadium as if I was standing on the turf myself.

Warren nodded at the seating area on the outside of the room, covered by a railing. "Seats are first come, first serve." He grabbed Amanda again and walked her over to the drinks by the sink and what looked to be a bar area.

"Of all the places I would expect to see you, this is not one of them."

I turned around, pleasantly surprised to see Ben.

"Me either," I looked away. "I got a lot of studying done last night."

He just stood there and placed his hands in his pockets. "I couldn't pass up seeing the rival's game in a private suite."

"I get it, it's gorgeous."

"Have you been to a game before?" he asked.

"We're going to sit down," Amanda interrupted us. She took notice of Ben standing there. "Ben, right? Annabelle's TA!"

I could see Warren grabbing some chips.

Amanda moved closer to Ben, flashed him her Cooper smile. "She totally deserves a good grade, she's like the smartest person I know."

"Excuse us," I quickly pulled her away from him.

"Amanda, I love you, but what are you doing?" I turned around to see Ben, still standing there, still watching us. "He's responsible for my grade."

"That's why I'm putting in a good word for you, he has to give you an A."

"I appreciate it." I looked back at Ben who was now talking to Warren. "But, he's the one doing me a favor and the last thing I want is to jeopardize my grade so can you please not bring up the fact that he's my tutor or that he's tutoring me or that I need tutoring while we're here?"

She smirked. "If you say so..." she stared at me for a little longer then looked at Ben, "interesting."

"What?" I asked her.

She shook her head. "Nothing." She grabbed my hand, and we walked back over.

* * *

"Game's starting again soon," Warren said to us.

The game was almost ending and dare I say, all of us were enjoying ourselves. It also helped that it was mostly the green jerseys crossing the touchdown line. We were so close to winning.

"Was this your first time coming?" Ben asked when we sat back down next to Warren and Amanda.

"Yes," I said. "You?"

"Believe it or not, I've never been before despite being a local."

"That's not that hard to believe."

"Why's that?" he asked.

I thought about it. "You're a bookworm like me."

He looked down at my clutch. "I think your phone's ringing."

I quickly pulled it out. "It is, my mom's calling." *Strange*. It was 9:30 PM on a Saturday. She should be watching something with her girlfriends and Lucy.

I stood up. "I have to take this."

"Say hi to Marie for me," Amanda said from behind me.

"Hi mom," I stepped out of the suite. "It's a little loud in here." I could barely hear her through the stadium announcements, but the halls were emptier now.

"I'm at the game with Amanda, the third quarter is starting soon, is everything okay?"

She raised her voice over the noise on my end. "I need to run something by you!" I heard another voice behind her.

"Is that Lucy?" I asked. "Say hi to her for me."

"She says hi," mom kept going, "how do you feel about spending Thanksgiving at the Coopers this year?"

"We are spending it with them, you told me we were."

"I mean, staying at their place for the week, sweetie."

"Why would we do that?"

"We have a couple buyers interested, at least a few who are ready to purchase if I do another round of upkeep around the house."

"If you're okay with it sweetie, the realtor wants me to do a final showing Thanksgiving weekend to really market the house, I'm thinking Black Friday? I need to let them know it's a yes so we can get moving on hiring the cleaners and do this soon...your thanksgiving break's coming up sooner than we think..." She paused, I could already picture her, penciling everything in the calendar. "There's no way we'll have everything done in time if we don't get a head start now."

I smoothed my hand over my hair, slowly sliding it down my hanging ribbon.

"I still have your room to go through, the basement." She let out a heavy sigh. "Your dad and I's...my room."

"Mom," my voice barely came out, "please let me go through my room."

"What did you say sweetie? I can't hear you too well over all that noise."

I suddenly felt tired, overwhelmed.

I don't know when it happened exactly, I couldn't recall a specific day. But when dad got sick, mom withdrew from being my mom.

"I can't hear you sweetie. Think it over, okay? I love you." Then she hung up.

"You're leaving already?" Amanda looked back at me when I walked into the suite. "We're winning!"

"I know, it's been a long day." I said. "I'm thinking of going back to Wolf before meeting up with Kevin."

"Okay..." Amanda hesitated. "We'll meet up with you at his house then."

"Bye Annabelle," Halle said behind me.

"I can walk out with you," Ben followed me.

"You don't have to do that," I quickly said.

"I don't mind."

He opened the door to the suite. Once we stepped outside of the arena, we heard the touchdown.

* * *

The air was crisp when Ben walked me back to Wolf. We walked in silence for a while. I looked over at him and he looked far away, somewhere else.

"How long have you known Warren?"

My question startled him.

"We're cousins." He looked at me. "Do you always wear the ribbons?"

Without having to say it, we were back to the questions, but I was still reeling in the fact that he was cousins with Warren and Gabe.

"Since I can remember, it's a family tradition." I said, while thinking of what I could ask him next. "What's your favorite place you've traveled to?"

"I haven't, those are all the places I want to travel to and hope to one day." he said. "Teach and travel, that's my dream."

"You've never been to any of those places?" I asked, confused. He had pins on multiple locations on the map behind his office desk. I just assumed they were pins of places he had gone to.

"Not your turn."

"Not my turn," I repeated.

"You're in SFC?" he asked. *He did notice me at Worship Night.*

"I joined one of my roommate's clubs, Daughters in Waiting. Have you heard of that group?"

"I have."

"Did you –"

"It's not your turn." *Right.* He looked at me, "I can make an exception."

"Don't take pity on me."

"Then I won't," he said.

He stared at me. I looked straight ahead.

"In your opinion," he looked at me again, "why do you think CompLit is looked at through multiple narratives at the same time?"

We were back to class mode, the point of the questions after all.

I thought it over. "It gives us a better understanding of different genres and how they originated."

"Right on," he said. We bounced questions back and forth, seamlessly, not once stopping.

"This is me," I said when we got to Wolf.

He dug his hands further into his pockets.

"Thank you for walking me back," I said to him.

"It was my pleasure."

I was halfway turned around when he spoke again.

"No matter what it looks like right now," he paused. "I have a familiar feeling that life is beginning all over again for you."

"With summer." I finished his sentence with a smile. "That's Fitzgerald, Gatsby. I love that book."

"Correct." He stood there for a second, completely unreadable. "It's nice to see you let go."

"Even nicer to see you smile," he said then walked away.

I stood there, thinking of the scent that lingered after him. *Mint*, definitely *green apple*. I knew I was close to being right this time.

* * *

"You're here."

Kevin looked surprised. "How did you get here?"

"I took the bus," I said over the music in the house.

"Why would you do that?"

Since Amanda and Halle texted they weren't sure they would still come, I had one of two options. Stay in my dorm and mope all night or pull the plug and come hang out with Kevin, before I also changed my mind. I also had a brewing desire to finally tell him.

"It's your party." I stood there. "I didn't want you to have to come pick me up."

"I didn't mind," he pulled me in, squeezed my hand, then lifted me up. "Anything for you." My heart fluttered down my chest.

"You know some of the guys already." He nodded at a few people who were also standing in the yard with us and introduced me to some of them. It wasn't a huge party when we walked inside the house. There were a couple of people there, some from the soccer team, and several girls standing around. Thankfully, the only guy I didn't want to see wasn't there. At least not anywhere near us.

He turned to me when we were back inside. "What do you want?" He nodded towards my left. "Food and drinks are over there, I know you don't care to drink though." I had a flash of that night when he came to pick me up in front of Warren's.

He didn't say anything for a moment. "Everything alright?"

"Yes," I looked at him, "thank you for inviting me."

"Doesn't seem like it," he shook his head and grabbed my hand, "let's go somewhere private where we can talk, you and me."

Kevin knocked on a couple of doors before eventually finding one that was empty. Despite the noise outside, the room was abruptly silent when he shut the door.

"Come here," he pulled me towards him so we could both sit on the bed. Then he caressed my hair and played with my ribbons. My mind wanted to resist him but my body didn't, so I let him kiss me on my lips then my neck. All of a sudden, my phone rang.

"Everything okay?" I asked when I picked up the call. Kevin continued to kiss my neck and attempted to remove my sweater.

I sat up. "Wait, Amanda's on the phone."

"Sorry we can't come!" Amanda said. "We're heading to Warren's."

"I got to Kevin's," I said.

"Is tonight the night?"

"Umm..." I looked at Kevin, who looked annoyed. "How did the game end?"

"We won!" Amanda said. "Is he next to you? Pass him the phone."

I looked at him, "Amanda wants to talk to you."

Kevin grabbed my phone and put it on speaker. "Listen Amanda, I want to spend time with my girlfriend tonight, is that okay?"

"Totally but only if you guys come hang out with us after," she said. "It's rival's weekend, come by the frat!"

"Enjoy it for all of us and have a good night." Kevin said and hung up.

"Hey! I didn't even get to say goodbye to her."

"You ever notice you're always under her shadow?" he asked, annoyed.

I winced. "I'm not under her shadow, and nd you haven't gotten the chance to know her that well."

He shrugged. "I've seen her a bit...now where were we?" He proceeded to kiss me again then lifted up my shirt. "Is it so bad that I want to spend all the time in the world with you?"

"No." My knees were numb. My whole body wanted him badly.

"Are you okay with me doing this?" he asked me in between kisses.

I wanted him to stop but I couldn't bring myself to. *How can something feel so right and wrong at the same time?*

I kissed him back – not wanting either of us to come back for air. Then Kevin attempted to remove my bra. He was successful at it and when he was about to kiss my chest, I stopped him. *I came here for a reason.*

"What's really going on?" he asked me, his deep brown eyes staring at me.

Heart pounding, I looked at him. "There's something I need to tell you, you deserve the right to know," I looked down, "and decide if that's what you want."

He sighed. "I'm listening, babe."

"I've never seriously dated anyone before."

He looked completely unfazed. "I know, you told me." He scooted closer next to me. "Is that all?" He chuckled then proceeded to kiss my neck. "You smell good," he looked at me, "and you look really good tonight."

I knew all I had to do was let it out. "It's not you, I'm just in my head about these things."

"Annabelle..."

"Wait." My knees were numb. I stopped him from kissing me again. "You need to hear me out."

He let out a frustrated sigh and moved away from me.

I stared at him, "look at me."

"I've never dated anyone before."

He rolled his eyes. "I know, you've said that already."

"No, Kevin, I've never dated *dated* anyone before."

He still looked unfazed. "And you're the first girl I want to be in a serious *serious* relationship with so who cares?"

"You don't get it, do you?" I asked him. He simply shook his head.

"I'm a virgin," I blurted out. I kept going before he could stop me. "I've never had sex, besides kissing one guy before you, I had never been with anyone else. I've never hooked up with anyone, I've never done anything remotely close to having sex."

He stayed quiet for a while, his head bowed down. I thought he was about to get up and walk out when he turned to me.

"This is what you're so worried about? Why didn't you tell me sooner?"

"I don't know," I looked down. "It was all happening so fast between us, I just...I could never figure out the right time to say anything."

"I've opened up to you in ways I haven't with any girl." He stared at me. "And you couldn't have the decency to tell me this sooner?"

I thought he would be the one to be caught off-guard. Instead, I was.

I looked at him. "You're an athlete, I thought..."

"Do you really think that low of me?" he asked me. "You thought it would bother me?"

"Of course not."

"I don't play around with my heart, Annabelle." He stared at me. "I thought you were the type not to either."

We both stayed quiet.

He slowly grabbed my hand then kissed it. "I mean it." He looked at me, "I like you and I don't say that loosely."

"Just tell me when you're ready," he said.

His dimple caved in. "I'm waiting for you, am I not?"

I looked at him, leaned in, and kissed him.

"Come on, I have to show you something," he stood up and walked me out of the room.

Seventeen

"WHERE ARE WE GOING?" I smiled at Kevin.

My eyes were fixated on him as he walked us out of the room – nodding at a staring Jordan – straight to the dance floor.

He drew me closer to me than whispered in my ear, "wait here."

I watched him walk over to the computer near us then pressed a few buttons. The music stopped. There were loud groans, shouts of complaints, but just as quickly, it picked back up again.

"Care to dance?" he asked me when walking back. The song was an upbeat song that everyone around us was jumping to, but Kevin closed the space between us and placed his hand around my back and led me into a slow dance.

I looked around at the crowd. "It's not a slow song."

"Uh huh," he smiled.

There weren't many moments in school when I'd slow-danced with a guy. Actually, there weren't any. I never went to any of the school dances, but I guess at this moment, I didn't care. There was no way they could compare to the way Kevin's eyes were fixated on me, or his thumb pressing against my back. I followed his lead as he swayed us back and forth, somehow allowing us to still follow the rhythm.

He leaned in. "You didn't have to hide your virginity from me, let me know when you're ready."

"Thank you for understanding."

He circled around me, then spun me around so my back could be against his chest. He placed both of his arms around my chest then whispered in my ear. "I'm okay waiting, Annabelle Wilson."

I thought he wouldn't let go. I didn't want him to let go.

When I opened my eyes, Jordan's eyes were glued on us and there was a hint of sadness in them.

I turned back around to face Kevin and placed my arms around him.

"You make everything better," I said to him and leaned against his chest.

* * *

Dear MGU Reader:
My fellow classmates
Ladies and gentlemen

I've got a big announcement. He knows and the world...surprise... surprise...didn't stop. He didn't care at all. Did I mention he's the greatest? Maybe he's the one I've been waiting for all along.

Thanks for all the support ladies and gents. Let's see how this plays out.

Kisses
...Or should I say hugs...
The Virgin

xxanonymousxx90: let us know how your first time goes if you lose it
dess_jamie_45: You'll 100% regret it

MaxShirla: Please don't lose it aimlessly. I still regret my first time

Singlegal: sex can be fun with the right person

sexycani: Get it over with

MGUFresh: You're so naive

juniorrr: I knew she would bail on us halfway through. Most virgins are desperate to lose it.

penelope_73: I've never met someone more desperate in my life

freshman11: Let her live! She's in college <3

* * *

That entire next week, I avoided thinking about mom and focused on normal things, college things, like tutoring, meeting up with the twins, and hanging out with Amanda and Halle. I focused on the best thing, hanging out with Kevin. I felt it all over again. His arms around my waist, his deep stare, his soft kiss. He took it so well, even Amanda was shocked but happy for me.

I felt the best I had in months. It wasn't about mom or the grief. It was about me finally, for the first time in my entire life, finding myself. I knew it was only a matter of time before I would get to know my dad for who he was here, the version of him I never got to. When he, too, was forever changed on this campus.

"Pay attention," Jaz said to me, bringing my focus back to the conversation at Daughters in Waiting. The twins were so kind and welcoming, I didn't think it hurt continuing to go. It also helped that I kept getting extra credit for it.

"Romans eight," one of the girls said. "That's how I know God loves me unconditionally."

"For me it's John three. He tells us that he loved the world so much that he gave his only son for us," another girl added. "That always humbles me, I don't know anyone else who loves me unconditionally like that."

"Sometimes I forget it," another girl said, "I find myself expecting a lot out of my boyfriend and family and I can forget that as much as they love me, they can't fit every need I have."

Another girl chimed in, "I think we can stop seeking it from other places when we truly understand God's love for us."

Kacie looked at a piece of paper in her hand. "I'm going to hand you each a copy of this before you walk out today, please consider what you want to bring to our purity discussion next week based on the conversation we had today and our previous ones."

I just looked at her and nodded when she handed me the paper when I walked out.

"How did the game go?" Rachel asked me outside of the library.

"It was a lot of fun," I said to them. "Your volunteering event?"

"Same as usual, we do a couple throughout the semester with SFC." Roxy said.

"Are you interested in doing any with us?" Rachel asked me.

"Sure, let me know any upcoming ones that come up." I told them. "By the way," I paused, "if you guys are interested, my friends want to do a girls' night of some sort. I'd love for you to come if you can?"

Rachel spoke up first. "We'd love that!"

Roxy agreed. "You have our numbers, let us know when and we're there."

* * *

Dear MGU Reader:
My fellow classmates
Ladies and gentlemen

Now, now, no need to get in a frenzy! I'll only have sex when I'm ready to. It's quite natural to want to lose it by now, but this virgin won't get pressured.

Kisses

...Or should I say hugs...
The Virgin

ava_yen: that's what we all say
_virgin409: slow down
nickrimma11: get it done with
Sandy5532: You can say that, but it's hard not to give in when you like someone!
marriegray: It's going to be a big let down for you
0virgin61: I'm the same way! Can't pressure me to do what I don't want to do <3 <3
Itsme__karine: I would follow the advice on here if you're still trying to wait
blake##: y'all are so harsh
sophomore44: we're looking out for her!
$virgingirl$: she'll be fine

* * *

"Ben!"

I felt bad for startling him, but I had to let him know. *He never rushes out of class*, I thought.

He looked like he hadn't slept in days and barely had the energy to acknowledge me.

"Hey," he nodded. "What's going on?"

I handed him the papers. "I got As."

He scanned through them, every single assignment grade and quizzes since tutoring had started. *I scored As on all of them.*

I stared at him for a minute. "I just wanted to thank you...it's working." I shook my head. "If I'm honest, I didn't think it would."

"You have a gift," he smiled a little, but it didn't reach his eyes.

"I still have a way to go but thank you, I just wanted to tell you that."

After a second, he handed my papers back to me. "Time and patience are the strongest warriors."

"Tolstoy," I whispered as he walked off.

* * *

"We're not staying here today."

Ben didn't give me a chance to walk into his office when he heard me knock on the door. I turned around to see him behind me, holding the red stress ball.

"We're going to another floor," he started walking, "same building."

I followed him to the floor marked, *Basement: Archives*.

"Watch your step," he opened the door and turned on the light. My stomach shrunk away. The room smelled like mold and aged dairy and only the long rays of bookshelves facing us made up for us being here.

"Are these all vintage?" I looked at him. "This might be the room my guidance counselor told me about."

He nodded. "Are you okay with us sitting here?"

"I don't see why not," I said as he threw the ball at me and sat down. His back leaning against the thin wall in between two shelves. I sat opposite him.

"What do you want to do with your degree?" Ben asked, kicking off our series of questions.

"Let's see...before my dad died, I wanted to be a writer like him, he was a journalist."

"So you –"

"Not your turn," I said and tossed him the ball.

"Touché," he said.

I thought of seeing him at Worship Night. "You believe in God?"

"Yes, I believe in him. I have all my life." He cocked his head, "Don't you also? Aren't you a part of SFC?"

I took a deep breath. "It sounds stupid and weird, but I joined my roommate's club to get to know my dad more, he was Christian."

"That doesn't sound stupid or weird."

I cleared my throat. "What's the one place you would go to right now if you could?" I asked him. "I know you haven't traveled yet but if you could choose one on the spot?"

"Japan."

Now, that was surprising. Ben wasn't an open book, but I wasn't expecting that answer. I so desperately wanted to ask him why right then.

"Do you have any siblings?" Ben asked me.

"It's just me and my mom."

I looked at him. "Why were you really there that night at Warren's?"

His stare was intense, forcing me to look away.

"I had a fight with my parents," he played around with the ball. I could see him tensing up.

"We've been arguing a lot about what to do with my brother and it's been tough. Warren reached out when he started at MGU and I figured why not, I'll go to his party. It's not my scene, but I wanted to go for a few hours."

"Is everything okay with your brother?"

He tossed back the ball. *Right, not my turn.*

"What are your thoughts on the texts Professor Lee compared in class today?" he asked me.

Bummer. I made a mental note to ask the same question next time.

* * *

Girls' night was Amanda's idea, but Halle commanded it. She reached out to all of us and asked us to get ready to squeeze in another one of her art projects. None of us knew what it was, but she reassured us that unlike last time, no one would get messy.

"Who's ready to get their asses beat?"

We were at the bowling alley in the mall near campus, staring at Halle, eager to know what this project was about and why it had to be during girls' night.

Amanda pointed her finger at Halle, "you totally are if we're bowling, I'm good at this."

She flashed her Cooper smile at everyone. "Since we're at the mall, I think it's only fair that the winner gets a shopping spree."

Halle chuckled. "Whatever."

"You wish," Roxy said.

Rachel shrugged. "She's the competitive one out of both of us."

"Then she might need to be on my team," Amanda said.

I looked to my right at Jaz and the Ngono twins, who were with us and were fitting right in. So were Amanda and Halle's friend, Jane, whom I had already met, and Gabriella, their big.

"How should we play?" Jane asked everyone. She looked at Halle, "When are we doing this project of yours?"

"Be patient," Halle said. "That's coming after this." Amanda and Jane rolled their eyes.

"We could play in groups," their big Gabriella said. "I'm down for whatever."

"I want to go first," Halle said. "Gabriella, want to tag team?"

"Sure." Gabriella said. Amanda, Halle, and their sorority friends decided to go first while the rest of us lounged. I sat in the booth next to Jaz and across from the twins.

"Annabelle, if you're still considering volunteering with us, there's a 10K fundraiser going on next weekend," Rachel said. We watched Amanda score a perfect strike.

"She didn't just talk a big game," Roxy said and turned to me, "SFC has a few members running for charity, we're helping with the refreshment stands."

Amanda overheard her and walked over. "My sorority's doing that!"

"Soon to be sorority," she corrected herself. "We're helping them fundraise for the environmental club."

"Amanda, come play!" Halle called out. Amanda walked back again.

"Ours is for SFC to help plant churches," Rachel said.

I looked at the twins, "count me in."

"I'm running this year, so I won't be working the stands, but Rachel is," Roxy said.

"How many people show up?" I asked them.

"A large amount." Jaz said.

"It's big, but it's only open to the student body," Rachel added.

"I totally sucked this time," Amanda came back and sat down with us again. "I was distracted."

Rachel smiled at me. "Annabelle, how are you liking the club so far?" I felt Amanda's eyes watching me.

"So far, it's not bad." I said. "You're all really nice."

"I"m happy to hear that," Roxy smiled. "We were worried about that, we're only sophomores but we haven't seen a lot of nonbelievers joining before."

Amanda made a face. "Nonbelievers?" I shifted in the booth.

"It means people who don't believe in God," Roxy quickly said. "I'm sorry, I didn't mean it like that."

Amanda looked at me. If there was a universal look for, I told you so, her stare would be that.

Rachel sat up. "What Roxy meant to say is that you're always welcomed, and we love having you join us, it's not every day girls are willing to join our group."

Roxy smiled at me, "exactly."

"We're all volunteering together then?" Rachel asked.

"I guess we are," Amanda said.

She gave me another look before walking off. When she got to Halle, she whispered something. Halle looked at me, shrugged her head, and turned back to watch Gabriella throw the ball.

"I didn't take it offensively," I said to Roxy, who still looked uncomfortable. "At all! I know you didn't mean it in a mean way."

"Have you guys thought much about the purity conversation coming up tomorrow?" Rachel asked us.

Roxy looked at me. "Rachel's in a serious relationship right now."

"I didn't know that," I said to Rachel.

She smiled, "We've been dating since high school."

"Is he at MGU?" I asked her. "Maybe we could do a double-date at some point."

She shook her head, "He's out of state." *That has to be hard.*

"It's going to be a tough one to discuss but that's why I love our group and SFC so much, they're really helping me," she added.

Amanda walked back to our booth. "It's your turn, we already put your names in."

She held me back when the others walked away. "I told you this was a mistake."

"What do you mean?"

"Annabelle, they're totally weird. It's social suicide, you can do better than them. Nonbelievers? Who speaks like that?"

"Give them a chance," I said. "They've been really nice so far. Please, for me? They didn't mean any harm by it."

She simply shrugged when Halle walked over to us.

I looked at Amanda. "Can you support me on this?"

"I've been supporting you, Annabear," Amanda said. "I'm just worried about you."

"I'm finally branching out, my grades are good, I have a hot boyfriend as you love to say, what's there to worry about?"

She stared at me. "A lot actually." Halle walked away.

"What are you talking about?" I asked her. "How exactly are you helping by making fun of the friends I'm making?"

"Friends?" She made a face. "They're acquaintances at best."

I could hear Halle and their friends whispering behind us, clearly eavesdropping in on our conversation.

I looked at Amanda, "I always give your friends a chance."

"What's so bad about my friends?" Amanda asked.

Halle walked up to us. "Yeah, what's so bad about us?"

I stared at her with the most disdain I've felt towards her all semester. I barely ever had one second with just Amanda without Halle being there.

"Can I just have one conversation with Amanda without you budding in?" I asked Halle.

"Can you relax?" Amanda asked. "Why are you getting upset? We're looking out for you, *I'm* looking out for you. They were being rude."

"No, they weren't. I'm not having this. Give them a chance or don't, but we came here for girls' night and to do Halle's project so that's what I'm going to spend my time doing." I looked at both of them. "Instead of judging your friends."

I walked away to play with the other girls. Roxy had the ball and was about to hit a strike when I noticed the name she was assigned. *Twin 1.*

"Let it go," Jaz said to me. "It's not worth it."

I didn't say anything back, I simply walked over to the board. *Nonbeliever*, I looked again. *Twin 2.* I felt my entire body would explode.

I walked back to the booth. "Who wrote those names?"

Halle laughed. "They're kind of funny."

I tried to keep my voice low. "Who typed that in?" I looked at Amanda. "Who wrote it?"

"What's the big deal?" Halle asked.

"Of course you wrote them." I spat.

"Actually, I didn't."

Amanda looked at me. Her voice was low, the lowest I've heard it. "I did."

"Why would you do that?"

"It was a *joke*, Annabelle," she said. "Lighten up."

When I started gardening with mom, she took me to a flower shop so I could buy my first seeds. I'd spent all weekend deciding which flower I wanted to plant, and eventually landed on the one that could help me make a wish. But mom just stood there and asked me to choose another one. She said the flower I wanted spread too quickly, it was wild, and our garden wouldn't be big enough for it. That summer was when I first named a flower after someone. *Dandelion*, I told Amanda, *you're my Dandelion.*

From a distance, you could never stop watching her. Amanda was always that girl, the girl who made you wish you were her, the girl who made you feel like you could be anything, anyone. Yet now, in this moment, I saw something else in her, someone else.

"It's not funny." I said to her, fighting back my tears.

"It's supposed to be funny," Amanda said.

Jaz walked over to me. "Don't worry about it, it's your turn."

I firmly repeated. "That wasn't funny, it was mean."

Eighteen

Amanda: I'm sorry, I meant it to be funny. I never thought it would upset you.

Amanda: It was meant to break the ice

Amanda: can you just come back and play?

Amanda: where are you?

Amanda: are you with them?

I PUT MY PHONE AWAY. Roxy, Rachel, Jaz, and I were seated at the food court, drinking our smoothies.

"I'm so so sorry that happened," I said, embarrassed.

Roxy shrugged. "It's okay, we're not really offended by it."

I stared at her dumbfounded. "How can you not be? I'm upset for you." I felt horrible. This was the first and only time I had invited them to hang out with my friends and this happened. "I don't get how you're not."

Rachel looked at me. "Annabelle, it bothers us, but it happens. She probably took offense to what Roxy said even though Roxy didn't mean it that way, we all make mistakes."

"I didn't invite you here to put up with that," I said. "It was so uncalled for."

Rachel just looked at me. "What good would it be for us to react the same way?"

Jaz spoke up. "I get why you're upset, but you can still forgive her if she apologizes."

Were we all in the same bowling alley?!

"You guys are being way too calm about this, I'm still livid."

They didn't respond to me for a moment.

Roxy looked at me. "I get it, but it wasn't enough to ruin girls' night over it."

"Don't be upset for us," Rachel said. "I promise you we're good."

"We promised Halle we'd help with her project," Roxy said. "Let's do that and call it a night."

I let out a heavy sigh and checked Amanda's new text messages.

> Amanda: I'm sorry!!! PLEASE come back

I looked at the three of them, "Are you okay with us going back?"

Roxy smiled, "Halle still has her class project to do right?"

Rachel agreed, "I'm down to go back if you are?"

"Fine."

* * *

Amanda, Halle, and their friends immediately hugged us when we walked back into the bowling alley.

"Truce?" Halle extended her hand for me to shake. When I did, she brought me into another hug before whispering, "sorry."

"You're right, it was a stupid joke," Amanda said. She looked at the twins. "I expected them not to come back so I'm totally happy they did."

She looked at me, "I was in the wrong."

"Stupid joke," I repeated.

That's when Halle clapped her hands for everyone to sit down.

She stood up to face us. "I have a class project to start pronto and you all agreed to be a part of it."

"Please get it over with," Amanda said.

"Alright, alright," Halle rolled her eyes. "My final project for my class is a digital mural. I have to interview a couple of people on campus that I hang out with about their semester and capture what my professor called 'the essence of the person'."

"On camera," she added.

"So how will it work?" Rachel asked.

"I'm still figuring out what I want the final project to look like," she looked into her bag on the table. "For you guys, I'm just going to record each of you and ask you a series of questions."

"Trust me on this, I'll make you look good for my project."

"Just make me look hot," Amanda said.

Halle looked at her. "Okay, I'll start with you."

While Halle made her way filming each of us for the project, we played a few more rounds of bowling.

"Annabelle," Halle said to me, "I'm ready for you."

I walked over to her, "I'm feeling nervous all of a sudden."

"Don't be, let's do a test run first. I won't record this time, but I'll go through the motions if that works for you?"

"Sure."

"You ready?" she asked me. I nodded.

She lifted her camera. "How would you say your semester is going if you could describe it in one word?"

"Fine so far," I said. "It's been a lot, in a good way."

She asked me a few more questions before stopping again. "Say what you just said but don't hold back and make sure to look directly at the camera."

I cleared my throat.

"Hi, I'm Annabelle Wilson...."

Halle motioned for me to keep going.

"My semester's going okay, it's different, it's not bad or anything. I've met some nice people." I kept going for a bit until Halle stopped me again.

"That was good, really good," she looked down at her camera then looked back up at me, "but we have to try again."

"Really? You said it was good."

"You forgot your boyfriend."

"Oh, sorry."

"On my count, we start again." She pressed the record button then lifted her finger to tell me when to speak.

* * *

The only time I had discussed not having sex for religious reasons was, well, never. I was a virgin because I wanted to be. I was waiting to fall in love and be loved and as Amanda put it, the impending *boom*. It was as simple as that.

An involuntary shiver ran down my spine when Kacie flowed her eyes around the room, once landing on me, then fixed herself to say, *can I ask you a personal question?* My body froze. Unlike the girls in the room, talking about my virginity publicly was as taboo as joining this club.

"How would you guys define purity?"

She asked it as casually as if she was asking us what our favorite snacks were, but that didn't stop the group from diving in, as usual.

"Purity's anything we do that keeps us in line with God's love for us...sexually, it's guarding ourselves until marriage."

"That's not purity."

It didn't take long before the conversation picked up.

"I feel like some people include kissing and others include anything outside of kissing and others say not having sex is purity. I don't know, I think not having sex is purity. People just make it more complicated than it should be."

"It is to me." The first girl repeated herself. "I think not having sex is the only definition of purity."

Another girl defended her, "Anything you don't do outside of marriage including sex, kissing, or any other sexual act is purity."

By now, I was clenched to my seat.

"Kissing is sexual?"

"Kissing leads to other things, it's definitely sexual."

"Sexual or romantic? That's two different things."

"Okay everyone," Kacie smiled. "Let's give each other the floor when we're speaking and can we tie this back to scripture?"

"I would say..." The girl next to Kacie grabbed her bible and in the split of a second, landed on a page. "Chapter four in first Thessalonians says that it's God's will that we stay sanctified, avoid sexual immorality, that each person learns to control their own body in a way that is holy and honorable and not in passionate lust."

"Based on that," Kacie looked at her, "what would be your definition of purity?"

"Honoring my body."

"I agree with that definition and first Corinthians seven," the next girl added to the conversation. "That each man should have sex with his own wife and the wife with her own husband, so I see purity as only having sex within marriage."

"God says that all other sins we commit are outside of the body, but whoever sins sexually, commits sins against their own body...I would agree that purity is guarding and honoring your body," Roxy agreed.

I looked away, suddenly conscious that I was in over my head joining this group. The more they spoke, the worse I felt. This was ridiculous and intense. My decision to be a virgin wasn't off some high moral ground, I simply chose to. I glanced over at Jaz who was watching me. I pulled out my phone and checked the time. *Thirty minutes left.* I let out a heavy sigh.

"I struggle with it," Rachel said. She paused for a second, then continued. "I know God's plan for me is to have a healthy sexual relationship within marriage, but my boyfriend and I are courting, and we have every intention to get married. Waiting's taking a toll on us since we don't plan on getting married before we're done with school."

She continued. "Purity is my heart posture towards God and what he has for me. I do it because I know it's the best thing I can do to protect myself when I'm dating."

"Do you and your boyfriend kiss?"

"We kiss." She responded to the girl who asked. "We're not rigid about it, sex and any other sexual intercourse is the only thing off the table."

"Anyone else?" Kacie asked us.

"What do you think?" Jaz asked me. I thought of telling her to mind her business, but I was distracted by the junior, a few seats away from me, who was now speaking.

"I'm not a virgin, but I've been judged by some people because of it."

As far as I was concerned, you got judged for being a virgin. Not for not being one.

"I got pregnant at sixteen and got shunned for it."

A tear rolled down her eyes. "I don't know what I would do without my daughter, I love her to pieces, but I would have waited if I could have." She paused to catch her breath. The student next to her patted her back. "You get shunned if you don't want to wait and you get shunned if you do.

"Purity for me now looks like abstinence, I'm not having sex with anyone until we're both in love and I'm clear on what I'm doing. There's a lot of risks that come from sex, I don't want to put myself through that again."

"I came across this article the other day..." Kacie filled the silence after a moment. "It was pretty eye-opening for me and I'd love to know where everyone stands on this. Raise your hand if anything I say applies to you, but please don't participate if you don't feel comfortable."

"Who in this room has never been kissed, never done anything sexual, never had sex, and is saving themselves for marriage?" Kacie asked us. Roxy and three other girls raised their hands.

"Thank you, ladies. Who here has been kissed, made out, or just done PG things without any sexual intercourse?" she asked. Rachel and five other girls raised their hands. I raised mine as well.

"Who here has hooked up with someone including sexual penetration?" Kacie asked and raised her hand. The remaining twelve girls who hadn't participated yet raised their hands as well.

"If you've been sexually active with someone, who here regrets their decision?"

Most of the girls raised their hands.

For a second, it looked like Kacie was about to cry. "I lost my virginity when I was seventeen to my prom date. It really broke me. I regret it so much, I wish I could take it back. We didn't end up together like I thought we would and looking back, I could have waited, and I chose not to.

"We literally get attached to other souls when we have sex. I don't want to go through that again with someone I was never meant to be with in the first place. I know my spouse and I won't be perfect, but at least we'll make vows to spend the rest of our lives together and honor that."

She let out a small exhale. "I'm choosing to protect my peace now."

Kacie's words moved me in a way I didn't expect them to. My heart softened to the conversation and the warmth of it filled me up.

"My biggest gripe with these discussions," the next girl speaking took a heavy breath, "is that everyone just assumes we get to choose," she lifted her fingers up to make imaginary quotation marks, "to be pure."

"We forget that...hey...sometimes, there's assault, there's divorce, you might even get cheated on." She looked at all of us. "It's not so black and white out here, there's multiple gray lines, especially on a college campus. Not all of us just get to wait for a spouse and joyfully experience sex after that." She took another deep breath. "I think the church needs to show some grace to people who don't have it so black and white."

The room was silent again.

"Thank you for reminding us of that." Kacie said softly, "I agree, it's so important for us not to condemn each other when it comes to this topic."

She looked around and stopped at me. I looked away.

"Anyone else?" she asked.

"The bible doesn't explicitly say that we can't have sex with each other outside of marriage." A freshman across from me added.

"It clearly condones adultery and premarital sex," someone disagreed.

"God told us in Genesis to be fruitful and multiply *after* he created marriage. It's supposed to be experienced and enjoyed in a union."

"What if I never get married? I can't have sex?"

"Have you guys seen the statistics with STDs these days?" Roxy asked, "no...thank you. I'm all for protecting my body."

"I second that!"

"Me too, I'm good on the hookup culture."

"I can't stand hookup culture, it's just a big waste of energy."

"My friend's dating a guy who told her he won't wait more than a month for a girl to put out."

"My discernment is so strong now, I can spot a player right away."

"We're going to wrap it up here ladies," Kacie said when the discussion was picking up again towards the end of the hour. The group slowly erupted into a laughing fit.

"I didn't mean it like that!" Kacie shook her head, "You all raised some really good points tonight. I think we should keep going with this one so bring as many questions, thoughts, and comments you have next week, and we'll pick up where we left off. Feel free to stay after if you want more details on any of the resources I shared at the beginning!"

* * *

"What are you thinking?" I asked Jaz when we walked back into our dorm.

"I should be the one asking you that." She sat on her bed. "You told me you were a virgin before."

I avoided her gaze and sat on my mattress. "Yes."

"Can I show you something?" she asked.

"Sure."

I held my breath as she walked over to me, sat on my mattress, and placed her laptop on her thighs. Then I watched her type in MGU Reader in her browser. I sat still, unsure of what she wanted to do.

"Some people have an easier time waiting because they know why they're waiting."

She looked at me. "Sex is more than a physical connection. It's emotional, mental, spiritual, you name it. They don't want to share that type of connection with anyone but the person who deserves it."

She browsed the website. "Look," she pointed at an article that was getting a lot of traction. "It's the article Kacie was basing those questions on."

I read the title out loud. "Seventy percent of college students at MGU regret their first time – research inspired by The Virgin's posts."

I looked away from the screen. I saw the post that week and tried not to think too much into it. The more I hung out with Kevin, the more I wanted to lose it.

Jaz pointed to the gender and age breakdown on the post. "Both guys and girls regret it, isn't that interesting?"

"That's why posts like The Virgin are inspiring," she said, then took a breath. "A lot of people are saying they don't like hooking up."

I could feel her gaze on me so I stared up at the ceiling.

"I can't say I agree with everything she writes, but I like what she's doing," she said, "I think it's cool and it encourages students, it also starts conversation."

She looked at me as if she knew. Not another word uttered from her mouth, but she knew I was the one posting.

She got up, taking her laptop with her. "I'm heading out, do you want anything?"

I cleared my throat. "No, thank you."

Before she could walk out, I stopped her, "Jaz..."

She turned around.

"I'm really sorry you walked in when Kevin slept over yesterday." We only cuddled, but she made a point to pack her things and go, leaving us the room all night.

"That's okay." she said, her hand gripping the door. She stood there so long, I thought she forgot why she got up in the first place. "Just remember your why, Annabelle."

* * *

Dear MGU Reader:
My fellow classmates
Ladies and gentlemen

There's something I need to tell you. Since I started writing here, I've been a little ashamed of actually writing here. The very thing I'm writing about is the very thing I'm embarrassed of. Most people in my real life don't even know I'm a virgin. You're looking at me as an inspiration and sometimes I wonder if I deserve that. A friend of mine said that my voice was needed on this platform. I've decided to take her word for it since she's ten times smarter than me and a lot more in tune with her emotions.

This same friend believes in saving ourselves for marriage. She believes that our bodies don't control us, we control them. What if I don't want to wait until marriage? If I choose not to? What if I don't get married? I never thought much about what it meant to hold on so tightly to my virginity or not have sex altogether and stay celibate for years. Like for religious reasons or some sort.

Our conversation got me thinking, sex shouldn't be some checkbox item we checkoff. It should be safe. It should be with the right person. It's knowing we're making the right decision for ourselves and our bodies. And I really think it should be special. It might even mean staying celibate forever. It's our choice to make regardless.

I'm going to keep writing here, because I think we all need it.

Kisses
...Or should I say hugs...
The Virgin

UserX48: At least you have a choice.
AnonymouSXX4: i'm down
Bluessclues: let's support each other :)
Green_thumb: I'm not a virgin but I support it
Purplehabbits: Count me in. I haven't had sex in months
Sweetbees: I'm waiting with you!
Misssrebecca: My girlfriends & I made a pact to stay abstinent this semester
SeniorBaby: I just lost mine and I feel numb. I worked it up to something it wasn't.
virgin12: proud to be a virgin. it's a gift & i can't just give it away to some random.
Footba11lfan: how many times do we have to tell you to just write in your diary?
An_On._33: I'm sick of seeing your posts on here.
cinannmon55: ur posts motivate me so much

MGUILoveYou: How else will you know you've found the one?
foreverkells: ^Do you even read her posts?
Linnn$$$: I just had a conversation with my friends about being a
virgin and everyone swore I was the only one and that no guy would
put up with that. Glad to know I'm not crazy for wanting to wait.

Nineteen

"STILL IN?"

Ben stared at me. I was so busy processing things in my head, I forgot he caught my toss.

We were back in the archive room in the basement. I thought of the question I wanted to ask him last time.

"Is everything okay with your brother?"

"You asked this before, but we ran out of time," Ben said. *He doesn't miss anything.*

He shook his head yes. "It is. Convincing my parents of that is another thing though." He flung the ball in the air and caught it when it came back down. "We don't see eye-to-eye on his treatment."

"You said you love to read because of your dad?"

"That's not really a question," I chuckled. "But, yes, I love a lot of things because of him. I used to get envious at how many books he'd read."

"What about you?" I threw the ball back. "Where does your love for reading come from?"

Technically, we had zero obligations to answer these questions, but we did it anyway. This was an easy question. The easiest I could have asked him. I wondered why he was taking so long to answer when Ben tensed up.

"It's one of those things that grew on me in high school," he finally said.

I could tell this was the truth, but there was more he wasn't saying. He tossed the ball back.

"Have you drafted the practice essay for the exam?" he asked. "It's going to be hard, we should review how to prepare for it."

Why am I disappointed? Exams were next week.

"Okay." Is all I could muster.

* * *

I've always wondered what guys were like when they were starting to really like you, maybe even fall in love with you. With Jordan, I never got the chance to experience it because it happened so fast. One moment, I was secretly crushing on him without any clue he had a thing for me. The next, he was sneaking into my bedroom and confessing his love for me. Two weeks later, he was gone, and four months after, the dreaded call happened.

With Kevin, I could finally hope for true love again. Kevin felt safe. Kevin *was* safe. Kevin was genuine.

"Come here babe," he pulled me in for another kiss in his house.

"We can't help each other study if we're not actually going to help each other study."

He scrunched his nose at me, "we can't?"

"I can't afford to fail any of my exams," I said to him. I was confident going into my exams before Thanksgiving break, but I couldn't take my chances. Aside from my tutoring sessions with Ben, I spent every spare time I had studying for them.

"Let's see," Kevin grabbed one of my class books and proceeded to ask me a series of questions related to the notes we had previously discussed. *I was so wrong about him before.*

"Like the view?" His dimple spread across his cheek when he noticed I was staring.

I bit back a sarcastic reply and kissed him instead. When we pulled away, his friend Seth was staring at us.

"Hey man," Seth said to him. "Can I talk to you for a sec?" Seth simply nodded at me and walked back to his room.

"Sure," Kevin reluctantly got up. He was halfway out of their living room before turning back around and giving me a gentle kiss on the forehead. Then he walked off.

Boom incoming, I thought, then leaned back on the couch.

He returned less than five minutes later with the biggest smile on his face.

"Babe," he sat down on the couch. "I gotta run something by you."

I slid my notebook back on the coffee table. "What is it?"

"Jordan's not back yet so Seth and I are trying to sort this out," he placed one arm around me and grabbed my hand. "How do you feel about me spending Thanksgiving in Blakely?"

"Huh?"

"Well, Jordan's twenty-first is coming up Thanksgiving Eve, we've been discussing this for months."

"During summer," he quickly added as if to say, *before we were dating*. "He hates being home so we're thinking of spending it with him, nothing special, but he's been there a lot for me and Seth."

I crossed my arms over my chest, trying hard not to not show my blood rising straight to my head.

He stopped. "You alright?"

I took a sip of my water. "Uh huh."

"Anyways," he went on. "We were planning on spending it at Seth's, but something came up with his family, so we won't have the house."

"We'll be out of everyone's way," he took a breath. "We're thinking of getting a hotel out there."

He stopped again. "Babe? You sure you're alright? You look like you've seen a ghost."

I took a deep breath, pushing the worry away. "I'm fine."

He grabbed my hand and kissed it. "Plus, I kind of get to hit two birds with one stone."

I looked at him. "What?"

He caressed my hand. "You haven't said much about it...but I figured having me there might ease up on...you know...the whole house stuff. Take the pressure off."

"Jordan told me your mum is selling your house, it won't be like it usually is anyways. I'm not going home until Christmas so...I got no plans for Thanksgiving besides his birthday."

I had a flash of my mom during our last phone call, her dreaded news.

"First," I sat up, both upset and annoyed. "That wasn't his place to tell you." I looked at him. "Second, you have to understand how ridiculous this sounds."

"Don't be mad at him, I pried it out of him. We were talking about his birthday and other things, and it came up. I was trying to figure out what your mum was like."

"Umm, you could have just asked me, and you've met her before."

"That was different, I wasn't your boyfriend then. You never talk about your folks or your mum with me. Every time I bring them up, you change the subject."

My stomach sank. I didn't know where to start. Talking to Kevin about my dad, mom, or family back home would be like pulling him into the world of sadness he was already taking me out of.

"I've known the Coopers my whole life, please don't take it personally. Jordan had no business telling you that."

"I understand, but I want you to let me in."

"I've been letting you in." I thought about it. "I don't think my mom would be okay with that."

"I wouldn't be staying with you." Kevin said. "We're thinking of getting a hotel."

We stayed quiet for a moment.

He looked at me, "I want to be there for you, if you'd let me."

I felt bad when I saw the look on his face. I placed my hand on his thigh. "It's Thanksgiving, I have to spend it with my mom."

"And the Coopers," he said.

"Yeah," I shrugged, "we're spending it with them, we do that quite a bit."

He looked away from me. "Exactly."

"It's different," I said quietly. "You've met my mom, not formally as my boyfriend, but you did meet her before."

We might be an easy distance to the inevitable boom, but spending Thanksgiving together felt soon, too soon, even for us.

He slumped. "So what? I come celebrate Jordan's twenty-first and I don't see you?"

"Lucy would never accept you guys staying at a hotel...did Jordan tell you she would?"

He shook his head. "Seth and I haven't told him Seth's place off-limits, we're figuring things out."

"Oh." *He somewhat has a point.* Thanksgiving this year would be different, and if it was anything like the spa retreat, worse. Having him there would be a welcome escape. I checked his face one more time.

His dimple caved in. "Babe, we'll already be in Blakely."

"Okay, I just have to ask my mom then."

I quickly grabbed my phone and dialed her number before either of us could change our minds. Kevin held my hands.

"Hi sweetie!" mom said in a hurry.

I started carefully. "Hey mom, are you busy?"

"I'm running errands with Luce, I placed a couple of boxes for you to look at in your room and garage, we have a lot to sort through when you come home."

My shoulders tensed up. I glanced at Kevin, who was giving me a look reminding me to ask.

"Mom," I tried to relax. "There's something I need to ask you." I put her on speaker. "Kevin's with me."

"Oh, hi Kevin."

"Hi Mrs. Wilson."

"Make it quick sweetie," she said. "We're swamped right now."

"Can Kevin spend Thanksgiving with us?" *Bandaid off.*

There was a pause. A *long* pause.

"Annabelle..." She sounded both surprised and upset. "You know I'd love to have him over or meet him eventually, again." I could tell she was carefully choosing her words. "But the Coopers are hosting this year, and we can't impose that on them. You and I have a lot to do with the house."

The more I thought of it, the more I desperately wanted him there.

"Him and his friend are thinking of coming to Blakely for Jordan's twenty-first." I said. "They were going to get a hotel so I figured..."

She didn't say another word. I heard shuffling noises and whispers.

Lucy grabbed the phone. "I thought Jordan was spending Thanksgiving at his friend's?" She sounded excited. "Ace, Kevin is more than welcome to come over again this year! We'd love to host him." she said, "I'll have to call Jordan now, I'm so excited!"

She paused. "The more the merrier Ace, our house is yours, say hi to Kevin!"

She handed the phone back to my mom and we fell silent again.

"See you both at Thanksgiving, and Annabelle?"

"Yes mom?"

"I'll still need you to set aside time to help me with this stuff, including the showing."

I cleared my throat, "of course mom." Then we hung up.

Kevin squeezed my shoulders. "Wasn't bad at all."

I watched as he walked back into Seth's room and came back, flipping his phone around his fingers.

"Good to good, Jordan's in."

My stomach flipped, in the worst way. "Fine."

"You hungry? I'll make us something."

I looked at him. "A little, but I was thinking of heading back to Wolf." I started sorting through my stuff. "Can you give me a ride?"

His gaze locked in on mine. "Why don't you stay?"

"I don't think that's a good idea."

"I won't try any funny business," he moved closer and kissed me on the forehead. "Except this."

"Babe, I can't stay." I tried to think of an excuse. "I don't have my stuff here."

"I've got you..." He rushed to the guest bathroom by the front door and walked out, an entire box of unused toiletry items in his hand. "My roommates keep a couple of things for..."

I stopped him. "Ugh, don't tell me."

He laughed. "It's their business."

Over the next hours, we ate with his friend Seth, studied some more, then watched a movie, before Kevin turned back to me.

"Ready for bed?"

I looked away, "sure."

When I was done brushing my teeth, Kevin walked me over to the room. He opened the door.

"It looks different," I whispered, trying my best to hide that I was uncomfortable.

"I bought new bedding." he said. "I got embarrassed after the tour I gave you last time."

He had new plaid sheets. New posters were hung up on his side of the room now. Posters of his favorite sports teams instead of the models from before. I tried not to look at Jordan's side which was still decorated the same.

"My roommates grilled me. Don't ask. Do you want to listen to something before bed or?"

"Let's go to sleep," I said. He wrapped his arms around me then kissed me.

I pulled away. "I'm only staying here if you don't try anything funny."

"I know," he smiled, then pulled me into bed. We fell asleep soon after. When I woke up around 5 AM to use the restroom and tell Kevin I really should head back to Wolf, he pulled me closer to him to stay. Before drifting back to sleep, I noticed Jordan's bed was still empty.

* * *

"He...what?!?"

Amanda asked me dumbfounded.

"Amanda! Halle! Get back to your stations." Their big yelled from the registration table at the 10K race. We were off to the side as Amanda and Halle took in what I'd just told them.

"He asked to come home with her for Thanksgiving," Halle repeated my words to Amanda.

"I'm totally pissed that Jordan's going to be home this year but," a grin spread on Amanda's face, "teach me your ways, Annabear." Her eyes gleamed, "you have the smoldering hot and perfect specimen of a guy asking to spend Thanksgiving with you and you haven't even had sex yet."

Halle laughed. "That's precisely why."

"Kevin doesn't care about that," I replied.

"Every guy cares about that," Amanda said.

"Hey guys," Rachel approached us and gave us each a hug.

"Amanda! Halle!" Their big yelled again.

"Gotta go. I guess these runners can't register themselves," Amanda said and walked away with Halle.

I looked at Rachel. "Is Roxy still running? I don't see her." I scanned over the group of runners who were warming up before the race.

"Yeah, she's here somewhere." Rachel looked around before

looking back at me. "Follow me so I can sign you in." We walked over to the refreshment tables where the SFC club members were huddled with Kacie.

"Hey ladies," Kacie greeted us. "I placed Annabelle on water and lemonade duties with you Rachel." She pointed to a table stand near the finishing line of the track. "You just have to fill the small cups with their beverage of choice when they walk up and that's all you have to do for the next couple of hours."

"Easy peasy," Rachel smiled.

A few moments later, Jaz joined us.

"Hey," she said. She gazed at me for a moment but didn't say anything. I could tell she was biting her tongue.

Rachel looked at the track. "They're getting ready to start." I glanced back at the start line and could see Roxy, wearing an SFC shirt. We waved at her, but she didn't notice us.

I watched as Rachel pulled out the stacked cups one-by-one and filled them with the drink options.

She looked at us. "This way, we have them set up before the runners come to us."

"Are you still liking our group?" Rachel asked me a couple of minutes in.

I filled the cup I was holding, "I do, I'm surprised everyone's so comfortable talking about...their sexual experiences."

Rachel shrugged. "It's important we are, some of us don't have these conversations outside of the group." She looked at me. "It keeps us connected...and accountable."

"You have a boyfriend right?" she asked. I avoided Jaz's glare.

"I do," I smiled, filling another cup.

"How long have you been dating?"

I thought about it. "Since the semester started."

For a moment, neither of us said anything. I really wanted to know what she was thinking.

"How long have you been with your boyfriend?" I asked her.

"Close to four years," she smiled at me, "we're high-school sweethearts."

I nodded, thinking about what she said during our purity discussion. How could they, after four years, both in love, still be virgins?

"Hand me that one please," Rachel asked me, looking over at the empty stack cups next to me. I quickly grabbed them and gave them to her.

"Thank you for letting me know about the race," I said to her. "It's nice to help, I can also use this for extra-credit."

"Same," she smiled. "I'll keep you posted for other ones."

We made small talk for a while longer before Jaz noticed Roxy.

"Roxy's coming," Jaz said.

"I see her," I said.

"She's so close to finishing," Rachel said.

Rachel turned towards the runners as well. We waved at Roxy passing us who was so focused on running, she didn't see us again.

"I didn't know Ben was running this year," Rachel grabbed another cup to fill. I looked over at the track, sure enough, Ben was also running.

"You know him?" I asked her.

"Roxy and I met him at our freshman orientation last year, he's in SFC."

"He's my TA," I told her.

"I'm not surprised, he's ridiculously smart," Rachel said, "they considered offering him the president position for SFC but he declined it. He has too much on his plate with home and stuff."

"He does?"

"You haven't heard?" Rachel said. "Him and his brother were in a tragic car accident a few years back."

"I didn't know," I said. Ben was always so composed, like nothing bothered him, I never would have guessed.

"He rarely talks about it." Rachel said. "He keeps to himself a lot."

I watched him as he ran, gliding seamlessly. When he ran past us, he noticed me, he slowed down a bit, then kept running. I slid my phone out of my vibrating pocket.

"Hello?"

"Hey babe, what does your mom like?"

"What does my mom like?"

"I'm out shopping with the guys, and I was thinking of getting your mom something."

My heart warmed up. "Babe, you don't need to do that."

"I don't mind," he said, "we're at the mall."

I didn't have to give it a second thought. "Ribbons...and gardening."

"I don't think I'll be able to pick any gardening stuff..." he paused. "Ribbons like yours?"

"She'll love that, that's really sweet of you babe."

"Done. How's the event going?"

"Not bad, I'm enjoying it." I said. "They placed me on drink duty."

"Glad coach had other teammates doing it. So, ribbons for your mom?"

"Yes, she'll love it!"

I hung up and walked back to the refreshment table.

"Everything okay?" Jaz asked me when I walked back.

"Kevin was calling me," I said and grabbed water for myself then looked for Roxy in the crowd of runners again.

"Shoot, did I miss her crossing the finish line?"

Both Jaz and Rachel shook their heads as Roxy walked up to our table, her shirt drenched in sweat. She grabbed multiple cups of water, held her fingers up as if to say, *don't talk to me until I've had all of these.*

When she was done, she let out a loud exhale. "You guys are rockstars, I needed this."

"We should be saying that to you," Rachel attempted to give her a hug then stopped. She gave her sister a high-five instead.

"You're one of the first to finish," I said to her.

She smiled. "Falbright and I made a bet."

"Ben?" I asked her and she simply nodded then grabbed another cup of lemonade. That's when I noticed him walking up to us, t-shirt drenched as well.

"Hi Ben," Rachel gave him a high-five. "You did good."

"Hi guys," Ben looked at me. He placed his hands in his pockets.

"Hey." I said quietly. Amanda walked over to us.

"Hey, long time no see," she said to Ben and grabbed herself a cup of lemonade.

"Hi Amanda." he said then looked back at me. I looked away again.

He grabbed himself a water cup. "I need to hydrate."

I looked at him, "You were pretty fast, you like running too?"

Roxy looked at him, "That's why I made a bet with him, I told him he couldn't beat me." She laughed and tapped him on the shoulders. "Glad I won."

"I just have to pursue the things I love doing," he looked at me, "and do them so well that –"

"People can't take their eyes off," I finished. "Maya Angelou."

"Nice seeing you all." he said then walked towards Kacie's table.

"What were you two talking about before I got here?" Amanda asked me while the twins were talking amongst themselves.

I organized the cups for the rest of the runners. "Nothing, he just showed up to grab a drink."

"I see the way he looks at you," Amanda said and gave me a sly grin. "Two boys in one semester, who knew Annabelle Wilson had it in her?"

"Stop," I pushed her away. "There's absolutely nothing going on there." We talked for a little longer until her big yelled out her name.

"I can't wait for this to be over." she said then jogged back to them. When she got to her group, I looked at the SFC table, Ben was talking to someone but staring at me. He looked away when I noticed him.

Twenty

I WASN'T JUDGING. Like everyone else, I was glued into the next conversation we were having about purity. It was too good not to pay attention.

"Alright ladies, last time was a little intense for us and before we get back to opening the floor for our discussion, I just want to say again that this is a safe place," Kacie said. "Anyone remember where we left off our discussion?"

"I think we were debating what falls under purity and what that looks like for each of us."

The girl next to her spoke up too. "My mom says that sex should be considered a gift from God and it's powerful in a marriage, but it's a hard thing to abstain from if you're not careful."

"Kissing turns to making out which turns into sex in the right setting and next thing you know, you're having premarital sex."

"It's not that easy to just not have sex."

"It can be."

I was surprised that even with this group, everyone's opinions were so divided on this.

"People forget that purity isn't strictly sexual," another student said, "it's first and foremost spiritual. When we give our hearts to Jesus, our bodies become temples to his spirit. We can't forget that. We can't just let any and every one into that sacred space."

"That's a good point, but how exactly do we do that practically?" The girl across from me asked.

"I go to therapy and pray."

"I study scripture regularly and I surround myself with people who share the same belief."

"I only date guys who are waiting until marriage."

"It's hard to do that on a college campus though."

"It's hard but doable and not impossible."

"My body's private, I'm only showing it to who I choose to show it to."

"Proverbs four tells us to guard our hearts because everything flows from it," one of the other freshmen in the group said. "We can't guard our hearts if we let everyone have a piece of it."

She kept going. "I pray a lot for God to guard my heart against people who shouldn't have access to it, I also pray the same thing for my body."

"What if you're not religious?"

The room suddenly stopped talking to look at me. It took me a good minute to realize I'd said one of my thoughts out loud. The hair on my arms rose and I felt a sudden burst of embarrassment. *What was I thinking?!*

I finally turned my attention to Kacie. "I'm sorry, I didn't mean to voice that."

"That's okay," Kacie smiled. "Go on, we'd love to hear your opinion."

I looked down, still processing my thoughts, still embarrassed at having said it out loud. I glanced at the twins then Jaz before turning back to Kacie.

"What if someone isn't religious?" I asked. "What are we... what are they supposed to do then?"

No one said anything, but Kacie's eyes darted between me and the rest of the group. Soon enough, she was smiling again.

"I will always point them back to seeking God, but the best thing they can do is wait. One of the big misconceptions we believe all the time is that we have to experience things to learn from them, Godly wisdom says the opposite. We don't have to have sex with someone to know in our gut that we shouldn't have sex with them.

"The hookup culture sucks...how many of us are give our bodies away for nothing...it's just meaningless sex, it's terrible for our mental health or health in general."

Roxy chimed in. "There's nothing wrong with us not wanting to have aimless sex."

Before I knew it, the conversation picked up again.

"Both men and women should be guarding their bodies but we're the ones who constantly get criticized for having sex."

"My freshman year of college, a lot of guys chased me down and went ghost as soon as we did anything," another girl added, "it sucked, and it really affected my self-esteem. People act like hooking up is okay and it's not."

"Agreeing to hook up with random people for sex is not dating," the girl next to Rachel said. "It's not even fun."

"I had a guy not tell me he was having sex with other girls while pretending to date me," someone else chimed in. "I was so mad when I found out!"

"Have you guys read The Virgin's recent post?"

I glanced around the room, refusing to make direct eye contact with anyone.

"I love reading her!"

"No offense, but she says a whole lot of nothing."

"I happen to love her posts," Rachel agreed.

"The comment section is where I get most of the good tips."

Roxy joined in. "My friends and I made a pact that we wouldn't have meaningless sex. It's kind of epic that she has the whole school discussing something that's otherwise taboo."

I could feel Jaz glancing at me. That's when I noticed her. The girl a few seats away from Kacie, across from me. She was staring at me, her eyes locked in. She always stood out to me because she usually stayed quiet during the discussions like me. Except this time.

"It's easy to drill purity this and chastity that down our throats but there are a lot of people who were forced into sexual acts they didn't want to be a part of." she said, "God is a healer and a restorer, I'm so over people guilt-tripping those of us who have sexual pasts we had no control over.

"We mentioned it last week, but I want to say it again. Some of us didn't get to choose how we lost our virginity. This group saved my life freshman year, I had no one to talk to about these things when I first got to college. My family didn't believe what happened to me and...it's not like we like to openly discuss sex and we really don't like to talk about abuse.

"I just wish everyone else in my life was willing to have these conversations. I can't count on my hand how many times I was made to feel small for what happened to me, what I had no control over. Jesus healed me from the pain I felt after that experience, he did. No one who has ever shamed me or made me feel small can even understand the pain that comes from having that choice taken from you.

"There's nothing I've gone through that he didn't heal and I'm so grateful for that. I practice purity by relying on him and him only."

The room was silent as her words sunk in.

Roxy spoke up first, "I'm sorry for what happened." Then, we heard the scraping of a chair against the tile. Kacie got up to hug her and, soon enough, we all did.

"It means the world we can be here for you," Kacie said in the middle of the huddle. She looked at all of us. "I honestly can't even begin to express how much these talks have helped my time at MGU. Aside from all the resources shared in this group, please know that I will always be here if any of you want to talk more about this. No matter what, I want you to keep praying, keep guarding your hearts, keep being a part of a loving community, including a loving church. You have me and everyone else here you can count on."

"We're sad you're leaving us after this semester," Roxy said.

I'd only been there for a few weeks, but even I could see that Kacie was good at leading the discussions. I couldn't imagine anyone else taking her place.

"It's time for me to pass the baton," Kacie smiled at Roxy, "but we still have a few weeks together after we come back from Thanksgiving."

I whispered to Rachel, "I thought Kacie was graduating in the spring?"

Rachel shook her head. "No, she graduates this semester, we're going to miss her though."

* * *

At the beginning of the semester, all I wanted was to come back home, to not have to leave my hometown and instead, spend some time there just *figuring it out*. Taking in what life meant now with dad gone. Now, the day we were leaving campus to head back to my hometown, I realized, I was scared.

I glanced over at my packed bag on my mattress. I'd managed to shower, throw on my clothes, and say my goodbyes to Jaz before waiting for Kevin to pick us up in two hours. Kevin and Jordan.

"Hey!" Amanda picked up when I called her.

"What are you up to?" I asked her, "I'm done with exams, killing time now."

"With the crew, come!"

I paused for a second. I hadn't been back at their house since the night I drank with them.

"We're just chilling, I'm going to wait here until Kevin's ready to get us," Amanda said.

"Okay," I put her on speaker and placed my orange ribbons around my ponytail.

"Sure!" I grabbed my purse, and the door slammed behind me before I could stop myself from going.

* * *

When I walked into the house, Warren had his arm around Amanda in their living room. *Still not official* but they sure looked cozy. Halle got up from the couch and walked towards me while I said hi to the few who were there.

For a moment, I just stood there. *Ben?*

"Hi," he said.

"Take my spot Annabelle," Halle said to me. "I have to meet up with my parents for a faculty dinner tonight." She gave me a hug. "Happy Thanksgiving!"

She leaned in and whispered. "Goodluck with the boyfriend."

Gabe got up as well. "I can give you a ride."

I looked at Halle and made the same expression on her face. "Goodluck with the boy toy." She laughed and walked out of the house with Gabe.

"Have a good Thanksgiving!" Amanda yelled after them.

"Help yourselves," Warren said to me and Ben when he got up with Amanda. "We're going to grab drinks."

Amanda looked at me and smirked.

Ben looked at them as they walked off. "Have you been in their backyard before?"

"No, have you?"

"I can show you if you'd like?"

"It's nice." I said to Ben when we walked over to the outdoor firepit that was set up.

"I'm now officially on break," Ben said.

"You and me both." I looked at my phone. "We're going back to Blakely in a couple of hours, this semester's going by so fast."

"As if you can kill time without injuring eternity," Ben responded.

"Thoreau. Just how many novels have you read?"

"Too many," he smiled which showed a softer side to him.

"Are you cold?" He took off his jacket. "Here, have this."

"No," I said quickly. "Actually, a little." I grabbed the jacket from him. "Thank you."

Not knowing where to look, I looked up at the sky. "I'm kind of surprised you can see the stars already."

He looked up as well. "You should see this view when it's pitch black, it's incredible."

"I'm sure," my voice trailed off.

I glanced at him. "Do you have big plans for the break?"

"Just hanging out with my family. How far is your hometown?"

"Not far," I said, "we'll get there by five."

"How did you come up with this question game?" I asked him.

"Hospital visits." he said, catching me off-guard. "My brother and I did this all the time. He's the only one I've ever done this with prior to trying it with you."

"You mean to tell me this isn't your usual tutoring routine?" I snapped my fingers. "I knew it."

He chuckled. "Building trust is the way I go about tutoring, but I usually tutor in a different way."

I teased him again in my best Amanda voice. "Totally makes sense."

He laughed. We paused for a bit. Both of us stared at the fire pit.

"Do you think you'll go on to be a journalist like your dad?" he asked me.

"Maybe...I don't know if I have what it takes to follow in his footsteps. When he was alive, I thought I could do anything, but now, I'm not so sure."

"I think you can," Ben said.

I rolled my eyes. "You're saying that because you almost have to."

"I don't."

When I looked at him again, he looked away. I stared at him for a second longer. Ben was cute. The kind of cute that grew on you after some time and made you notice things you may not have noticed before, like the tiny mole next to his left eye.

"What happened with your brother?" I asked him a bit too quickly. "I'm sorry."

His brow raised up, as if he was contemplating answering me.

"We were on our way home from a competition for my speech and debate team my sophomore year of high-school. I got my license a couple months back." He stared into the fire pit, "My brother's always been my biggest fan and always wanted to tag along with me so I figured I'd drive us instead of riding in the school van with everyone.

"On our way back from the competition, a truck slammed into us and pushed us off the road into a massive ditch. I was in a coma for two weeks and woke up to find out my brother was paralyzed. That's when I started reading. Prior to that, I hated it. I never saw the point of it until a teacher recommended this book to me about being there for a loved one when they're hurting. That's all I could do to get rid of the pain and guilt I felt. I can't count how many novels I read that year alone."

Ben stopped talking. He stared at me, without attempting to look elsewhere. "When I met you at Warren's party, I recognized that stance you had very well. It's the same one I had that entire year."

He didn't have to say anything anymore because I knew what he meant. I realized what Ben felt was a grief I wasn't sure how one could learn to heal from. It was a grief that stayed around and constantly reminded you of what happened or didn't. A grief that didn't have a finality to it like my death did. I was at a loss for words, but Ben didn't allow either of us to feel pity for the other. He kept going.

"How did your dad pass away?"

Months ago, maybe even weeks, I would have felt resentment

at having to answer this. This time, he felt like the only person who could understand me.

"Cancer." I said. "He passed away this year. One day I was planning what to present for my senior class project and the next, he was gone. I still can't wrap my head around it.

"He was sick for close to two years, but we always thought he would make it. Actually, I don't think we ever thought he wouldn't even though we used to joke that cancer had its mood swings."

He lifted one brow in confusion.

"Dad's health changed all the time when he was battling it," I said, "one minute he was healthy and full of energy and the next, we had to take him to what ended up being his final hospital run."

"I was so certain he would beat it," I looked away from him. "He wasn't there for prom. He wasn't there for my senior pictures. He wasn't there when I walked with my graduating class. He also wasn't there to see me off to college."

Ben didn't interrupt. He kept listening and watching me.

"Everything reminds me of him. The worst is I feel like I didn't just lose my dad, my mom's hurting too. She's hurting a lot and I don't know how to handle it, I don't think she does either. I wanted to take a gap year and be there for her, but she didn't support it. She didn't want me to disappoint my dad. They both graduated from here."

I looked at Ben, desperately hoping he could make sense of this for me. He was smart. He'd read all these books most people couldn't get around to. He was someone who looked like he knew the answer to everything, even this one.

"If there's a God, why didn't he heal my dad?"

He didn't flinch at my question. He shifted in his seat but kept my gaze as he spoke.

"I can't tell you why God heals some people and not others or why he answers some prayers and not others...I asked myself that all the time after my accident then just came to the conclusion that all I could do was trust in his character. He's done a lot for me over the years and he's been there for me in ways no one could ever have. I have to trust that he'll work all things out like he says he will."

He let out a deep sigh. "What I can tell you is that scripture is true in this regard, he's absolutely near to the broken-hearted."

"Why are you asking?" he asked me. "Don't you believe in him?"

"My dad grew up in the church, he had me baptized when I was young. We only went to church as a family two times, for my baptism and when he was first diagnosed. He went a lot more by himself, even more when he was sick."

"My mom's not religious, she doesn't believe in God." I shook my head. "She also didn't understand how God could hurt him after he prayed to him so much."

I could hear loud sounds of laughter coming from inside.

I looked at Ben again. He stared at me attentively. He didn't try to change the subject or say something positive.

"How can you believe in a God like that?" I asked him.

"Because he changed my life." he said. "It's not something I can convince you of, it has to be something you seek for yourself. Annabelle, if your dad was saved when he passed away, I trust that he's now at peace. Can I ask you one more question?"

I looked away. "It's your turn."

"What about you Annabelle? You told me what your parents think and believe. What do you think?"

I met his gaze, admitting something I never told to anyone else. "I prayed to God twice before. My dad and I went on a trip together and I wouldn't go to church with him that day. I ended up sneaking out when he fell asleep and went by myself. No one knows this, I was desperate.

I answered his question directly. "I think I believe he's up there. My dad meant everything to me. My dad and everyone else can't be crazy to think that there is one. I just don't think he hears me or wants anything to do with me."

I thought of the gift dad gave me before he passed away. "I also don't understand the bible."

I'm not sure what I expected at this moment, but it wasn't Ben's sudden burst of laughter. He couldn't control himself as he let out a deep laugh, one I wouldn't have expected from him.

"The face you made just now was ridiculously cute," he said. I looked down to hide my smile.

He went on, unfazed. "God always hears us. You don't have to pretend to be somebody you're not to seek him so don't ever let anyone tell you otherwise."

"James four eight," Ben said, "it became one of my favorite scriptures after the accident. It tells us to come near to God and he'll come near to us, I can personally attest to that."

"Hey!" Kevin walked up to us.

I got up and gave him a kiss. "What are you doing here?"

"Are you not getting my calls?" Kevin held me, "Amanda said you were here, I'm driving you back to Wolf to get your stuff."

I looked at my phone.

"We were going to walk back," I said to Kevin. "Thank you for coming to get us!"

"You don't have to walk now." Kevin kissed me again then he turned to Ben. "Sup man. I hear you're helping my girl pass her classes."

Ben looked at me then back at Kevin. "She's doing that all on her own."

"Then what does she need you for mate?"

I pulled away from him, "babe."

He kissed my forehead then looked back at Ben. "I'm just saying."

Ben rose from his chair.

I handed him back the jacket he'd given me. "Thank you for this."

"Sure," Ben said. "I should probably get going too."

My heart was beating out of my chest as we made our way back into the house.

"Thank you for everything," I said to Ben.

"Anytime." Ben said. "Happy Thanksgiving." He looked at Kevin, "same to you."

I immediately turned to Kevin once Ben was out of Warren's house. "What was that babe?"

"Let's go, we need to get back to Wolf to get your stuff," he said. "Jordan's waiting on us." He walked out of the front door.

Amanda pulled me back before we walked behind him. "You're in deep trouble, miss."

"For what?"

"That look on your face." She ran a hand through her hair then gave me her Cooper smile. "The one you had at the football game, the one you had at the 10K, the one you had tonight." She stopped, another smile spread on her face. "I've never seen you with that look."

"What look is that?"

"The boom, Annabear," she smiled. "It's the *actual* boom."

She leaned in, "I'm sure of it."

Part 3

Twenty-One

THERE WERE WORSE things than being stuck in a car ride with your first love, your boyfriend who happened to be his best friend, and his sister who happened to despise him. Yet, I would have chosen them. For the first time in my life, I dreaded coming home. Had it not been for Amanda and Kevin arguing about the better playlist, surely, I would have had a nervous breakdown right here in this seat.

It felt like we drove a thousand years when Jordan stopped at the intersection known for alerting drivers that our hometown, Blakely, Massachusetts – *charming seaside in the heart of history* – was only a mile away.

Kevin whistled, "to have grown up here," he looked at Jordan, "you're lucky."

Amanda held my hand and mouthed. "We've got this."

I whispered a thank you and went back to brainstorming my options. If I wanted to change mom's decision to sell our home before the showing on Friday, three days away, I had to think of something fast.

Heart pounding, I looked out my window, drowning out the newly started music dispute between Kevin and Amanda. I clenched my seat as Jordan passed the *Welcome to Blakely* sign and held my breath while we drove through the colorful cottage homes overlooking *Seaside Lake and Beach Community*. I forced myself to look away briefly when he drove past the giant parking lot below *Cooper Wealth and Investment Agency* and again at the *Blue Lighthouse* tourist attraction. I almost stopped breathing altogether when we turned right at the exit instead of left which would have taken us to *Blakely Memorial Hospital*. My final exhale of discontent was let out when we entered our families' shared neighborhood, *Rockville Residences*.

Kevin turned around from the passenger seat with his eyes resting on mine. "I'm happy to be here babe."

"Me too," I simply whispered back.

I accidentally caught Jordan's stare and looked back out to the rows of cobblestones we were driving through. It was hard not to feel a way when we drove by the same colonial homes, the same high-pitched roofs with their oversized chimneys, the same long driveways and gated yards. Blakely and our neighborhood looked the same. It seemed everything looked the same except for what mattered most. The two people who made this place home for me, my parents, were gone in their own way.

"We're here," Jordan said and parked the jeep in the Cooper's driveway.

"Finally!" Amanda unbuckled her seatbelt. "I need *out* of this car." She stepped out to greet mom and Lucy who were standing out front, arms waving, right next to Jacob. Kevin stepped out of the vehicle next.

"It's nice to see you again, Mrs. Wilson." I heard Kevin say and watched him hand mom her gift.

"You didn't have to do this," mom said with a smile on her face that showed she didn't mind him doing it. "Thank you, I love it."

"Annabelle must have told you it's a family tradition," she added.

"She did, it was my pleasure."

He hugged Lucy next just as Amanda was taking some stuff out of the car while catching up with Jacob.

"Are you coming?" Jordan asked me, still in the driver's seat.

"In a sec," I whispered. Thankfully, he stepped out next. I watched Lucy excitedly greet him then ask if he could help Kevin bring the bags inside.

"Where's Annabelle?" mom asked, a bag also in hand and halfway to the front door. I waited for everyone to walk in then I stepped out of the vehicle.

I stared at the front door, tall enough a horse could probably walk in without having to duck. The front lawn that we always enjoyed playing soccer or tag on was trimmed as usual. I could see everyone pacing around through the high-arched windows, like my family's house, but painted blue instead of brown. It was the classic New England home that most houses in our neighborhood looked like. But theirs was a three-story home instead of two like mine.

I looked away from the silhouettes of Jacob and Lucy that were now in the kitchen. It dawned on me at this moment, I wanted to be in the basement archives playing another round of questions or maybe seated in the library room listening to everyone else speak.

"Everywhere and else," I heard myself whispering.

"Sweetie," mom came rushing out of the house. "What are you still doing out here?"

"Hi mom, I was just grabbing a few things."

She didn't say another word. She just grabbed me and held me for a little longer before we both went inside.

* * *

"Please make it quick!" Mom yelled when I hurried up the steps to Amanda's room. "We're on a time crunch."

I opened Amanda's door. *Even her room's the same.* The same turquoise walls filled to the brim with posters of her favorite girl groups.

Amanda closed her blinds and looked at me. "You should come out with me tonight, I texted a few friends to meet up later."

I sat at her vanity desk and looked at the massive bulletin board with pictures of her and her friends that hung over it. "I don't know, Kevin needs me here."

"You could bring him," she said. After three seconds of silence. "I'm joking, but if I were you, I'd show him off around town."

There was a sudden knock on her door.

"It's Kevin."

Amanda opened her door and he walked in.

I got up to kiss him. "Are you okay in the guest room?"

"Never been better, you alright?"

I shrugged. "I'm good enough."

"Mind if your girlfriend joins me tonight?" Amanda asked. "I would invite you too, but you know...girl night and all."

He simply looked at her, "not at all." He looked at me. "Seth's pulling up in the morning, so Jordan and I are just hanging out here tonight."

He kissed me again. Just his presence alone made being back here ten times more bearable than it would be otherwise.

"Thank you for coming," I said to him.

"Anything for you."

"Okay Romeo," Amanda said, "Juliet and I have to get ready."

He gave me another kiss and walked out.

Amanda shook her head. "Are we in the Twilight Zone or what? Your mom's selling your house, Jordan's home, and your boyfriend's spending Thanksgiving with us, before any of mine."

"Definitely twilight," I responded.

"How did we go from you having zero boy toys to this?"

"Beats me, Mandabear."

"You know what else I've noticed?"

"What?"

"My dad's not here. He should be here, he's always here before dinner time."

"Maybe he's out golfing," I tried to convince both of us.

"Sure." She applied her lipstick. "Whatever, I'm totally getting wasted to put up with all of this."

* * *

"Aces," Lucy said to us in her kitchen. "We need your help with the pies before you meet up with your friends."

Mom looked at us, "Luce and I have a meeting with the caterers in an hour for the showing."

"Annabelle, I placed your boxes in your room, it's best you sort as much as you can before you head back to campus. The other ones are in the garage for you to look at."

"I'll start tomorrow," I told mom.

Lucy looked at me. "Mare and I did a lot of the work so you can relax during the break."

"It's all easy from here," she continued. "This way, you have *more* time enjoying your holiday and less time helping clean stuff."

Amanda looked at mom. "What happens if someone wants to buy at the showing?"

Lucy responded instead. "They already do, it's a great property."

Mom immediately looked at me. "We have a few buyers interested as you know. Friday's showing is really for the last bidding. If all goes well, the couple I'm leaning towards wants to move in right after the New Year."

"After the New Year?" Amanda dropped the wooden rolling pin. "Why the freaking rush?"

"Amanda." Lucy said through gritted teeth.

Mom stared at me, about to say something, then stopped herself.

"Is Kevin okay with everything?" Lucy changed the subject.

"Yes, he likes it here."

Amanda looked at mom, "He says we're lucky to be from Blakely."

"You are!" Lucy grabbed cream out of the fridge. She shot me an innocent look. "You two are lovely together."

"Thank you for letting him stay here," I said to Lucy.

"I love a good sleepover," Amanda said.

"It'll be like old times," I added.

Amanda looked at Lucy. "It's great being back home but where's dad?"

"At the country club with his buddies." Lucy handed mom the cream, "The recipe calls for this one for the filling."

My eyes narrowed on Kevin's gifted ribbon wrapped around mom's wrist. I watched her move past Amanda, sorting through the list of ingredients to put inside the mixing bowl. It was finally hitting me. Like my *Daughters in Waiting* group, this was the way she was choosing to heal and turn the page, at any cost.

* * *

"Marie's not changing her mind at all."

Amanda stopped abruptly. We were on our way to her friend's house, which was also in our neighborhood.

"You're all welcome to join!" Amanda asked, mimicking mom and Lucy who had spent the past thirty minutes giving the guys the full rundown of the showing happening on Friday. "You have to do something, Annabelle. You can't just watch it happen and not say anything."

"I'm trying to, but I can't think of anything yet."

"I can't imagine your dad would have wanted her to do this."

I stopped my tears from welling up. "Don't mention it."

"What's the actual reason?" she asked me. "Is it financial issues?"

"Of course not."

"Thought so, boredom then?"

"Definitely not, Lucy's here."

She rolled her eyes. "Then, what is it?"

"I don't know, Amanda."

"Get to the bottom of it so you don't leave me here," she said. "I can bug my mom about it if you want?"

"Why didn't I think of that before?" she asked herself. "Why haven't you asked me to?"

"Don't say anything to your mom," I said quickly. "Mom and I need to have a real talk without you or Lucy or anyone else there. We've both been avoiding it, but I'll try to talk to her soon."

"Do it fast," she said. "I can't lose my best friend to Florida."

"You love sunny weather."

"Only on vacation."

"Or the lake house!" We both said at the same time. She linked her elbow with mine and we started walking again.

"You remember Michelle from school, right?" she asked me, a few feet from Michelle's house.

"I didn't hang out a lot with you guys...I don't want to intrude."

"She won't mind, just...be cool."

Before she had the chance to ring the doorbell, Michelle came running out of her house.

"I want to hear all about MGU!"

"Tell me about BU!" Amanda said back to her.

Michelle stopped in the middle of their embrace to look at me.

"You're here."

"Hi," I said to her.

She turned back to Amanda. "Gang's downstairs."

I stared at them walking in together before pulling out my phone.

Annabelle: We promised mom and Lucy we'd
be back by eleven

Amanda: We're having a movie night ;)

Amanda: We can totally hang here longer!

Michelle handed Amanda the open bottle of Tequila when we met up with the others in her room.

"You were taking forever so we started without you," Michelle said.

Amanda grabbed the bottle, took a chug, and handed it back to one of her other friends.

Michelle sat across from us on top of her bean bag. "The guys want us to show up around eleven," she said. I resisted the urge to text Amanda again.

"We need to hurry up and catch-up then," one of the girls said. Suddenly, they all looked at each other and let out a simultaneous squeal.

"BU is soo much fun!"

"I'm dating the richest guy at MGU."

"I don't miss high school at all."

"I'm thinking of transferring somewhere out of state."

"Guys!" Amanda spoke over everyone. "We can't all talk at once. I'll go first. I already sent you the stats on him. He has the nicest house on campus, and he's loaded."

"Has he asked you to be his girlfriend yet?"

"Not yet, but he's about to, I can tell, we hook up all the time. Ask Annabelle, he's totally glued to me. I'm kind of happy it's Thanksgiving so I can take a break from him."

"I bet he has the hots for you," Michelle said to Amanda. "You always got the best guys."

"And you always get them to fall in love with you," her other friend added. She looked at me, her eyes shrunk. "What about you?"

"Annabelle's dating one of the hottest guys on campus,"

Amanda said. "You guys should see them together. Every girl's jealous of her."

"Really?" Michelle asked. "What's his name?"

"Kevin," I said.

"He's been here before." Amanda cut in. "Remember the hottie who came over for Thanksgiving before?"

"Oh yeah...I remember that," Michelle said, still looking confused, "the college guy? What's he like?"

"He's..."

"Smoking hot," Amanda answered her, "and romantic."

Michelle didn't look convinced. "How did he ask you out?"

"Gosh Michelle," Amanda grabbed the bottle again. "You want to know his social security too?" The other girls chuckled.

"I think BU guys are hotter than MGU," Michelle spoke again.

Amanda glared at her. "How would you know that? You've never been to MGU."

"I've seen the pics you've sent me, we totally have the hotter guys."

They started to one-up each other on how their college lives were going. I don't remember exactly when in the conversation, but eventually, I made my way back outside and called Kevin.

"Hey babe," he said.

"What are you doing?"

"Hitting the sack now, I wouldn't mind seeing you when you get back."

I paused for a moment, trying to figure out if my response should be flirty.

"We'll see each other in the morning babe."

"Not sure I can wait that long, is girls' night helping at all?"

"Not really, but I'm happy to be getting fresh air." I looked at the time on my phone. "Also, I miss you."

"Miss you too babe."

"When will you be back?"

"It's supposed to be at eleven, but I have a feeling Amanda wants to stay out longer."

He hesitated. "Can I ask you something?"

"Uh huh."

"Do you always do everything she tells you to?"

"Who? Amanda?"

"Yes, Amanda. I've dated you for months now and you do everything she tells you to."

I tried not to get offended. "Kevin, we're extremely close, we're kind of like a package deal."

"Tell her that."

"You're being rude."

"I'm looking out for my girlfriend."

I liked his protectiveness, I really did, but I couldn't help but feel that he was out of line.

"The more you get to know her, the more you'll like her," I said, immediately wondering if Jordan had said something to him.

"She may not get along with Jordan, but you shouldn't judge her for it."

"You kind of have to get along with her babe," I added. "It's our golden rule."

"What's that?"

"Amanda and I have to get along with each other's boyfriends otherwise we can't date them."

"Ah." He said, "I can't picture you getting along with Warren."

"He's not her boyfriend yet."

He chuckled. "Since that's the case, I can't picture you getting alone with any of her boyfriends."

"I don't mean to be rude," he said after a moment. "I'm just looking out for you."

My voice lowered. "I know."

My stomach was in perfectly tangled knots now. The good kind you didn't want to untangle and instead, made you want to run home and kiss your boyfriend. It was nice to have a guy who wanted to protect me.

"I like that you care," I said. "Stay up, I have to show you something." Michelle's front door opened.

"Gotta go, Kevin. Stay up!"

"I know we said eleven," Amanda flashed me her Cooper smile. She didn't have to say it, I already knew what she wanted to ask.

"The party's not too far from here, it's in this neighborhood. Everyone back home is doing something, they won't even know we're not back in time. We'll be there one hour max."

"I can't this time," I told her.

She raised her eyebrows.

I stared at her. "If you come back first, you cover for me if they ask."

Twenty-Two

"THANKS FOR MEETING ME HERE."

"Thanks for letting me," Kevin looked at our landscaping. "Nice house." This was never the way I'd pictured bringing a guy home, but I knew he would like what I was about to show him.

"Don't touch anything," I said to him.

"Are you sure it's alright I'm here?"

"Yes," I said. *I need you here.* "I want to show you something."

I grabbed his hand and entered the code to the garage. When I turned the lights on, it was totally and completely quiet. But it wasn't the boxes stacked on top of the others that caught me off guard. Those I expected. It was the new furniture in the living room when we walked inside the house, the fliers that were laid out in almost every room on our ground floor, and all the family pictures that were removed. Even our kitchen cabinets were emptied.

Kevin didn't say a word, he just kept holding my hand. I walked with him past the laundry room, adjacent to the kitchen, and stopped in front of the door to the backyard.

I took another deep breath and walked us out. "This is what I wanted to show you."

"Whoa." That was all he said at first.

It was a sight. A rare sight. Anyone who wasn't used to it usually had that same expression because our garden was impressive and took up a good chunk of our backyard. *Totally a masterpiece,* Amanda once said.

I walked him to the sign mom and I placed at the front of it when we first started to build it – FOLLOW THE LILIES. The flowers rotated throughout the year, but the sign always stayed there.

"Babe, this looks straight out of a fantasy."

Slowly, I walked him into the garden, following along the path that zigzagged its way around. Along the entrance, yellow and red coneflowers were lazily moving against the wind. Right next to them were the rows of roses. First the red ones, then the white ones and then the pink ones. We passed the new batch of daisies and lilies behind the pink roses. There looked to be hundreds of them. Then we stopped in the white gazebo – completely encircled by the sunflower plants – in the middle of the garden. When the sunflowers were in season, they always looked like they were saying, have a seat or dance. Either way, you're welcome here.

I took another deep breath and walked him past the gazebo to the other side of the garden.

"What all is here? I've never seen anything like it."

"The strawberries are here," I pointed to our right. I turned to our left. "Lettuce, Brussel sprouts, green onions, cucumbers, and of course our peppers."

I kept walking, "We get the occasional yard stealers trying to eat it." A slight grin spread on my face. "Mom and I don't mind." I pointed to our right again. "Raspberries and cranberries are here. Very occasionally, we'll have blueberries too."

I stopped a few feet later and spun around. "Grapes over there and the few remaining plums."

I pointed straight ahead. "Our lemon, lime, and orange trees are over there. They're delicious when we can pick them."

Kevin didn't say anything for a while then finally turned to me. "No wonder you don't want her to sell this place." I grabbed his hand and walked him back to the gazebo.

"I can sort my stuff out another time," I said when we sat down on the bench. "I have all week anyway."

Kevin smoothed out the ribbon dangling against my neck and dropped his forehead to mine. I closed my eyes, taking in how happy I was to have brought him here.

He wrapped his arms around me and kissed my neck first and then my cheeks. "We have about...an hour and a half to make out."

"My alarm will let us know when to stop."

He grinned and kissed me again. I kissed him back, both excited and relieved that he was here with me. That he wanted to be here with me.

"How long did it take you to do all this?" he asked after a moment.

"Since I was little, I knew she wouldn't get rid of this. We've built this for years. If we move, I hope whoever gets this place wants to keep it." I stared at him. "You're the only guy I've brought here Kevin."

His dimple caved in. "I'm honored." He trailed his hand down my arm. "Does this mean it's a date?"

"Maybe."

He smiled. "Look who's the romantic one now."

He kissed me again and there was an instant bang in my chest. Maybe his too because I could hear his heartbeat as my pulse quickened.

I had to unwillingly pull away, "I think your phone's ringing."

He blew out his breath. "Hold on, I need to take this." He stared at me. "Don't go anywhere."

"I'll try not to," I said. He quickly fumbled in his front pocket to pick it up. I could see the name on the screen. *Jackie*. Kevin got up and walked outside of the gazebo, further away from me – not realizing that the sounds in the garden echoed.

"Hey babe," I heard him say. "Not much, hanging out with the mates."

I sat there, unsure of what to do while he spoke to the unknown girl. It hit my heart like a mallet and pulled it out of my stomach. I dropped my head and closed my eyes. *She's probably just a friend.*

"I had fun last weekend too." There was a pause. "Send me those pics." Then a small laugh. "You know I fancy you in blue." Another pause. "I'll hit you up when I'm back on campus."

I looked at him, casually strolling back into the gazebo. It made no sense to jolt myself into a state of jealousy. *She must be a friend.*

"Who was it?" I asked him.

He looked away. "Jordan wants me back at the house."

I simply stared at him, then said, "I have a bunch of boxes to sort through."

I could tell he wasn't sure what to do.

"Kevin, you can go. I won't be able to sleep anyways with everything I need to do," I calmed my breaths. "You saw that garage."

"I don't want to leave you here."

"It's my home," I said. "It's the safest place where I can be."

"Fair." He kissed my forehead. "Call if you need me." He kissed my lips, "anything for you."

* * *

I walked out of the garden moments later, but instead of going back to the Cooper's, I made my way back inside my house. I stepped into the shadows of the living room, careful not to make any noises despite knowing that no one else was in there but me. My footsteps were heavy on the wooden floor when I walked upstairs, passing the bathroom, forcing myself not to look at the hallway leading to my parents' door at the end of it.

I didn't expect to feel this much hurt, but I knew at this

moment, only one thing could help me. Like the garage, my bedroom was filled with boxes. I suddenly felt like I could hear everything. The crickets outside. The wooden floor squeaking every step I took towards my bedroom closet. The loud beating in my chest when I grabbed the gray memorabilia box my dad gifted me for my sixteenth birthday. It was metal with its own lock and key, and I kept everything dear to me in there. I placed the box on my closet floor to open it when I received a text.

My heart shattered a million pieces when I realized it wasn't Kevin texting me.

> Jordan: Are you up?

> Jordan: How are you?

> Jordan: I'm here if you need me.

Being here, back in my room, back in Blakely, it was like being forced right back to everything.

> Annabelle: Thanks

My phone immediately rang.

"You're up," Jordan said. "I saw Kevin came back, he mentioned he was at your place."

"Everyone's sleeping, Jordan."

"Not us," he said.

"How do you think it went with your mom seeing Kevin?" he asked. I was quiet for a moment.

"Are you happy he's here?" he asked nonchalantly, but I heard something else in his voice.

I thought of the most careful answer I could give him. "It takes the pressure off that he's been here before." Jordan didn't say anything back to that.

"I'm sorry for the way our call ended last time," he told me.

"I'm the one who hung up on you."

"Don't worry about it."

I was just about to say goodnight when he spoke again.

"What does it look like there? Do you need my help with anything?"

"Mom's packed up almost everything."

"Brutal."

"Tell me about it, thank you for asking."

"Tell me if you do." He stopped for a moment. "I want you there today, you should come out with us."

"Kevin said your birthday was a guy thing."

"There's no one else I'd rather spend my birthday with than you, especially in Blakely."

"I would love it if you could come," he added. I could hear him pacing through the phone.

"Can I count on you to be there?" he asked.

"Hello?"

"Annabelle, you there?"

"I don't think it's a good idea, Jordan."

There was a long pause, an unbearable pause.

I let out another sigh. "I'll only go if Amanda can come."

"That I don't care for," he said, "at all."

"Then I won't come. She's worried about your parents, Jordan. You should tell her if something's going on."

"It's not my place to tell her." he said flatly. "Goodnight, get some rest."

Minutes later, I was lying flat on my bedroom floor. My eyes fixated on the fan spinning circles over my head. When I grabbed my phone to check the time, I saw Jordan had texted me again.

Jordan: Thanks for picking up my call.

Jordan: I mean it, tell me if you need me.

Jordan: I want to be there for you

Jordan: If that's what you want

I stopped myself from opening the memorabilia box and walked out.

* * *

In a way, I was glad it was Wednesday, Jordan's birthday, because family breakfast meant I didn't have to dwell on what I'd heard in the garden. I was also wishing it was a stupid mixup on my part. From a third party's point of view, like Kevin's, breakfast must have looked peaceful and fun. We all seemed to be getting along, but the heavy truth was that dad wasn't here, we were still waiting on Jordan to come down and celebrate, and Mr. Cooper hadn't come home the previous night.

"Who wants the next batch of pancakes?" Lucy asked inside the kitchen. I drew in a calming breath and walked back in.

"Do you want anything to eat?" mom asked me.

I shook my head. "No, I'm not hungry."

Jacob grabbed a plate. "I'll take some."

Kevin pulled out a dining chair so I could sit next to him.

"When are you and Amanda heading to the house?" mom asked me.

"After breakfast," I answered her.

"Please don't touch anything but your boxes," she flipped the bacon in the frying pan. "Luce and I will drop by this afternoon after my realtor meeting."

Amanda rolled her eyes. "Ditto."

Kevin watched me silently. "Should I come babe?"

Mom and Lucy stopped what they were doing.

I grabbed his hand. "If you want...but, I think you should hang out with Seth and Jordan since it's his day."

"I don't mind." He stared at me and wouldn't look away. He was always there, willingly, and always showed me he cared. I knew at that moment not to panic about this Jackie.

Amanda stopped him. "Don't you dare say it."

"Anything for you," she mocked, then threw a piece of bread across the table at us.

Kevin caught it. "You beat me to it."

"If you two keep this up, mom's going to want all the people we're talking to to show up for Thanksgiving every year."

Lucy looked at her. "How many people are you talking to, young lady?"

Everyone laughed except mom who was hyper focused on the new pieces of bacon she was placing in the pan.

"We won't be at the house long," I said to Kevin. "Enjoy your day with the guys."

Lucy smiled at Kevin. "When is Seth getting here?"

"Any minute now actually," Kevin said.

The kitchen door opened but instead of Jordan, Mr. Cooper walked in. He was a tall and slightly heavy man with peppered hair that always drew attention to himself.

"Dad," Amanda got up to hug him. "I finally get to see you!" He hugged her back before turning his attention on everyone.

"Morning," Mr. Cooper said. He walked over to Kevin and shook his hand. "Great to have you here."

"Thanks sir," Kevin said.

Mr. Cooper looked at me and gave me a hug.

"How's school treating you, Annabelle?"

I cleared my throat. "Good."

He stood there for a moment before patting my shoulders. Mr. Cooper and my dad weren't the closest, but they got along well enough.

He walked over to the coffee station. "Where's Jordan?"

Mom and Lucy exchanged a look.

"He's trying to make his beauty entrance," Amanda said.

"Ace," Lucy looked at her. "Must I tell you again that it's your brother's birthday today?"

"Please no, don't torture me."

Mr. Cooper shook his head and poured coffee for himself. I was suddenly reminded of the funeral and the heated exchange I saw between him and Jordan. I looked away from him just as the kitchen door opened.

"Happy birthday!" Jacob, mom, and Lucy all said at once to Jordan.

Mr. Cooper walked over to shake his hand. "Happy birthday son." There was an awkward pause before Lucy spoke again.

"I made all your favorites," she said.

He ran a hand through his hair, "thanks mom."

Kevin gave him a high-five. "Happy birthday mate."

Lucy frowned at Amanda so she would stand up.

"Consider this your one hug for the year." Amanda said to Jordan. "Happy birthday."

"Thanks," Jordan said. He assessed all the breakfast food on display then lifted his eyes away from the kitchen island to the table, then to me.

"Happy birthday," I said quietly. The doorbell rang.

"Must be Seth," Kevin said as Jacob rushed to open the door. A few seconds later, he walked back into the kitchen with Seth.

"You're the last of us three to turn the big two one," Seth said to Jordan after greeting everyone.

"It's a big deal mate," Kevin added.

"Can't go wrong with unlimited pool and wings." Jordan smiled, "Billiards won't know what hit them tonight." He looked at me again. I looked away.

Mr. Cooper stared at the boys. "Don't get crazy, Thanksgiving's tomorrow."

"Dad," Jacob looked at him, "what are the chances you let me go tonight?"

"Jordan wouldn't dare invite you to hang out with his friends," Amanda said. "Don't worry though, you're not missing out."

"Amanda." Lucy said. "Would it kill you to be nice to your brother today?"

Amanda took a bite of her pancake. "Totally."

"You can come eat wings with us," Jordan said to Jacob. He

looked at Amanda and sighed. "Even you." He paused at me. "You too, Annabelle."

I wasn't sure what to do or say and I was glad that no one else did either. We were all frozen in place.

"Wow," Lucy leaned against the island, "that's a great idea." She looked at mom who was also stunned.

"It's very thoughtful of you Jordan," mom said.

Amanda looked at Jordan, "You haven't come back for any holiday in two years and now you want me at your birthday party? What the heck's going on with you?"

Lucy looked at her, "*Ace.*"

Mr. Cooper and Jacob stared at Jordan.

"What is it you like to say mom?" Jordan shrugged. "The more the merrier."

"You want the girls to come?" Seth asked him.

Kevin put his arm around me. "I don't mind it." Seth just gave him a look.

"Jacob's staying home," Mr. Cooper said.

"That's not fair," Jacob said.

Jordan ruffled his brother's hair. "You have all day with me." He looked at his friends before looking at Amanda then me. "I want you there though." Both Lucy and mom looked really pleased.

"Your room's already set up." Lucy said to Seth, breaking the next wave of silence. "Jacob, do you mind showing Seth the second guest room?" Lucy looked at Amanda again. She gave her a look that said, *please do this for your brother.*

"Ugh." Amanda said. "I'll celebrate his birthday with him. Why should he have all the fun anyways?"

Twenty-Three

I STILL HAD to figure out a way to ask Kevin who Jackie was even if I knew I was anxious for nothing. I must have gone through a dozen flowers in my mind trying to think of a replacement for him if it ever came down to having to change his.

"Zinnia." I muttered under my breath. *Finally*. Pretty much anyone could grow them. I opened my eyes to the table staring at me.

I shifted in my seat. "Nothing."

Kevin removed his arm from around me, "this is delicious."

"You're eating these wings like it's Thanksgiving meal," Seth joked.

"I took you here before," Jordan said to Kevin. As strange as all this was, Jordan was seated next to Amanda, seated next to Seth at our table at Billiards. A couple of Jordan's high-school friends occupied the other one.

"It feels like my first time," Kevin said mid-bite.

"There's a joke in there somewhere," Amanda said.

Jordan grabbed his beer. "You're not as funny as you think."

Amanda shrugged. "Funny, I've been told the opposite." Kevin chuckled and grabbed another wing.

Jordan extended the basket of fries towards me so I could grab them. I shook my head no and he brought it back to himself. I caught Seth staring at me and he looked away. He was the only guy who didn't seem to care that me and Amanda were there.

I felt a kick under the table.

"Bathroom break?" Amanda asked me.

"I don't really need to."

I felt another kick on my leg.

"Sure."

"You can't possibly hate being here as much as I do," she said as soon as we walked into the one-stall bathroom.

"You don't look like you hate being here at all."

"That's because the bartender took my fake ID," she smiled. "I totally needed those shots after the day we had going through those boxes in the garage. It's hard work, that alone should be reason enough for Marie to stop this. Good thing you want to do your room by yourself."

I adjusted the ribbon around my bun. "We were only there for a few hours."

"That my friend, was a job reserved for your knight in shining armor."

She flushed the toilet, "or soccer jersey."

"I wanted you there. It was kind of Kevin to offer, but I can't impose that on him, he didn't come here for that."

"Annabear," she walked over to the sink, "it's cringe watching him try to impress you, you've barely paid any attention to him all night."

"I haven't said anything."

"Exactly, you're the only one not talking," she dried her hands, "what's the matter? The grumpy attitude is totally unbecoming."

I could tell her right now what I heard in the garden, but I could also picture it. Amanda waltzing out of the restroom and going to give Kevin a mouthful.

"It's just a lot being here," I said. "Does it look that bad?"

"Awful, stop looking so uncomfortable."

"I wish Halle was here to help me talk some sense into you," she added. "She says hi by the way."

I felt relief, but I wondered if she looked away from fixing her hair in the mirror, she'd notice my face and put two and two together, that something was up with Kevin. Amanda always knew these things even if she was the one that never got hurt.

"I scored an invite to another party tonight."

It was a sad moment. We always put two-and-two together.

"It's Thanksgiving Eve, you told the boys you'd drive them back," I said.

"Mom pressured me, I can't end my night like this. It's the busiest night of the year."

She pulled out a flask from her purse. "Help me think of an excuse to bail." She took a sip. "Movie night again at Michelle's?"

I grabbed the flask from her and walked to the toilet to pour it out.

"That was expensive vodka!"

"I don't care. I get it, you like to party but you're always drinking now. It's too much."

She straightened herself up and rinsed her mouth over the sink. "Now I totally have to go out tonight."

"You don't have to go out, you could just stay home with me."

We stood there silently.

"A proper sleepover," I smiled. "Like old times."

She grinned. "Proper? You're sounding like your boyfriend."

I shrugged. "He's rubbing off on me."

"You sure you don't want to come out for round two tonight?"

"No, Mandabear."

"Then help me think of an excuse."

"I won't do that," I poked her. "But I'll probably put on a great movie that you're going to miss out on because it'll probably be one of our favorites."

"Annabelle," a grin appeared on her face. "Tonight, *this night,* is the night to take the next steps with Kevin and I don't mean taking him on just a midnight tour around your house."

I rolled my eyes. "What happened to waiting on the boom?"

She shrugged. "Yeah, well, it can clearly happen with anyone. Not to mention, I totally thought you'd be ready by now."

"Think about it, Kevin can't keep his eyes off of you and you have the whole house to yourself."

"I don't," I said. "The house is packed."

"I don't mean our house." She smiled, "I mean yours." I looked down.

"What are you waiting for? It's not every day you get to lose your virginity to a hot college guy like Kevin," she unlocked the bathroom door, "I promise you, it doesn't get better than this."

"Boys!" Amanda walked over to the table. "Who wants to take us home?"

Kevin looked at me. "You're leaving?"

"Yes," I said. He came out of the booth to kiss me.

I exhaled a sharp breath and crossed my arms around me. "I'm heading back with Amanda."

Jordan looked at Amanda with contempt. "You said you'd drive us home."

"How about..." She pointed to the other side of Billiards where a group of girls were staring at us. "You get one of those girls to give you guys a ride."

"I don't mind driving Amanda home and coming back later to get you," I offered.

Kevin moved closer to me and kissed me. "You're not doing that."

"I'll drive them back," Seth said. He looked back and forth between me and Amanda. "Grab your stuff." He walked out.

"Good, this party blows," Amanda followed behind him.

Kevin rubbed his hands on my back. "Will you be up when I get back?"

"I should be," I said. "Text me." *I'll ask him tonight.* He kissed me again passionately then released me.

Jordan cleared his throat. "They're waiting on you."

"You sit up front." Amanda whispered to me when I joined her and Seth outside. "He's worse than my brother."

"Ready?" Seth asked us when we got inside his truck. I nodded. He couldn't be anymore different than Kevin and Jordan.

"Seth, do you mind doing me a favor?" Amanda asked him in her most flirtatious voice while twirling her hair. "Mind dropping me off at a friend's house not too far from here before dropping off Annabelle?"

"You're something else." Seth said under his breath. "I'm taking you guys back to your house."

"Whatever, can you at least put the radio on?"

"No."

"Do you ever get that stick out of your ass or is this why you and Jordan are such close friends?"

"Only on special occasions."

"You do have a sense of humor." Amanda said. "Ugh, how do I have to pee again?"

* * *

Even with the two of us outnumbering Seth in his car, Amanda and I stayed silent. Seth kept to himself. More in a *I can't be bothered to entertain you* than *I'm contemplating life's biggest mysteries*. It was easy to tell he wanted nothing to do with us.

Amanda faked a cough. "It's nice of you to do this, I totally didn't think you were the type."

I knew better than to turn around and give her a look. We had no idea what Seth could or would do at this moment. He looked like he wanted to drop us off the side of the road.

Seth looked at her from his rearview mirror. "I know you were sneaking drinks in there."

"I was using the toilet," she responded. "That's what restrooms are for."

"Sure you were," he said. His hands were firm on the steering wheel like it was taking all of him not to stop us on the side of this road. No one said another word until he pulled up in front of the Cooper's.

"I really have to pee!" Amanda rushed out of Seth's truck and ran into the house before I could get out.

"Wait," Seth said to me. *Why do I feel like doing the exact opposite right now?*

I sat frozen, one leg already out and ready to dash.

"You're dating Kevin," he said. I stared at him.

He continued. "You and I both know Jordan has feelings for you. Even if Kevin refuses to see what's going on with you and Jordan, you should make up your mind."

"Umm, I haven't led anyone on."

"I don't care to see my friends getting hurt," he insisted.

I stared at him. "Kevin and I are fine and there's – you don't know anything about me and Jordan." I stepped down. "Thank you for the ride."

I was still shaken up when Amanda left less than an hour later to meet up with her friends. I spent my time in her room thinking over my exchange with Seth and getting more upset by the minute. Maybe, I thought, he didn't mean anything by that. He was perceiving things wrong. This was just a big misunderstanding wrapped up as a Thanksgiving holiday.

"Hang up man," I heard Seth tell Kevin when he picked up my call. *Not a misunderstanding.*

"I was just calling to tell you goodnight."

"Night babe."

"Hey Kevin?"

"Yes babe?"

"Do you really like me?" I kept going. "I can make more of an effort hanging out with your friends when we're back on campus...if that's what you want."

He didn't say anything.

"It's just...if you want me to, I can."

"Of course I like you," he said after a moment, "you don't need to do that."

"Are you sure?"

"Babe, I don't care, don't stress about it," he said. "I like how things are with us, we're in a good place."

"Me too, but you'd tell me if weren't?"

"Hundred percent." He laughed. "I gotta go babe, goodnight."

I could hear girls giggling in the background.

"Night." I dismissed the pang in my chest and hung up.

* * *

Once again, I was back in my own home at midnight. Mom was so busy preparing for the showing with Lucy, I barely saw her. To think both of us were in and out of our home without the other, it felt wrong. It felt like the opposite of what dad would want. It felt like I was right all along. *We're avoiding each other.*

Jordan: Are you up?

I threw my phone on the bed and stepped back from the boxes I was sorting through. I walked over to my closet and pulled out my memorabilia box again. The only one who could have the perfect words for me right now would be my dad. So, I opened the box. Staring right in my face was the necklace Jordan gifted me years ago before leaving for MGU. I placed it to the side and lifted the ivory bible dad gifted me for my seventeenth birthday. I moved my fingers alongside my name that was stitched at the bottom left corner. I hadn't read it when he gifted it to me. *I didn't even care to read it.*

I grabbed the letters dad wrote me next, each addressed to a specific moment. I placed them on the floor and read the designations on each of them. *Before your wedding, before your first job, before your graduation.* It's like he knew when he was first diagnosed that he wouldn't beat it even though he made us believe he would. I stopped myself from opening all of them and held just one.

My breaths were heavy, scared, as I finally opened the letter I wanted to when he first handed me this box and letters. Now felt like the right time, more than ever, to read it. *Before you fall in love.*

* * *

My Dearest Daughter,

Happy sweet sixteen!

This milestone in your life is one to celebrate, but I want you to know that you will always be my little girl. I can still remember holding you in my arms in the delivery room and promising your mom that I would do everything in my power to protect you. You will always be my little girl who runs up to me and begs me to read her favorite books with her or runs up to me screaming "everywhere and else" just so I can pick her up and spin her around the room.

Now that you're in your teenage years, I can see you growing into a beautiful, intelligent, and wise young woman, and I find myself nervous when you ask me questions about boys. I can't imagine any man who will love you and cherish you and want to protect you as much as I do, but I trust that you'll make the right decision before you give your heart away. I want these letters to support you so you make the right decision when I'm not there to verbally answer you. I hope you know that, no matter what happens, dad is always here to guide you through all the stages you'll go through in life.

When the timing is right and you're ready to give your heart away to that special someone who deserves it, I hope you remember this:

It's okay to take your time with things. You're a lot like your dad in that way so try not to rush into falling in love, because that special someone should be kind, caring, and patient with you. He will make sure to wait until you're ready and if he doesn't, he doesn't deserve your love. He will make you smile and laugh and he'll be there when you cry. He'll want to spend his time with you talking about your interests and he'll show you through his words and actions that he loves you, values you, and respects you without needing you to be anyone else. He'll enjoy all those little quirks about you and he'll take an interest in your hobbies. He'll put in the effort it takes to make your love last and he won't shy away at letting you know he wants to.

Before you fall in love Annabelle, please don't forget that there's nothing wrong with wearing ribbons in your hair and there's nothing wrong with your desire to spend all afternoon reading multiple books and the next afternoon discussing them. There's absolutely nothing wrong with your love for gardening or wanting to spend your summers watching your favorite flowers bloom. There's nothing wrong with spending a week straight at the library so you can learn all you can about lilies or some other topic that's fascinating you for the month. Sweetie, there's also nothing wrong with your love for dessert and stuffing your face with them on occasion.

If a guy you date makes you feel like any of this is wrong, please remember what I told you, he's not the one to fall in love with. That special someone will want to protect you and he will protect all those things about you that make you unique and he'll love you all the more for them.

I have tried my best to set an example for what that love should look like with the way I've treated your mother. My hope is that you fall in love with the one who loves you as deeply as I have loved her.

I love you,
dad

* * *

There was a knock on my window. I quickly wiped away my tears and pushed the box and all of its belongings back into my closet. I scooped up, noticing Jordan staring at me.

"Please let me in," he knocked again. I opened the left window frame.

"What are you doing here? It's one in the morning."

He stepped in. "You don't sleep, I figured you'd be here."

I stared at him, puzzled and irritated. "You shouldn't be here."

He looked around. "What can I do?"

He stood there, staring at me, hands in his pockets. "I'm perfectly coherent."

"I'm trying to be a friend," he added.

For a moment, I didn't say anything. A dozen thoughts flooded my mind.

Eventually, I sighed with resignation. "Anything not intact goes into the donation pile by the door." I walked over to the box labeled *Middle school books* and gave it to him.

"Sure thing," he grabbed the box from me.

We were all work and zero conversation, not even an attempt to. He'd pull out an item from the box and ask for my input and I'd point towards the door. He'd shake his head and place it with the rest of the donations. Then we repeated the process.

"You're really giving all of this up?" he asked me a few boxes in. "You spent years collecting these."

"I don't have a choice."

"Your mom's never been the impulsive kind."

"I guess we've all changed."

"There's nothing you can do to talk her out of this?"

"That's the problem, we haven't talked, and I can't think of a single thing to do to stop her."

"That's it? She sells the house, and you leave just like that?"

"Yep," I sat down and opened another box near him. My own tongue felt thick. "It's Florida for our future."

"You can't be serious."

"No, but my mom is." I pulled out a few more items to donate. "It's her way of handling everything."

He sat down next to me and grabbed another item. "Keep or donate?"

"Donate."

"Just looking at all this stuff sucks," he threw the item across the room, and it landed perfectly in the donation box. "It's almost like your dad was the glue to everything."

"It feels like it, doesn't it?"

We both took a break and looked around my room.

"Florida's really not that far from Blakely," he stared at me. "It's only a ride or plane away."

"How are things with you and Kevin?" he asked. I avoided his concerned eyes. *He's offering to be a friend.* I shouldn't feel nervous talking to him about this.

"Do you know a girl named Jackie?" I asked him.

He blinked at me. "No, who is she?" *See, it's nothing.*

"I'm not sure, just wondering."

He turned a little and stared straight at me. I caught myself staring at his appearing smile and looked away. Another small smirk touched his mouth. Suddenly, it was pitch black again. Back to that night he told me he was in love with me. Back to the start of...*nothing, you have something special with Kevin.*

When I opened my eyes again, he was still there, watching me.

I stood up. "Come on, you offered to help. Two more boxes and we call it a night."

His face reddened. He stared at me, not moving, then lifted his hand for me to help him up. He stood up inches away from me.

"Your lead," he said and grabbed the next box I handed him.

Twenty-Four

Dear MGU Reader:
My fellow classmates
Ladies and gentlemen

Can you love two people at the same time? Before you say it, I
don't mean having your cake and eating it too. What would you do
in those shoes? Stick to the new or go back to the old?

Gobble. Gobble. Happy Thanksgiving.
I won't bite more than I can chew.

Kisses
…Or should I say hugs…
The Virgin

Baseballguyx : if you like someone else, u never liked the 1st one
that much
SweeetMaggnolia77: love is too complicated. Enjoy your time with
your family 😊
AnonymouSXX4: Happy Thanksgiving!
Singlegal: u can't love two people at the same time

 MGUjuniorrr : says who? I love them all 😊
KawaiiGirl: rule of thumb is to never go back
Rachel59: Happy Thanksgiving, Godbless!
Imnothere: who do you like more?
Massachussettsbabe: Happy Thanksgiving
SammyWorks: Happy Thanksgiving <3 enjoy the holiday!
FuntimeSunTime: Happy Thanksgiving!!
Lacie_Sm: Aren't you a whole girlfriend now??
MGUGal: she's all over the place
Sarah_Lee95: Happy Thanksgiving!

* * *

Rachel: Happy Thanksgiving!

Roxy: Happy Thanksgiving!

MY HEART WARMED up to their messages. I imagined they were having a much better break than I was. Last night was a close call, but I was happy to be able to look at Jordan and not cave. *My future's with Kevin.* I snuck away from the conversation in the lounge and went inside the kitchen just as Lucy was walking out with a dessert tray. She squeezed my shoulders and walked past me.

I lingered there silently, observing mom take one of the pies out of the oven. I kept watching her face closely, the way I did at the funeral, hoping to see her eyes light up again.

Her shoulders tensed up. "How are you feeling?"

I walked over to help her. "I wish dad was here, but dinner didn't go as badly as I thought it would."

The conversation was lighthearted and easygoing, and Mr. Cooper hadn't said much.

"It wouldn't have, the Coopers are family," mom responded.

"Jordan says dad was our glue." I paused. "I think he's right."

Her voice was flat. "Your dad was gifted in that way." She was quiet for too long. "We just have to get through it one day at a time, he wouldn't have it any other way."

"Mom, there's no way I can sort through everything in my room this week."

"I can tell," I could hear the trace of disappointment in her voice. "I walked in this morning."

She looked at me. "I thought Amanda helped you with some of that stuff."

"She did." I knew this was not the moment, but I didn't care to stop. "I thought about it mom...what if we just hold off on selling the house and grandma comes up here for a few months while I'm in school? I can even spend New Years with my cousins here, they told me they're dying to come up again...." I kept going when she didn't respond. "That way you're not alone while I'm in Blakely, grandma can be here, and I can still have time going through those boxes."

"I appreciate it sweetie but pushing it off isn't going to stop this from happening."

"That's not what I'm saying."

"We'll discuss this later, sweetie, everyone's waiting on us for dessert," she grabbed the pie and walked out.

"Annabelle!" Amanda looked up at me when I walked into the lounge. "Please tell mom Warren's friend is a great big for me for the sorority. You met her at Girls' bowling night remember? Gabriella?"

I shook my head. "She was nice."

"I"m trying to convince Amanda to go with the daughter of someone that I know would be perfect for her and Halle." Lucy said. "But she won't listen."

"You should listen to your mother," Mr. Cooper said to Amanda. "She's done this before you."

Amanda rolled her eyes. "Years ago, trust me on this mom, Warren's friend's the better option."

I grabbed the seat next to Kevin, across from Seth, Jordan, and Jacob.

"How long have you two been dating?" Mr. Cooper asked Kevin. Everyone stopped talking and Jordan sat up.

Kevin squeezed my hand, "not that long." He smiled at me. "Since September, so about three months now?"

Mr. Cooper smiled at me then looked at Kevin. "This thing you have going on, is it serious?" Mom and Lucy drank their wine.

Amanda threw her head back. "Just when I thought we were having a good Thanksgiving."

Mr. Cooper ignored her. "Annabelle's a bright young girl like my daughter, I would assume you'd know that."

Kevin cleared his throat. "Yes, sir."

"Remind me again what your plans are after college?"

"I want to go into politics, sir."

"That's smart of you, you can't go wrong with that." Mr. Cooper turned to Seth. "What about you?"

"I'm in finance, sir," Seth said. "Same major as Jordan."

Jordan clenched his jaw. I panicked at the thought of a heated argument between him and his dad, because I knew, if Mr. Cooper kept going, there would be one.

I got up to serve myself dessert and Amanda followed me.

"I'll reel dad in if he gets too crazy," she whispered while giving me a slice of pie. We both knew no one except my dad could ever *reel* Mr. Cooper when he went into one of his tangents. Although a funny guy when he wanted to be, he was set in his ways.

"Please do," I whispered back to her.

"Has Jordan told you we hire college interns over the summer?" Mr. Cooper asked Kevin and Seth.

I scanned the room before sitting down and thought to myself, if Mr. Cooper didn't have his condescending tone, this would be less awkward for everyone.

"It's easy money, you won't have to do much."

"Maybe they want to do much dad," Amanda joked.

Lucy took another sip of her wine. "Can we not talk about the family business right now, Bill?"

"It's what affords this lifestyle, one more year and Jordan can help me run it."

I squeezed Kevin's hand when I noticed the same expression on Seth and Jordan's faces. A wave of anger and discomfort flared through my body. Kevin came to one Thanksgiving before, but that was before Jordan completely fell out with his dad – for reasons that were still unknown.

"Their great-great-great grandfather built Cooper Wealth and Investment Agency from scratch." Mr. Cooper added sharply. "This family's legacy is because of them."

We all sat silently for a few moments. Then he furrowed his brows. "How's school going for you son? Your sister's making the most of MGU, are you?"

Amanda smiled, "thanks dad!"

"Yep," Jordan mumbled to his dad.

"You're sure about that?"

Lucy looked at Jacob. "There's another pie to heat up, why don't you go do that and bring it back out when it's done?"

Mr. Cooper placed his drink on the stand next to him. "You boys may love your soccer, but that's not a long term plan." He focused on Jordan. "I assume we're clear on that."

"What happens if we're not?" Amanda asked. Both Jordan and his dad gave her a look to stay out of it. She took another bite of her pie, "I'm joking."

"You have the family business waiting for you, son. The same business that affords your upbringing. Your only responsibility is graduating, working for us, and getting your masters."

Jordan scoffed. "That's more than one."

I suspected he would eventually say something, and I think Seth and Kevin did too because they didn't look surprised.

Mr. Cooper's head tilted in that familiar way when we knew he wasn't going to drop this. "Mind telling me what you were doing in New York?"

"Who was in New York?" Amanda asked.

Lucy flung back. "Ace, can you please stay out of this?"

I groaned and moved closer to Kevin. I did my best to not glance at Jordan again so I turned to watch mom. Her eyes were closed and she took another sip of her wine.

Mr. Cooper directed his question at Seth and Kevin. "What was he doing in New York?"

"Leave my friends out of this."

Mr. Cooper folded his arms. "You're coming back this summer to start getting the hang of things, that's a direct order."

And then, finally, it was over. Mr. Cooper had his final say. Or so we thought.

"I'm not joining your company," Jordan said.

Mr. Cooper simply laughed. "If you think I'm letting you ruin your future, you have another thing coming."

Jordan repeated himself to his dad. "I'm not working for the family business."

I was the first person he ever told it to. In a way, I was glad he was finally standing up for it.

Amanda looked at Jordan, "have you lost your mind?"

"Ace!"

"What mom? It's totally not the time and place to have this conversation!"

I wanted to tell her to say it to her dad, but I didn't. Jordan looked at me pointedly and cracked a faint smile. I glanced at mom, her eyes were flashed with fury. I knew what she was thinking at this moment, *if dad was here, he would have stopped things from escalating*. Then I grew angry again. *We* didn't have to be here.

"Jordan...you don't mean that," Lucy said quietly.

He looked at her, his expression cold, emotionless. "That's why I went to New York since dad wants everyone to know. I took the LSAT and I'm graduating early next year. I already signed on to intern at a law firm in New York."

Lucy chuckled, a sound of disapproval.

Mr. Cooper glared at her. "Was this your bright idea?"

"Our son's perfectly capable of making decisions on his own," she snapped back.

"My son has responsibilities and you're steering him in the wrong direction!"

"*Our* son," Lucy spat. "Our son."

Jordan sat up straight. "Mom has nothing to do with my decision."

Amanda gasped. "You want to be a lawyer? Since when? You really thought now was the time to let us know?" Seth and Kevin exchanged a look.

"Ace, stay out –"

"Ugh, I know mom," Amanda said.

Mr. Cooper stood up. "I won't watch you make this mistake."

Jordan looked him square in the eyes. "Like I've watched you have an affair on mom for years?"

I saw the heated flame dance around from Amanda, to Lucy, to mom, to Jordan, right back to Mr. Cooper.

"What did you just say to me? You may hate me but leave your mother out of this."

For a moment, no one spoke. Until Jacob came out and said, "the pie's ready."

Kevin looked at me and Seth. "Should we go?"

Jordan's eyes were wide now, he stood up.

"Jordan," Lucy whispered.

Jordan kept going. "Dad couldn't force my hand in private so he's trying to do it in public."

"That's enough Jordan," mom whispered. "Please, let's all calm down."

Seth stood up too and looked at me and Kevin. "I think we should leave."

"Annabelle, you and I should..." mom said but was interrupted by Jordan again.

"I'm sick and tired of pretending this family's something to be proud of," he looked at his dad. "Are you finally going to tell Amanda and Jacob what's going on?"

Amanda froze. "What are you talking about?" She looked at her parents, everything sinking in. "What the heck is he talking about?"

Jacob looked at his dad. "What's going on?"

Mr. Cooper shook his head. "We're not discussing this now."

"Just tell them the truth dad!" Jordan yelled, "Tell them you've been separated for months and stop lying to them about the affair!"

Kevin and I exchanged a look and he got up. I noticed Seth staring at Amanda. Jordan looked at all of us, stopping at me quickly, before continuing with the rest.

"Is this really true?" Amanda asked her dad, her eyes were covered in tears. "Is what he's saying true?"

Mr. Cooper's eyes softened when he looked at her, "honey..."

She got up too. "Jordan's right, why can't we be a regular family for once?" She ran out of the room and I got up as well.

Mom stared at me. "Annabelle, we should get going."

"I can't leave Amanda like this," I said.

"I know, but..." she shook her head, "we should go home."

"What home?" I asked her, then walked off.

* * *

"What did I ever do to deserve this?" Amanda asked.

By the time we walked over to our neighborhood's park, we were both fuming. I was sad for her, but angry too. Angry that mom thought it was a good idea to spend Thanksgiving there, knowing what was going on with Amanda's parents. She put Lucy first, because Lucy needed her. I found myself sad all over again.

I sat down next to Amanda. It all seemed unreal, like suddenly, the host would pull the curtains up and tell us this was all an act, *we won the prize afterall.*

"What do you want to do now?"

She shook her head. "I want to get the hell out of here. Jacob's the one I can't stop thinking about. We're at MGU, he's here all by himself."

She took out her phone. "I'm texting Halle, I'm heading back to campus today."

"Now?"

She stopped. "Yeah, now. I'm not staying here. You can't possibly expect me to be there for that showing."

"I'm not." I knew asking her to stay was an unreasonable request.

"No offense but I want nothing to do with our moms or anyone back in that house, especially Jordan." She put her phone away, "I'm going to drive my car up." She suddenly remembered. "Ugh, I don't have a parking spot."

"We can figure something out."

"So you're coming with me now?"

I winced. "I can't, but Kevin and Seth are heading back, I'm sure they'll take you. I really can't leave, Amanda." I thought of all the conflicts that were brewing under the surface for years. I had to do everything I could not to create an even bigger one with mom.

"Are you serious right now? Your mom hasn't cared about how you feel with her selling the house, tell her to do it alone for all I care."

I looked down.

Her eyes bore into me. "What about Kevin? You can't possibly let him leave like this?"

"They were heading back tomorrow, he said they don't mind at all."

"Annabelle, we can't stay here! Please come back to campus with me."

"Mom would be livid with me. I have to stay...I want to stay, I also have to speak with her."

"Everything sucks." I let out. "This entire year sucks."

"I thought I hated Jordan before..." she shook her head, "I don't even know what to call it now."

"We can go back to my house," I said. "Whatever you need, Mandabear."

She looked upset. "Yours is being sold, remember? We'll stay here until I figure something out."

Bright headlights pulled into the park's lot. Kevin and Seth stepped out of Seth's truck. Kevin walked up to me and grabbed me.

Seth walked up to Amanda. "Are you okay?" She shrugged.

"We just got done talking to your brother," Kevin looked at us. "Seth's driving us back to campus now."

"What about Jordan?" Amanda asked. "I'm not driving anywhere with him."

"He's staying back." Seth said. "How much time do you need to pack?"

"I'm good to go." She turned to me, "Are you sure you don't want to ditch?"

"I'm sure." I squeezed her hand. "Call me first thing when you get to campus." Seth nodded at me and walked Amanda to his truck. Kevin stayed back.

"Can we sit?" he asked.

"I'm sorry about everything," I said right away. "Things aren't normally this bad with them."

"You have nothing to apologize for, this wasn't your doing." He closed the distance between us. "So you'll head back on Sunday?"

I kissed him. "Yes, I need this time alone with my mom."

"I understand."

"I wish you could stay," I said. "But you need to be as far away from here as possible." He kissed the palms of my hands.

"Seth and I had a talk with Jordan." he said. "It wasn't the way to go about things, but he's fed up."

"I don't know how our families will bounce back from this."

"It's not your job to figure it out." He lifted my head up and kissed me again. "You weren't joking when you told me your year's been a whirlwind."

"You've made it better."

"My pleasure."

Still holding his hand, I finally asked him. "Umm...I've been wanting to ask you something before you go. I know it's nothing, but who's Jackie? I saw her name on your phone in the garden."

Kevin just stared at me. "You didn't tell me you heard that."

"I didn't want to jump to conclusions."

He didn't answer.

"Is she your friend?"

"I can explain later."

"Why not now?"

It was written all over his face. It pained me to have to ask him. "Are you talking to other people?"

"It's only been a few months Annabelle, give me a chance to prove to you I'm not that guy."

"I never asked you to prove anything to me."

"I really fancy you babe, really, I do. I don't want this to end."

He looked down. "You're not ready to get there with me and I told you I was alright with that." He shook his head. "I don't ever want to force you into anything."

"You're assuming things that aren't true," my voice quivered. "You told me you were okay waiting."

"I am babe." he said. "I don't want to lose you."

"Stop saying that! You're not losing me, Kevin. I'm not going anywhere."

He looked down, "neither am I."

I stared at him confused when my heart dropped. I finally understood it, why this whole time he didn't mind waiting with me, why he was so confident he would.

"You're only waiting on me because you're hooking up with other people," I said out loud.

"Come on babe," he put his arm around me. "When you put it like that it sounds..."

"True."

"We're all just talking about the truth today, aren't we?"

"Are you...hooking up with other girls?"

"I'm not hooking up with anyone." He looked at me, "You're the only girl I care about."

"But you want to even though you told me you were okay with taking things slow with me."

"I meant it, I'm dating you seriously aren't I?"

"I trusted you," I could barely see him with the tears gushing out. "You asked to come to Blakely to be there for me. You said you didn't play with your heart, you said it! You said you were in this with me. You can't just hook up with other people and date me at the same time."

"Annabelle –" His voice broke. "This waiting thing is hard for me, I'm doing this for you because I don't want this to end, but it's been hard."

After a minute, he released my hand. "People don't just wait around to have sex in college, you date, you hook up for bloody sake." He wiped his eyes on his sleeve. "I've tried all I can to make it work with you."

And there it was, the fifth moment. The fifth moment where you could predict the future. The one you never wanted to have to go through again. *The boom*, I thought, was never happening for me.

"You have a lot on your plate." He wouldn't look at me as he spoke. "I want to keep dating you but I'm afraid I rushed into things too much."

He finally looked at me and placed his arm around me. "Maybe down the line, things will make more sense for us."

Here it was, again. The moment the boy you were falling in love with broke up with you.

"I'm sorry," he whispered. "Please don't hate me, I'm always going to be here, Annabelle. I want to be here, but I think it's best we slow things down."

He lifted his hand and wiped my cheeks.

"I'm sorry, Annabelle," he whispered gently and walked away from me.

There was something so much more painful about this moment than the words that weren't being said. It destroyed you and despite that, you had to pretend that everything was fine. As I watched him walk away, I was reminded of how it felt when Jordan had ended things. It hurt with Kevin. *Really hurt.* I convinced myself all semester that he could be the one if we just took our time. I wanted to stop the tears from flowing or run to him and beg him to change his mind, but I couldn't work up the courage to.

Amanda opened the passenger door and ran out to me. "Did he just break up with you?"

She threw her hands in the air. "Are we cursed? Is this what this is?"

Amanda sat down and hugged me. "Do you want me to stay?"

I shook my head. "I can't ask you to do that, you get out of here, I'll be fine."

"Annabear," she held me so tight, I thought she wouldn't let me go. Then she finally pulled away. "Trust me, he wasn't that hot."

"There'll be other boyfriends, I promise," she said.

I wiped my tears. "I'm okay, really, you need to get out of here."

She stared at me. "Someday, some incredible boy's going to sweep you off your feet, and it won't end like this."

I hugged her tightly again and watched her reluctantly get into the back of Seth's truck. Kevin wouldn't look at me as the three of them drove off. Months of dating him and trusting him, destroyed in a single moment.

Twenty-Five

"WHERE WERE YOU?"

Mom asked me when I walked into our house. She was seated on the living room steps, staring at me. Her eyes filled with concern.

She stood up. "I've been worried sick. Why aren't you answering my calls?"

"Amanda left hours ago." She looked at the clock. "It's almost 9 PM."

"I was at the park," I mumbled while passing her and making my way up to my room.

"Stop." Her tone was short. I turned around to face her.

"What happened tonight was unexpected and I hate that you had to deal with that." She lowered her head, "after everything we're going through."

She walked up to me. "Tomorrow can be just you and me, we can do the showing by ourselves."

"Mom, come on." I said. "Enough with the showing. Today sucked for all of us! That was horrible and you guys kept that from us."

"Look Annabelle, I know you're upset," she started to say but I stopped her.

"No, I'm livid." I took a step down. "I'm not okay with what you're doing, and you don't care."

"How many times do I have to tell you that this is for our good, our future. If anything, tonight showed you that –"

"Dad knew what was for my own good," I said. I ran up the stairs to my bedroom and shut the door.

Mom walked in right after me. "No matter how much it hurts." She let out a deep breath. "I have to pick up the pieces for us."

I looked at her. "Before dad died, you used to ask me how I was all the time. You used to make time for me. It's been so hard being back here with all my things packed into boxes. Why can't we get through this together?"

She walked over to me. "I never thought your dad would pass away, but he's gone." She sighed. "He's gone and I need to make sure we're both okay."

"I'm not, mom. Not with this, not with you selling the house." I looked at all the boxes around us. "You used to come to me. You used to have tons of stories to share. We used to do everything together as a family.

"You've barely been present with me. Why can't we just talk like old times? Why is it so hard for you to come to me?"

She placed a hand over her chest, "I miss your father. I miss him so much; I don't know what to do with myself. Every time I see you, I see him. I see the way it's affected you, and I feel guilty because we have no family here."

She remained still, like it was taking all of her to keep herself up. "We can't lose ourselves in this town."

"We're not, mom. This home's the only thing stable in my life."

"Sweetie," she lowered her head, "your dad wanted us to move out of Blakely before he passed away."

There was nothing to say when your whole heart shut off. I couldn't respond at first or at all.

"I tried to talk him out of it," she stopped. "He saw this all coming from a mile away." She moved closer to me. "You love this place so much, but he never wanted you to be influenced by it." She paused. "Like I was."

"Annabelle," her voice was straighter now, her face relaxing, "we're moving before you start your next semester. Grandma and the rest of our family are waiting for us in Florida."

I said nothing for a moment, but I knew what she was expecting from me. I also knew mom was never going back to who I needed her to be for a while, maybe ever, and I couldn't live with that.

"What if I want to meet dad's family?"

I took a step back and pulled out the picture of my parents I'd placed in my pocket. They were at a campus event, arms around each other, and both smiling with dad wearing his SFC shirt. His parents were right behind him.

"Mom, I joined that club," I gave her the picture. "Dad's wearing their shirt."

She looked at me, startled.

"They're really nice," I whispered. "They're nothing like I expected them to be."

She didn't say anything for a while. She just stood there, staring at the picture.

"This was such a long time ago." I could tell she was reliving a distant memory as she spoke. "We look so young." She handed me back the photo like she was telling me to keep it away from her. "You know how we feel about that."

"They're the only people who genuinely made me feel okay this semester or even close to him." I dismissed the thought of Kevin. "Who took me away from all of this."

She walked over and gave me a hug. She held me a little while longer then walked to the door.

"There's a meal downstairs for you," she said. "I'm meeting with our realtor tomorrow and I'd love it if you could join us. Showing starts at 5 PM."

I watched her fingers tightly curl around the handle. I held my breath, hoping she'd turn around and tell me she'd consider changing her mind, that we would figure something else out. But she didn't.

* * *

Jordan: Are you up?

I heard my phone going off and woke up. All the photo albums from the boxes were spread around me. I sat up quietly and looked at the time. *Eleven*.

Headlights came near my window, illuminating my walls. The car stopped and a door opened. I heard sniffling.

"Mere, I don't know what to do." I could hear Lucy speaking to mom in our driveway. "I never wanted them to find out like this." More sniffling. "I need you, please stay with me. Bill's gone with his parents and Jacob needs us, me." Even more sniffling. "All the catering stuff is sorted right?"

The car doors shut again, and the headlights drifted away.

It's not like I had a significant reason as to why I texted him back, I simply needed a friend.

Annabelle: yes

* * *

This is nothing. We were old friends. We've done this many times before. I heard the knock on my bedroom window and quickly walked over to open it.

He stepped foot into the wooden floor. "I was at Billiards, I can't go home. I can't leave here without talking to Jacob, he wants nothing to do with me right now."

"Is your mom here?" he asked me.

"No, she's with yours."

"Oh, dad left the house." He ran a hand through his hair.

"The way I see it, I kind of did us all a favor...I shouldn't have said it that way, that was a jerk move, but now everyone knows. We can finally move on."

"You're right."

"What?"

"I said you're right." I repeated. "You were a complete jerk today."

"Annabelle," He stopped. "Dad and his family are the jerks."

"You swore you would never be like them." I stared at him. "Amanda didn't deserve that, and Jacob certainly doesn't. They should have never found out your parents are separating that way.

"You were wrong, Jordan. Your dad and grandpa have always been like that. You know it, I know it, everyone knows it, but you always said you'd be the exception. You were exactly like them today."

We were quiet for a second before he sat down against my bed.

"I screwed up," he said.

I sat down next to him. "You did."

"I've tried calling Amanda all day," he looked down. "Jacob won't speak to me."

"Jacob I understand, but why didn't you tell Amanda before?"

He shrugged.

"It wasn't your place." I looked at him. "Why do it now, why this Thanksgiving? Why couldn't you just freaking wait?"

"I couldn't stand to see the look on my dad's face after what he's done to mom."

I held back my tears. "I wish it happened another time, you ruined Thanksgiving."

"I'm sorry, I get this was tough on you and your mom."

He looked at me, "Seth and Kevin gave me a mouthful just now."

I looked away.

"They called me." he said, "Are things good with you two?"

A lump formed in my throat. "No, we broke up."

He stared at me. "He never deserved you."

"I was interviewing for the internship when I went to Manhattan," he said. "During your first date, I almost dropped everything when I heard you were going out with him."

I didn't say anything back.

"It's all so stupid now, but that's why I ended things with us. When I found out about dad's affair, I got scared. I caught him with her when he drove me up to school freshman year." He lowered his voice. "He made me promise not to tell anyone. All my life, people told me I'd take after him with the business, with everything."

He looked at me again. "I wanted to be nothing like him, so I distanced myself from you. You were the one person I never wanted to hurt. I knew if I stayed away, there was no way I could ever hurt you."

"You have to believe me, Annabelle. It broke me to see you hurting and not be able to be there for you like I wanted to. You hated me because you thought I abandoned you when all I thought about was you."

"Then you chose to come to school this fall, I was forced to face you. I thought maybe we could give things a try, but you gave Kevin a chance."

He said to no one in particular. "He always thought you were cute."

Jordan grabbed my hand.

"I had no right to stop you from dating him, but you have to know how hurt I was. What was I supposed to say to you? Don't date him because I'm still in love with you?"

It was like a whimper, but it escaped my lips, "yes."

We both didn't speak. He sat back next to me.

"You're wearing it," he said after a while.

I slowly ran my fingers along his necklace. "I want things to go back to what they were, just for a moment." *I want to rewind time.*

Back to when he was my Middlemist Red Camellia. Back

then, dad was still here. Our families seemed normal, we seemed happy. Back then, I was happy.

"Things don't have to change with us," he said. "I don't want them to."

I tried not to let his words sink in.

"I can't stop loving you, I haven't stopped loving you, and I don't want to stop loving you," he added.

It wasn't just the way he was staring at me. It was everything. We were both hurting and barely hanging on.

"Do you still feel this between us?" Jordan grazed his fingers down my arm. "Tell me you do, tell me I'm not crazy for still feeling this way about you."

He whispered in my ear. "Tell me you want this."

He sat still, staring deeply into my eyes, anxiously waiting for my answer. I couldn't deny how desperately I wanted things to make sense again. Considering my suddenly rapid heartbeats, I couldn't deny that he still had a part of my heart.

"I want this," I said.

Just about every emotion ran through my heart as Jordan kissed my lips and our bodies magnetically pulled towards each other. He grabbed my shirt and lifted it off.

"Is this okay?" he asked.

I shook my head yes. He lifted me up and placed me on the bed. I quickly pushed away the thought of Jaz, the Ngono twins, and the whole *Daughters in Waiting* group. *This is my decision to make.*

He kissed me again.

"Are you sure about this?" he reached for something in his pocket.

I looked at him again, took a deep breath, and whispered.

"Yes."

Twenty-Six

"SWEETIE, ARE YOU AWAKE?"

Mom knocked on my door. Jordan and I rose up in a frenzy.

I felt numb with shame. I felt scared. I felt every emotion I thought I wouldn't be feeling. I felt complete and total remorse. *I lost my virginity.* Instead of the army of butterflies I expected to feel after, I was crushed with disappointment.

"Annabelle, are you awake?" Mom knocked again and attempted to open the door.

"It's locked mom, please give me a sec!"

Jordan put his clothes on while I quickly pulled the covers up over the sheets.

"One second mom," I said. "Didn't you have a meeting this morning?"

"I did," she paused. "Everything okay?"

"Yes, I just need to get ready!"

I looked at Jordan. "You have to get out of here."

"Listen sweetie," she said. "I know you're mad, but I have something to say to you. Meet me in the garden whenever you're ready."

A few seconds later, she was gone.

"You need to leave before mom notices you were here," I said to Jordan.

He rushed to my window then stopped. "Wait, come here."

"I love you, Annabelle," he pulled my face towards his and kissed me. "Can I give you a ride back to campus? I want to take you back with me."

"Yes," I kissed him again and rushed him out. "Go."

* * *

I wasn't sure how long I huddled in the bathtub, but I let the water wash over my skin. I sighed quietly and closed my eyes, cursing myself for feeling regret.

Mom knocked on the bathroom door, "Annabelle, are you okay in there?"

"I'm coming out soon," I said.

"Okay," she paused. "Meet me outside sweetie."

I stayed in the bathroom a little longer until I could find the strength to get up. Eventually, I brushed my hair and tied one of my larger ribbons around my ponytail. A few minutes later, I met mom in the garden.

She rested her back against the gazebo's bench and motioned for me to sit next to her.

"I met with the realtor today," she said. "I canceled the showing."

"I won't sell the house, not right now...or soon," she added. "We have a lot to discuss first."

I sunk into myself.

"I thought you'd be happy about that," she added.

I could feel her trying to hold back her tears. She stood up and walked around the bench, standing behind me. She slowly untied the ribbons on her wrist.

She placed the first one around my ponytail. "I love that you never stopped wearing these."

"What you told me last night and at the spa breaks me, but it's faultless," she added.

"I haven't been your mother," her voice cracked. "I was so busy taking care of your dad when he got sick that I stopped taking care of you."

Slowly, she tied the next ribbon. "I can't make up for those years Annabelle, but I'm proud of you for not giving up on yourself."

The tears gushed down my face, so I let them.

"Sweetie," she softly ran her hand flat against my ponytail. "I love you and I'm sorry I neglected that you needed me too."

I couldn't speak, I couldn't move, I couldn't even gather myself. She placed her arms around me and with the lowliest whine I've ever heard from her, said, "I'm sorry I haven't been strong enough."

Before I knew it, she was back around, facing me.

"I will always love being your mother. I will always be here for you, I'm sorry I never made that clear to you after he passed away."

I don't know after which hospital visit it happened. It could have been the third or fifth, but mom came out of the hospital room and asked me to head home and make dinner for us. Then to do laundry and clean the house. *Write it down*, she said, or *read. Maybe garden*. She didn't have to say it explicitly, but it was clear. *Do anything but come to me for help*. There was a point in her lists of requests when I stopped expecting her to be there for me.

"I love you too, mom," I slid into her arms. "I will always love being your daughter."

She squeezed me tight and cried into my arms while I did the same in hers. The tears felt like we were regaining every second we lost apart from each other – when we were the ones we needed most.

I dropped my arms from her and stood up. It seemed the best moment to take the advice she'd always given me in accepting the apologies that came. I walked over to the entrance and grabbed our gloves, dragging the garden hose with me.

I walked back into the gazebo and looked at her.

"Let's start with the lilies," I said.

We spent all morning, practically all afternoon, just plucking and watering. Once in a while, we'd stop and simply smile at each other. The pain didn't go away instantly. It didn't go away at all this time, but it meant the world that she was there.

* * *

"Mom, that's a good picture of you and dad," I handed her the next album. "I want to hang this one up."

She handed me another photo. "How about this one?"

"Let's do both of them," I said and glanced down at my phone vibrating.

> Jordan: something came up

Before he texted again, I knew it would be bad news.

> Jordan: So sorry to do this Annabelle.

> Jordan: Can you catch another ride?

"Is it Kevin?" she asked.

I shook my head. "No."

"Mom," my voice barely came out. "Did you ever make a mistake in love before?" I fought back my tears. "How did you know you loved dad and he loved you?"

She shook her head. "Many of them until I met your dad. None of the guys before him were even worth dating." She thought about my question for a moment. "When we gave up everything to make our relationship work, your dad and I always chose each other."

"Breakups are hard sweetie, it's okay to be sad about them."

She touched my cheek. "You know your dad and I rarely argued with each other? The only time we did was about how to raise you. He was very close to his family, and they thought I took him away from them. I won't stop you from getting to know them if that's what you want. But if you have any questions about your father, please come to me first, okay?"

I nodded. "Mom." The tears gushed out again. "Can you please take me back to school?"

"Of course I will," she grabbed me, "of course, sweetie."

* * *

Dear MGU Reader:
My fellow classmates
Ladies and gentlemen

It pains me to write this today. I was supposed to be the one girl on campus you looked up to. The one who kept her virginity and waited for the time to be right, the person to be right, her heart to be right. I'm sad to say I lost it and I feel worse than I ever thought I would. I wanted so badly to get it over with. Just for a brief moment, I wanted to feel like my old self again. Now, it hurts too much. I regret letting you down. I regret letting myself down. My heart won't stop hurting.

Kisses
…Or should I say hugs…
The Virgin

Virgin_7890: sorry you're regretting this
Freetoroam: Don't beat yourself up. Most of our first times are terrible.
nuella44: I guess it's true, you live and you learn.
Gamerboy11: chin up
Emily1: My first time was in the back of a car. I hated it.

Daisylyra: My first time was horrible. I don't even speak to the guy anymore
SammyWorks: My first time sucked soooo bad!
StreamQueens: I'm surprised you lost it recklessly
Nerdyyygirl: I'm still keeping mine
Anon200: I hated losing my virginity

My keyboard hovered on the last comment. I read it again and again. As if my heart couldn't break anymore, their words destroyed me.

virgin23: thanks for showing me how not to lose your virginity

* * *

The pit in my stomach was tamed on the ride back to campus. I had no interest in discussing Jordan or the mess that happened at Thanksgiving. Mom wasn't in the mood either. We spent the ride catching-up on family and my college experience. Our time together made things clear – both of us wanted a clean and fresh start.

Florida sounds good, I said to her. We could go on this vacation and take the house off the market. Mom was shocked to hear me say it, but up close, all I could see was how hurt she was with everything that happened. I hadn't noticed it before. How intertwined everything was with the Coopers. How much we needed to deal with our own mess and not theirs. How isolated we were from family. We *both* needed out of Blakely, at least for a little while.

"See you later," Jaz said to me after class. "Don't forget Halle's thing!"

I grabbed my bag and rushed out of CompLit48, hoping no one would notice me and really hoping not to run into Kevin. I was almost at the exit door when I heard Ben calling my name. I stopped and turned around.

"Still on for tonight?" Ben gave me a thumbs up. "You left me hanging last week. Final exams are coming up, don't quit on me now."

I couldn't muster up the strength to return his smile.

"Sure." I agreed.

The expression on his face quickly switched to concern. "Are you sure everything's okay? You've been off the past few days." I half-expected him to say another literary quote for me to guess. Instead, he placed his hands in his pockets and stared at me.

"I'm here if you want to talk," he waved his hand. "Forget all this. I know what it's like to feel like you have no one to talk to."

I noticed Kevin walking towards the exit door and looked down. I resisted the urge to cry again. It sucked that Kevin never bothered reaching out or calling or texting and neither did Jordan. The entire week back to campus, I didn't hear from either of them. I couldn't shake the feeling that Jordan got what he had wanted all along. The only thing that kept me going was knowing that soon enough, mom would be back on campus, to drive me out of here.

"I need to go," I said quickly to Ben. "I'll meet you at our time."

* * *

"I think it's only fitting that I take you to our favorite spot." Ben immediately tossed me the ball outside of his office. We went in silence, he walked ahead. When we got to the archives, no one spoke. He sat down against a shelf. "Before we start, I meant what I said earlier."

Being here, the tutoring, had been helpful and an escape for me all semester. We were both vulnerable. Not backing down from our emotions. Not letting the weight of our worlds affect us.

"How was your break?" He kicked off the series of questions.

"Short version, it didn't go well. Long version, my mom's not selling our family home."

"Both of those are short."

"Why Japan?" I asked, remembering what he'd told me before about it being the number one place he wanted to travel to.

He rubbed the back of his neck, "There's an English teaching program there I really want to do. It goes on all summer and my brother would be able to come with me. He really wants to travel there too."

"But your parents won't let you."

He looked at me, his eyes confirming I was right. "How was your break, really?"

I tossed the ball between my hands. I was aware of it; how much Ben and this game inspired me. I couldn't say it to him, but it felt good to say what I thought and not hold back.

"It was hard being back home, but my mom and I finally had a breakthrough. We're going to start therapy together, we've never done it before, but we think it'll help us."

I paused. "I made a decision during break I'm still regretting. I thought it was the right time when I made it, but I haven't stopped regretting it since it happened. The more I think about it, the more I hate myself for it. I kind of wish I could take it back."

I knew what to do. *Keep going.* I avoided his gaze and asked him my next question. "Is it hard living at home with your parents?"

Ben didn't say anything. He stared at me for a while, not breaking my gaze. I noticed a flicker of compassion in his eyes.

"No," he shook his head. "I can't leave my brother at home and live on campus. He won't ever get to experience campus life so it's the least I can do. Having me home helps him. I don't feel like I'm missing out at all, it helps that I already live in Greenspring."

"Do you ever feel like you're drowning despite seeing the shore?" he asked.

I didn't have to think long to answer it. "You mean like your head can barely stay afloat yet somehow...you're still floating? All the time."

I tossed the ball back to him. "If you could keep one thing with you for the rest of your life, what would it be?"

"My faith," he shrugged. "I don't know what I would do without it."

He stared at me. "What's your favorite memory of your dad?"

The last time I'd shared any memories of him was during his eulogy. I looked away from Ben, not wanting to give him a fluff answer.

"My dad loved the outdoors. We went on a lot of trips together around the country, that was our thing. One of the trips I went on, I saw the most beautiful flower there so that became my souvenir for every trip. I'd buy flower seeds from the places we'd travel to and bring them home so my mom and I could add them to our garden. Some flowers couldn't grow once they were planted, this state doesn't exactly have the best climate year-round."

"Being home brought back so many memories of my dad, before he got sick," I looked at him. "What's your favorite memory of your brother before the accident?"

Ben gripped the ball. He was staring through me, somewhere off in a distant memory. "You know," he said after a moment. "We used to watch the discovery channel nonstop. It was *bad*. Think spending eight hours a day or more on weekends just binging their shows. One day, my brother and I built this outdoor fort in our backyard and carved out territories on the grass. We pretended each territory was one of the different countries we were going to travel to." He stopped then looked at me. "I hate that he'll never get to do it the way he wanted to."

"My parents barely let him leave this town." Ben tossed me back the ball. "Have you started drafting your answers to the final exam practice questions?"

He had switched course. We were back to focusing on the class. I answered him then asked my next question. For the first time in days, I smiled.

Twenty-Seven

"Okay, get up!"

I groaned at Jaz. "Please let me sleep in a little longer."

"If you don't get up, Halle's going to come here herself and drag you to her project release."

"I physically can't."

"Seriously, Annabelle." She grabbed another top off the ground. "You spent all week comforting Amanda, but you need to take care of yourself asap."

"You can't stay in bed all weekend," she added.

She pulled the covers away from me. "Check your phone."

> Halle: I'm showing my final project at GRUB
>
> Halle: Room 203 at 2PM.
>
> Halle: Be there.

"I slept through it," I quickly texted the twins. "I forgot to let you guys know."

The last thing I wanted was to get dressed and leave my dorm, but Jaz was right. Halle would be upset and rightfully so. She worked on this project all semester since bowling alley night and if anything, this would be a distraction from all the worrisome thoughts floating through my head. I hadn't heard from Kevin or Jordan. I needed to calm down and stop thinking about how bad I felt.

"You're still thinking about that, aren't you?" Jaz asked

Jaz was the only one who knew I was The Virgin on MGU Reader and when I came back from Thanksgiving break, she knew something was wrong. One conversation led to another, and I told her what happened.

"I feel absolutely horrible."

"Listen to me again," she said. "You made a mistake, and you'll have to accept that things happened this way and ended badly. Obviously, you can't take it back, but that doesn't mean you have to keep making it or keep reliving it. You can't change this Annabelle, but you can learn from it. Just think about the decision you'll make next time."

"It hurts so much Jaz," I felt stupid for even asking her, but I was hoping she'd say yes. "Should I reach out to Kevin? Or Jordan? What if they're the ones waiting to hear from me?"

"You know the answer," she got up, "shower, get dressed, and meet me in the lobby so we can go to Halle's thing."

* * *

Jane was the first girl highlighted in the video. Her voice was strong, resonant, and bubbly. She was full of feeling, excited to share about MGU and what her year was like. Rachel went next then Roxy then Amanda. Halle's final project for her art history class was well shot. It was incredible really.

Our eyes were mesmerized to the TV watching it. It was apparent to everyone in the room that Halle put a lot of effort into this. She captured the essence of every girl well. Something unique, deep, that we wouldn't have noticed otherwise had she not filmed us. I knew that when she'd get to me, I would see what I was confronted with at Thanksgiving.

My voice echoed around the room.

"Hi, I'm Annabelle Wilson. I'm a freshman in the English Department." My eyes were swollen, and I couldn't seem to look straight at the camera. "My semester's going well. My grades, umm, not so well right now, but I'm working through it."

A small *go* from Halle was heard in the background.

"I came to MGU, because…" I looked away from the camera again. "Honestly, I didn't think I would, but I'm a little glad I did. I'm figuring things out as I go. I've met some incredible people so far. At least I showed up."

The video ended and I could tell Halle cut the part of me mentioning Kevin. She got up and turned on the lights to a silent room.

"Sooooo," she looked at all of us. "What do you think?"

"Totally brilliant," Amanda said before the rest of us got up to complement Halle on her video.

* * *

I'd never put it all together before, but I couldn't deny what I saw on that screen. I gave the idea to mom on our ride back to campus, and she hadn't been opposed to it. In any case, I now knew, I was going through with it.

Dr. Gatz looked up when he saw me walking into his office.

"Ms. Wilson, what brings you here?"

"I was wondering if I could speak to you about something?"

He pointed at the empty chair across from his desk. "Have a seat!"

"Is it final exams? Tutoring's been helping I thought."

"No, that's been going well," I took a deep breath. "I've thought long and hard about this and spoke to my mom."

My voice sounded so small and scared. The truth was, I was scared, but mom confirmed again that she would support me on this. I was so relieved when she agreed. We'd go to Florida for a bit, do therapy, and spend time together. Then, I would start again at MGU next fall.

"I'd like to take a leave of absence," I told him.

Dr. Gatz rubbed his head. "Your grades are stellar; you've impressed us all this semester. I have no doubt you'll pass final exams next week."

"It's not that Dr. Gatz, I'm so grateful that you gave me another chance...I just...I need to do this for myself."

He sighed. "You know, I can't say I'm too surprised."

I looked up.

"I lost my mom in grade school, it'll be alright, Ms. Wilson."

"I'm sorry." I couldn't help but think of how many of us were hurting silently. "Did you ever stop grieving her?"

He shook his head. "Never, but it's more docile now."

"It will be alright, Ms. Wilson. We're more than happy to welcome you back when you're ready. I'll *personally* make sure of it."

* * *

"Are you ready for our final session?"

Ben asked me. We were meeting in front of the library instead of the basement archives. He wouldn't tell me why, he just said I'd be happy about it.

"Follow my lead," he said. We walked up to the librarian.

"How are you?" he asked her. She didn't hesitate to smile at him.

"How's my favorite student doing?" She looked back and forth at us. "I haven't seen you around in a while."

"I've been super busy this year."

She smirked, already knowing what he was about to ask. "That's reserved for *senior* faculty and library personnel only Ben, and you must be supervised to go in there."

"Please let me do this," he smiled. "I practically work here."

"How much time you need?"

"Two hours, maybe more."

She peeked over at the room behind her and looked back at him.

"I'm only doing this because you remind me of my grandson." She grabbed a key under her desk and handed it to him. "Third floor and to your right as you know, don't touch anything that you're not supposed to and..." she looked at me, "you kids have fun."

"She's worked here for over thirty years," Ben said to me while leading me to wherever he was taking me. "I came here a lot last year, before I had the office."

"She seems lovely."

"She's great." He opened the door. "After you."

We stepped into a brightly lit room. It wasn't really a sight and didn't seem like it held anything of value. Just a bunch of shelves with boxes on them, each numbered.

"Why did you take me here?"

He smiled. "You'll see."

He walked us over to a section in the middle. "You said you wanted to know more about your dad." He grabbed a box and placed it on the top of the table near us. "I looked into the school's archives and searched your family's name and found this. They do a good job of tracking everything here."

He lifted the lid and showed me what was labeled at the bottom. *SFC*. Ben sorted through the stuff in the box before taking out a folder.

He handed it to me. "I think that's him."

If only I could bottle up this feeling. I flipped through the copies of my dad's papers, the articles he wrote for the school's newspaper, even the pictures. I stopped at the one I had an exact copy of. My dad was wearing his SFC shirt with mom standing right next to him, smiling.

I swallowed back my tears and looked at Ben. "It is, that's my dad."

"They have a ton of stuff on him here," he pulled out more

documents and pictures from the box for me to look at. "He was club president at SFC his junior year. If you check the date and some of the other archived documents, they mention it. He wrote an article on SFC his sophomore year."

"Thank you." I whispered. "You've done more than enough for me."

"I geek out on this stuff." He cleared his throat. "You can't take any of this with you, but we can make copies. There's a copier here."

"We can make a pile of what you want photocopied," he said. "I also brought this." He pulled a camera out of his messenger bag. "I don't mind taking pictures for you."

"You're into photography?"

"It's one of my hobbies."

"What else do you do?"

"Not your turn."

I shook my head and smiled. "So, we're starting."

"How long have you dated him?" Ben asked while adjusting the lens on his camera.

Startled, I glanced at him. He stared at me in a way that made me nervous, happy, or both.

"Not long," I placed another document at the top of the pile. "We unfortunately broke up." I waited for him to say something else when I realized it was my turn to ask.

"Why don't you just go?" I asked him. "Go to Japan, get an internship, get out of Greenspring, take your brother with you. Why don't you just do what you've always wanted to do?"

"It's easier said than done." He stopped what he was doing. "Are you speaking to me or yourself?"

"Since you mentioned it...I'm taking a leave of absence next semester."

For the first time since we met, I could tell I shocked him.

He cleared his throat. "Don't be a stranger."

"Stand still." He snapped a picture of me and walked on the other side of the table to show me.

"Not bad," I said.

We stood there, staring at the picture he'd taken, while I waited for him to ask me the next question. I could smell his cologne again. This time, *cinnamon*. I couldn't fully tell the rest of the scent just like I couldn't figure out his flower despite trying to all semester. I realized then, I wouldn't be able to because this was Ben. He was direct yet hard to figure out. As if on cue, he moved away from me again, back to the other side of the table. It seemed like the right time to thank him for all the help he gave me.

"Final exam on Monday," he said. "Are you ready?"

"I think I have this one in the bag," I answered his question.

Like every tutoring session I spent with him, an hour felt like seconds. And three hours, like minutes.

Twenty-Eight

"You'll never guess what just happened!"

Amanda barged into my dorm. She extended her phone for me to look at the text messages on the screen.

> Warren: wanna do a test run?

> Amanda: for?

> Warren: let's try this out

> Amanda: What are you asking?

> Warren: I'm talking bf & gf

It was only a matter of time. Amanda always got the guy.

"He's lucky to date you," I said.

"Seriously! Who wouldn't date me?" she said. "You know what this means right? I just snagged the richest guy on campus! This is good for me, *really* good.

"See how this works, Annabelle? It's *too* easy. Halle and I are planning on spending New Year's with them. We're thinking NYC or Boston, we'll see what everyone's up to. Jane and Gabriella are down, what about you?"

"Oh...Annabear..." Her smile slowly faded. "I already told you! You'll find someone else in no time. Just have your pick from Warren's frat."

"I'm happy for you, Amanda. This is what you wanted. I'm not surprised he caved."

"Me either."

"Mandabear strikes again."

"Don't worry, soon enough, you and Kevin will be nothing but a distant memory," she said.

She sat at my desk. "How many exams do you have left?"

"Just one and I'm done. I have Kacie's farewell dinner after. I'll organize my stuff for the rest of the week before mom comes to pick me up." I said. "Amanda, I went through with it."

"You're really taking that leave of absence?" She shook her head. "I don't want you to leave."

"It's for the best, I really need to do this."

My laptop dinged, causing us both to look at it and the text messages coming through.

"Don't!" I quickly tried to shut the screen, but it was too late. She was holding my laptop in her hand, scrolling through the text messages Jordan was sending.

"Why is my brother saying he's sorry for what happened? What is he talking about?"

The blood rushed to my face.

"Annabelle," her expression changed from confusion to sadness in the beat of a second, "why is Jordan saying he doesn't want you to regret what happened and that he doesn't?"

I tried to grab the laptop from her, but she held it tighter to her chest.

"What are you hiding from me?"

All I saw was our friendship flashing before my eyes.

"I can explain, Amanda."

"Explain what? You're sneaking behind my back to see him? The only person in the world I freaking hate?"

"I know you hate him, that's why –"

She took a step back. "You're defending him?"

"No, I'm not defending him!" *Nothing is coming out right.* "It was a mistake; I can't take it back. We didn't mean to, all of it was a mistake."

"We?" She took another step back. "You're *we* now?"

"Please listen to me, I was the stupid one! I never meant to hurt you. I didn't want you to find out this way."

"You never meant to hurt me by talking to my brother and lying to me this whole time?" Her eyes shifted to a look of fury. "Were you doing this behind Kevin's back? Is that why he dumped you?"

I risked our entire friendship and said out loud, "I had a crush on him for years and we dated...not really, but briefly. I thought he was the one. Please give me the chance to explain everything to you."

"Aren't you a freaking virgin? Jordan doesn't date girls like you," she said which sounded more like *I now hate you too* or *how pathetic.*

"Please don't do that, Amanda." A sudden sharp pain pierced through my chest.

"Do *what*?"

"Do that thing you do when you act like I'm the weirdest friend you have."

"Don't you need to worry about saving your virginity for one guy? You have to add Jordan to the list of options? You don't even know how to date anyone, you had to be coached into it! Did you consider how this would make me feel?"

With this, I knew. Leaving MGU, leaving Massachusetts, could also mean leaving Amanda.

"It's not always about you," I said. "Can you for once hear me out and not make it about you?"

I thought she would stop and let me explain everything to her, but I knew she wouldn't. Because Amanda always had her punchline.

"Of course I make it about me, you shut everyone out!" She

yelled. "I had to convince everyone in school that you weren't some weirdo. Turns out, you are!"

"You're the one partying your entire life away instead of taking a single thing seriously!"

"At least I have friends, Annabelle! I get to live in reality while you pretend like everything's fine when it's not."

"Everything isn't fine!"

"Big freaking deal, that didn't give you the right to date my brother!"

"We didn't really date! If you'd give me a second to explain things to you, I would, but you guys are one in the same and you know what, I never saw it before. It's always about you and what you both freaking want!"

"Excuse me? I'm nothing like Jordan. How do you think I feel about our friendship?" She approached me. "Ever since your dad got sick, you shut me out. For two years, I had to beg you to do anything with me!" Her eyes filled with tears. "I had to buy you clothes for school and stuff because you couldn't get out of bed to do anything with me."

"I never asked you to do that."

"I did it because I care about you!"

I glanced to my left; my phone was vibrating. I looked at Amanda, who was staring at the call appearing on my laptop. I didn't have to look to guess who it was.

"Pick it up," she said.

My breaths were short, sparse, "Please give me the chance to explain this to you calmly."

"I was totally blind," she said. Her mind was made-up, she wasn't forgiving me for this. "Mom begged me to hang out with you those last years of high school. You were a complete nightmare to be around. You barely ate or hung out with anyone, you left me and only remembered I was there when your dad died."

I stared at her in disbelief. "Take that back."

"The Annabelle I knew would have never lied to me,

especially about Jordan," she insisted, "maybe we've grown apart."

"Maybe we have."

"Don't look at me like that."

My heart was in my throat. "I'm not looking at you like anything, Amanda."

"You think you're so perfect." It wasn't venom anymore, it was something else. "You're not perfect, you're not even special. The only thing unique about you is your virginity."

"Yeah, I was, so what?"

"You mean are," she spat.

"No, was! I chose to lose it to your asshole of a brother!"

"At least you got to choose!" She stopped. "You lost your virginity to Jordan?"

Her words hit me as if I was standing in the way of a freight train. The same words that haunted me for days after I'd read them under one of my posts. *I thought it was the girl from the group.*

"You're userx48."

"How do you know that?" she asked me. "How could you possibly know that?"

Amanda didn't move. She didn't say anything else. She just stared at me. That was the second time I saw my best friend speechless.

* * *

"Please Amanda, just give me a moment to explain everything to you," I reached for her arm, but she was already out of my dorm.

The student walking down the hall stopped to stare at me speeding towards Amanda, who was already in the elevator. I rushed down the stairs.

"Amanda, let me explain!" I caught up with her outside of our dorm building. "Give me ten minutes!"

"You're The Virgin? You?" She pointed her finger at me. "I

asked you that night at the spa and you lied to me. I never want to see you again."

She ran away before abruptly turned around again. "What else are you hiding from me? It's not enough to lie to me about sleeping with my brother, now you're the one behind that stupid poster too? What else do you need me to know?"

"We're angry at each other right now and it's all coming out wrong," I pleaded with her.

"How should it come out?" she asked.

"Like Jordan at Thanksgiving or maybe you want to go and write another post? Dear MGU Reader, here's how to betray your best-friend. I was so stupid to give you the benefit of the doubt. I knew it was you! My gut told me it was you, but I thought, *no*, not my Annabear. She wouldn't lie to me. You've lied to me all semester about Jaz so I should have just stuck to my gut."

"I never lied to you about Jaz." I stared at her. "I beg you to hear me out, please."

She snorted a laugh. "I have my issues, but you have to sort through yours." She walked away from me, stopped, then turned around. "By the way, Jaz doesn't exist so when you come back to reality, remember that!"

The first thing I did was run back to my dorm.

"Hello?"

"Hi Kacie, I need to ask you something if that's okay."

"Sure! What's up?"

"Do I have a roommate?"

I could tell she didn't know what I was asking.

"Umm, I mean...I was just wondering if I did have one?"

"If you were *assigned* one?"

Up until now – like at all this semester – I hadn't considered that the school said I wouldn't have one.

"I thought you were happy with not having one," she answered, "I figured with your dad and all, the school could, you know, help you out in some way, give you the dorm to yourself. Students love that! I should have checked again when you came to campus for orientation. Do you want one now? If you want one, I can make sure you have one next semester. The new resident supervisor's the nicest and I'm sure she can work with you on finding someone you'll get along well with!"

"I was just wondering," I whispered.

"No worries, see you at my farewell."

The phone dropped out of my hands. I couldn't do anything but fall to the ground and weep.

* * *

I knew this feeling all too well. The ruminating. The desperately wishing you could rewind time. I paced around campus for hours until I finally made my way back to my dorm. Jaz was there, sitting on her bed.

"You're not real?" I asked her. She shook her head no.

"How?" I looked around our dorm. *My dorm.* "I talked with you all semester, you walked with me everywhere. You took me to the club meetings. How can you not be real?"

"Who are you, Jaz?"

"Sit down, Annabelle."

"You have to be real!" I said. "I see you!"

She walked over and sat on my mattress with me.

"Remember your junior year of high school? In your hotel room?"

Crescent City.

"No, no, that's not possible. This isn't possible, is this some kind of sick joke?"

Still, she kept her eyes on me while speaking. "You prayed that God would heal your dad if he was real. Then you went to campus, and you saw the group flier in your dorm on your first day of orientation. You prayed again for the second time.

"You prayed that if God was real, he'd send you help, because your dad wanted you to go here and you wanted to make him proud, but you didn't have the strength to go on since he didn't.

You prayed that entire day and night. Annabelle, you stayed in your dorm for so long, you missed all the activities that day."

"You showed up the next week."

She wiped my eyes. "I showed up for you."

She extended her hands, and in an instant, a screen appeared in front of us showing my dad and I walking around in Crescent City.

"I was sent to spend the semester with you."

I shook my head. "You're not an out-of-state student?"

"Not in the traditional sense."

"What are you?" I dared not ask what I wanted to.

"Yes, I'm an angel."

My body shivered. I closed my eyes, wishing that when I'd open them, she'd be gone. But she wasn't. She was still there, sitting next to me.

"What about the Ngono twins? I talk about you all the time to them and Amanda, Halle, Kevin was in our dorm." I said. "Hasn't he seen you? They probably think I'm crazy."

She shook her head. "Did you ever notice he never looked at me? None of them can. No one can see me except you, but they don't think you're crazy."

"Amanda does."

"She's mad at you, that's why," Jaz said. "Your friends just ignore it when you mention me because they've never met me. They think I'm a busy roommate and we don't really get along."

"I never drew attention away from the conversations you were having when I spoke with you in public."

She extended her hand again and like before, another screen appeared. I could see the two of us at the welcome reception for my college. She whispered something to me at the dessert table, but no one else could see her or even notice her. It looked like I was just enjoying my own company, eating the desert, until Kevin joined me.

"This whole time you weren't real."

She extended her hand, once more, another screen. Each of

the screens showed our interactions during the club meetings, our walks, even the bowling game we played for girls' night. Jaz was there, but unnoticeable to everyone, only me. No one even paid attention to her. Except Amanda who never saw her, but whose ears I had talked off about Jaz.

"She'll never forgive me for hurting her," I told Jaz.

"That's not true. You two will get past this," Jaz said. Her skin was now glowing and looked fluorescent. She looked at me as if to tell me not to be scared, that this was still her.

"I have to leave you now, my time here is done," she said. "You're going to be okay."

I attempted to hold her hand, but my fingers went through her skin.

"Please don't leave me Jaz, not you too."

"You thought God didn't hear you Annabelle, now you know he does, he's here. Now you know we're here."

"You'll go on to do great things with your life. Don't stop taking care of yourself." She stood up. "Your dad's taking care of and you have the rest of your life and many beautiful things to experience." She smiled. "You and your friend will be okay, eventually."

"Take that leap of faith you've wanted to. Don't stop praying, we're here for you," she said then disappeared.

* * *

"I'll be there in a few," I said on the phone to Roxy and Rachel before making my way to Amanda's dorm.

"We're saving you a seat," Rachel responded. They were already waiting for me at the restaurant for Kacie's farewell dinner.

I walked over to Amanda's dorm, her apology bag in my hand. It was nothing, only a small start. The bag included the newer album from one of her favorite artists, a brand-new DVD of the recently released romantic comedy that was all the rave on MGU

Reader, a bunch of savory snacks, and my seven-page apology letter that I was desperate for her to read. We hadn't spoken in three days since our fight, but I was leaving campus tomorrow. I couldn't leave without attempting to talk to her again.

"If you're Annabelle Wilson, I want nothing to do with you." Amanda called out from inside of her dorm after hearing my knock.

I leaned against the door. "I know you want nothing to do with me, but I'm sorry. I'm deeply sorry, Amanda." I stepped away and placed the bag down with the envelope underneath it.

"Well, well, well." Halle opened the door. "If it isn't the number one traitor herself." She turned to face whom I assumed was Amanda. "Want me to throw these out?"

"If you say so..." Halle looked at me, "I won't throw it out then."

I briefly saw Amanda before Halle shut the door.

* * *

"Hi ladies!" Kacie handed each member of the group a gift bag.

Roxy looked at her. "Kacie, we're the ones treating you tonight."

"I wanted to do something special for each of you, open them!"

We pulled out earmuffs with our group's name stitched on them and shirts with the SFC logo in the front.

Roxy got up to hug Kacie. "We're going to miss you so much." She handed Kacie her gift from all of us. The flowers and visa card for her 'big girl' apartment she was moving into after graduating.

"Can I tell them now?" Kacie asked Roxy. Roxy nodded.

"You're looking at your new group *and* SFC club president," Kacie said to the group.

Roxy deserves this.

"Congrats," I said once she sat back down next to me. "You'll make the best leader."

A pit formed in my stomach.

"You leaving doesn't mean you're off the hook," Roxy smiled at me. "We're expecting you to phone into our meetings like we agreed on."

"Well," I cleared my throat. "I'm going to need all the details now that you're president."

"And we're going to need to compare notes with you on Florida," Roxy said.

"Please keep in touch," Rachel added.

"I will," I said. "I'd love to."

Kacie said something, and our attention went back to the group. I looked around the table, at the different girls speaking to each other. I had every intention to keep in touch with them. This group had become like my family on campus, all because of Jaz.

"What are you smiling about?" Rachel asked me, also smiling.

"Nothing."

Twenty-Nine

I KNEW I NEEDED TO, I owed it to everyone who supported my posts all semester. I couldn't leave without doing it. So, I wrote my final post.

*   *   *

Dear MGU Reader:
My fellow classmates
Ladies and gentlemen

This post will be my final one. It's something I want to share with you, because I think it will help you. I hope it helps you.

My father took me on a trip when I was eight – out to Crescent City, California. This trip was the start of our annual tradition of traveling together once a year. My mom and I had our gardening and my dad and I had our excursions and adventures. He was all about the outdoors and he was the reason I wanted to become a writer and journalist. Every time I tagged along on one of his work trips, I was so giddy.

I couldn't stop talking about Crescent City for weeks when we came back from this trip. It was the first and only place I traveled to with him that left me speechless. We spent most of our free time together hiking and seeing the most beautiful flowers there. That's when I discovered lilies.

I wandered away from him and he said he spent a long time looking for me. He said when he finally found me, I was stuck in the field of lilies – taking in all the colors around me. He said I had the most mesmerized look on my face watching them. I begged him to hang out in that field for an extra hour. I loved being there so much, we went there a second time during my freshman year of high school. I came back from that trip researching all I could about lilies, and we went again a third time during my junior year of high school, right after my dad was diagnosed with cancer.

When my dad's cancer grew worse, I stopped researching lilies altogether. It reminded me too much of our time in Crescent City and how perfect it was. But my dad called me out on it and told me not to stop. He said I shouldn't stop doing what makes me happy just because he got sick. So, I promised myself I'd cherish that memory just between me and him. I went to the hospital after school during his chemo treatments and read to him books about lilies and all the fun facts I could find about them. It became our thing that we shared. I didn't care how strange it looked, because the more I read to him, the healthier he got. I brought even more books and I read those too. Soon enough, the doctor told us that he was healed. Until he wasn't again. The chemo treatments picked back up.

One day, I fell asleep in the hospital room, and I dreamt that my dad and I were back in Crescent City on that field of lilies. In front of a house with the most gorgeous yard out front. The lilies were even brighter than I remembered them. I couldn't believe how beautiful they were, I couldn't stop staring at them. I couldn't move so my father held me and told me to wait out in this beautiful field. That the lilies and all the flowers needed me including the ones back home in my mother's garden. He said someone had to take care of them and I was the perfect person to do it. Then I woke up to the sound of my mother screaming, the monitors beeping, the doctors pushing me out of the room. I woke up to finding out my dad passed away.

I closed my eyes again, desperate to see the lilies we saw in Crescent City again, but I couldn't. No matter how hard I tried, I couldn't. Until the start of this semester when I met my roommate Jaz. She came from Crescent City, can you believe it? I told her I had gone before, and I knew where it was.

Some of you always asked me how I did it – how I stayed a virgin for so long. It's because I followed lilies until I didn't. Until my dad passed away and I didn't know how to follow them anymore. I didn't know how to guard my heart anymore.

Do you know that lilies hide and keep to themselves? They don't shine their beauty just for anyone. It takes a while for them to bloom, and you might even have to wait years to see some of them blooming. I think that's the coolest fun fact about them. They're not like other flowers. They're special and unique and they don't care who doesn't appreciate them when they're off-season. They're only blooming when they're ready to.

The day my dad died, I read a bunch of how-to guides on how to grieve. They helped me when I needed it, so I hope this helps you too. Here it is.

How Not To Lose Your Virginity:

First, don't make the mistake I made.

Don't lose it when you're hurting or when you're in pain. You're not thinking clearly, and you need to sort through all your emotions first.

Don't lose it when you're not in love, because otherwise, you can't trust that they have your best interest at heart.

Don't lose it quickly or just to brush it off, because like me, you'll probably end up regretting it.

Don't lose it just because your friends are having sex, because we all have our own journeys and yours is yours alone.

Don't lose it because of social pressure, because in the end, we all have a choice, and you'll have to live with yours.

Don't lose it when you're immature or you can't have an honest conversation about sex and your relationship goals. don't lose it when you haven't found your voice.

Especially, don't lose it when you're heartbroken. No matter how badly you want it to, it won't mend your broken heart.

But if you did. Lose it, that is, I hope it doesn't stop you from continuing to protect your heart and body. You can still do it. Moving forward, I want to wait for the guy who's worth waiting for and I hope he's willing to wait for me too. If he's not, he just can't be the one for me. Before I have sex again, I'll make sure we're both in love and together.

Truthfully,
Your Classmate

P.S. Keep following lilies.

* * *

All these years, all I wanted was the one thing I ended up regretting most. Growing up, I always thought Amanda chose the wrong guys. They were rude, dismissive, and didn't deserve her. Yet I was the one who had chosen the worst of them all and didn't notice until it was too late.

I bolted up when I heard the knock, and the door slowly creaked open. Amanda walked in.

My heart raced in disbelief.

She avoided my eyes. "Hey."

"You came."

"You've left so much stuff in front of my door; it's starting to look like I'm running a business." She stood by the door. "You're also annoying to Halle. I happen to actually have a roommate."

Even if she was angry with me, she still came. *Maybe it's a start*, I thought. I grabbed her hand and sat down.

"Don't think for a second I won't stay mad at you."

"I get it. I'm sorry, Amanda. I'm really sorry."

"My brother, Annabelle? Seriously?"

I looked away. "I'm sorry. There's nothing else I can say or do to take this back."

"I can't believe how stupid I was." She stood up. "I thought about it and all of it makes sense now. He *always* favored you! The constant rides he gave us when he hated my guts and him always asking about you. He's always been a totally different person to you than with me."

"You really love him?" she asked me after calming down.

It was rhetorical, but I knew not to answer it.

Her next question was less accusatory.

"Why did you keep it from me?"

She stayed quiet, observing me. I wiped my tears. It was now or never. She already hated me, and I had already lost her.

"Jordan was the first guy I ever opened up to. He made me feel seen and beautiful, I thought all those times we spent together meant something long term to him. I thought it meant that he was the one and I was the one for him. I was wrong. I wasn't that special someone for him. I was just someone who was always going to be around. He never wanted me like that, he just like that I was a fangirl over him. He liked the effect he had on me, and he liked knowing that I was waiting on him.

"I didn't want to lose our friendship. There was no way to tell you and not to lose you...the few secret dates he took me on which now seem like nothing compared to the ones I went on with Kevin...they don't even seem like dates anymore. Jordan barely made an effort back then, but I took everything he did like he was really in love with me. I was so naive. I would do anything to take it all back, anything."

"I'm mad at you, but I should have seen you hurting," she said.

I looked up, surprised.

"You were crying out for help, and I wasn't there...not like a friend should have been. You were right, I was too busy partying."

"No Amanda, this is my fault."

"It's because of me you didn't take your gap year. It wasn't just to please your mom," she said. "You didn't want to let me down."

"I chose to come here."

"I pressured you to come, I guilt tripped you. I only thought about myself because I didn't want to be at MGU without you."

"I wouldn't have met Jaz if I didn't come."

"That's always been you," she wiped away her tears. "You always see the best in me, even when I don't deserve it. You're always quick to apologize to me when I'm the one who also needs to be there for you."

"You lost your dad, your favorite person in the whole world, and all I could care about was how I wanted to come to college, and party, and meet all these new boys on campus. I'm sorry too, Annabelle.

"Yes, I'm mad about what happened with you and Jordan, I still can't wrap my brain around it, but how many times have you covered for me? I've asked so much of you, and you're there for me! You've shown me how selfish I've been in our friendship. From now on, we can't hide anything from each other. I don't care what happens next, you're my best-friend and that's what friends are for.

"It sucks you lost your virginity that way. We don't have to talk about it, but I know that's not how you wanted to."

The tears streamed down both of our eyes.

"Aman –"

"Shhh, it's okay." She pulled me near. "You'll get over this."

"It hurts so much."

"It'll take time, but it'll stop eventually. Boys come and go." Her eyes were blurry, she was somewhere else now, but talking to me. "Remember Landon Sweed?"

"Our high-school quarterback?"

"He never asked me. I kept saying no, but he never asked."

"What?"

"He made it seem like it was all me the week after in school, like I was the one who wanted to hookup. He knew no one would believe in me. Why would anyone believe me? I'm the party girl, the one who always wants to have fun. The one who couldn't possibly still be a virgin her junior year."

I held her tightly, "I'm so sorry, Mandabear."

"He didn't even ask me, like it was nothing for him. I thought maybe if I experienced it with other guys, it would take the pain and memory away. I left home that weekend and didn't tell anyone where I was except you, because I needed to get out of Blakely. That's why I said you had a choice under that post Annabelle, I envied you so much. I hated him for taking that away from me and here you were, my best-friend, and you were getting to happily wait for it."

"You can't let him get away with that Amanda, you have to say something. I'm so sorry you went through that alone."

She shook her head. "It's too late now."

"No, it's not."

"Trust me, it is." she said, "No one will believe me, I don't exactly have the best track record."

"I believe you so don't think that way. Please tell me you'll consider it."

"I don't know."

"We'll get through this together, I don't care if we're miles away."

She lifted her pinkie up. "Promise?"

"I promise."

"Mom's not doing that well," she said after a moment. "I spoke to her yesterday, but I haven't talked to my dad yet. He's moving out of the house."

"Do you think they'll work things out?"

She shrugged. "Who knows."

We could hear the girls in the next dorm, watching a show. They seemed a million worlds away from us.

"Can you tell me more about Jaz?"

"You want me to?"

"I do, I read your letter." she said. "She also sounded amazing whenever you spoke about her."

"She wasn't perfect or anything, she was just...so peaceful and kind." I said. "I never felt judged by her, like ever. She knew all these things about me, but I never felt like she looked down on me. You know what she told me? She said she was an angel sent down to answer my prayer."

"Really? That's impossible."

"I thought so too, it still sounds so crazy, but she knew all these things about me and my dad that no one else knew. Well, I guess no one else but me and God."

"That's totally insane."

"I know."

"Do you believe in him now?"

"A little, it's hard not to now."

"I don't, but I support you."

"That's okay."

We sat in silence a little while longer, listening to the girls next door laughing about whatever show they were watching.

"You're leaving MGU," Amanda said. "I'm going to miss you so much, it sucks you won't be in Blakely for Christmas."

"I'll miss you more, you should come to Florida for the New Year. I think the twins might."

"I'll ask mom."

The sound came out unexpectedly. I thought it was the girls next door then I realized it was Amanda. She was laughing, slowly at first, then it got louder and louder.

"What's funny?" I nudged her. Amanda couldn't stop laughing. "What? Tell me! What's funny?"

She finally caught her breath mid-laugh. "I can't believe this semester! I'm Warren's girlfriend, dad's been having an affair for years, and your roommate was an angel." She held her stomach. "You had sex with my brother and now you're leaving MGU and going to Florida."

Suddenly, I started laughing too.

"You forgot to add that I was flunking school."

She pointed her finger at me, "until you started tutoring!"

She clutched her stomach like she couldn't handle it anymore. Tears streamed down our faces.

"I still stand by what I said Annabear, he totally likes you."

"You think that –"

"Every guy I *think* has a crush on you actually has a crush on you," she finished my sentence. "Have I been wrong?"

"He was just helping me out."

"There it is again!"

"What?"

"That look," she said. "The boom."

"If you hadn't told me about Jordan, or even dated Kevin, I would have thought it was Ben you were actually falling in love with."

"Ugh, don't remind me." Her words sunk in. "I'm leaving anyway."

"Not for long," she said. She stood up and walked around my dorm, tracing her fingers along the study desks. "What do you think Jaz would tell you right now?"

"You want to know?"

"I want to know everything I missed out on, Annabear."

I stood up and walked over to grab something out of my purse. "I have a feeling it'll revolve around this."

She stared at the bible my dad gifted me and flipped through the pages quickly. She looked at me skeptically then sat on Jaz's bed, still holding onto it.

"Keep it for me while I'm away," I said. "The girls are great. Rachel and Roxy are amazing, and if you give the club a chance, I think you'll like them too."

She didn't say anything back.

"I don't know for sure, but," I sat back down next to her, "I think Jaz would tell us not to lose this friendship."

* * *

"Take your time ladies," mom said from the driver's seat in front of Wolf Hall, after we donated my dorm items. Our car was filled for our mother-daughter road trip down to Florida.

I hugged Amanda again.

"How many times are we going to cry this week?" she asked me.

"As many times as it takes to say goodbye," I said. "Lucy's driving you back home this weekend?"

I knew the answer to this, but I was stalling. Getting into mom's car meant that for the first time in our friendship, I had no clue when we'd truly see each other again.

"Yep, we need that time alone." she said. "Halle says goodbye again."

"I'm happy you have her here. The twins told me they want to keep in touch with you next semester."

She smiled. "They texted me."

We hugged each other for the hundredth time before I finally got in the car and mom drove off. Amanda was still standing there, waving at us, until we were no longer in her sight. Immediately, she texted me.

Amanda: I already miss you!

Amanda: YOU BETTER KEEP ME POSTED

Amanda: daily! <3

Amanda: Think about all the hot guys you'll meet in Florida

Amanda: or Ben ;)

Annabelle: I love you so much!

Annabelle: I'm calling as soon as we arrive

I stopped texting Amanda and knew I couldn't leave just yet.

"Hey mom, can we stop at my college building? I have one thing left to do."

* * *

"Come in."

I took a deep breath and walked into his office. He'd emailed me to come in to see him before leaving campus.

"Hey." He took off his glasses and grabbed the box on his desk and gave it to me. "For you, consider it an early Christmas gift."

"Thank you."

I cut through the wrapping paper, my heart beating a mile a minute. I pulled out the set of cotton and handmade indigo paper and landed on the note at the bottom. *Take any slipcase you want from the shelf.*

I quickly looked at him. "I can't do that."

"Why not?"

"Because you've done more than enough for me, and you won. I passed my classes! Every single one of them."

"It's a gift."

"No, Ben, I can't accept this."

"If you don't choose..." He cleared his throat. "I'll be forced to give you one myself and I have a feeling you want your own choice from this collection. You and I already a ton of books, I don't think you want a third copy of one you already have –"

"Okay," I stopped him.

He grinned. "Your pick."

I walked over to the second bookshelf, stopping at the slipcase set that I would have chosen had he lost. The one he'd gushed so much about.

"I don't need the whole collection." I grabbed the vintage Fitzgerald copy I never got around to reading with my dad. *This side of paradise.* "This one's enough."

He grabbed it from me and placed it in the box he gifted me.

"Why did you give me a pep talk that night?" I asked him my next question. He'd answered it before, but I knew it wasn't the full answer.

His eyes cut through me. "I knew you would ask me that eventually."

"Then why did you?" I asked.

"Not your turn."

"Right."

He positioned himself against his desk, arms folded, leaning back. "I never thought it was that weird that you were a virgin, and I didn't get why you were so up in arms about everyone finding out."

"You told me you felt that way."

"I never thought it was weird because I'm a virgin too."

I was left momentarily stunned. Ben did what he always did and moved on.

"See you soon?" he asked me his next question.

"See you soon."

He walked me out of his office. "Take care, Annabelle."

All I had to do was go back to the car, but I couldn't. Not yet. He had to know how much I was going to miss him.

"Whatever our souls are made of, I think yours and mine might be the same."

"Brontë." I heard him whisper behind me.

Annabelle's Bookshelf

To Kill a Mockingbird by Harper Lee

The Great Gatsby by F. Scott Fitzgerald

War and Peace by Leo Tolstoy

I Know Why The Caged Bird Sings by Maya Angelou

Walden by Henry David Thoreau

Wuthering Heights by Emily Brontë

This Side of Paradise by F. Scott Fitzgerald

Thank You for Reading

Annabelle's story is just the beginning. Inspired by my own journey, this series follows the ladies you've met as they navigate life's pressures, confront their pasts, and explore love in all its forms. There's so much more to come!

If you enjoyed the book, please consider leaving a review. It helps more than you know.

Keep reading for a short excerpt from book 2 in the *How Not To Lose Your Virginity* series.

A Sneak Peek Into The Next Book

"What's the juice?"

"Divorce papers are officially signed."

"Congratulations Amanda!" Halle says, "I'm on my way to that dinner in Brooklyn I told you about. Meet after at Jordan's?"

"Yes! Bring the new man."

"You'll like him, he's a refresher from all the others."

I'm happy for her. At least one of us is ready for love and wants to date the opposite sex right now.

"We totally deserve it," I say to her. "See you tonight."

I hit the next number on my call log. "Hey mom, I'm officially divorced."

"He finally signed them? Honey...do you want me to come and see you?"

"No, I'm good." I stop the car abruptly and let the pedestrians walk by. "I'm celebrating with Halle tonight."

"Amanda, this is a big deal. You were married to Warren for five years, are you sure you don't want me to come back up?"

"I'm sure, how's the trip with Marie?"

"It's going well, I always love visiting her in Florida. Have you heard from Annabelle?" *You know the answer to that.*

"No."

"Mare tells me she just came back from a journalist job out of the country."

"Mom, there's bad reception here, I'll call you back okay?"

"Oh, okay, A –" *Ace. You want to say Ace.* "Okay honey, call me later."

Eight years ago, Annabelle would have been my first call. I press the next number on my call log before realizing the light turned green again.

BEEEPPP!!!!

"Don't you see the traffic? It's Manhattan!" I roll down my window to yell at the driver behind me. "I'm going as fast as I can!"

I roll my window up again. "I'm officially divorced, Jordan."

"Good, the guy was a tool. Are you on your way?"

"Yep, I'm almost at your apartment."

"Why don't you take the metro like a normal East Coaster?"

"That's because I'm an upstate East Coaster and we don't take the metro."

"You're staying in Greenspring after the divorce? Amanda, if you need a place to crash for a while, stay at mine."

"You've offered before." I'm grateful our relationship did a one-eighty over the years, but I can't impose staying at his place. "Thank you, I don't know what I'd do without you during this time."

"You're my sister, that's what I'm here for."

"Okay, the driver behind me is so annoying."

"City drivers are awful, they won't hesitate twice before honking at you," Jordan says.

I make a turn on the street leading to his building.

"Do you need help with the hors d'oeuvres for tonight?" I ask him, prying my eyes away from the truck behind me.

"I hired people for that," Jordan says.

"I can't believe you got it Jordan, totally proud of you!"

He worked his way up and could finally celebrate becoming the youngest vice president at his law firm.

"I'm going into your garage," I pull into Jordan's building. "It's weird, the truck behind me is coming in."

"How big is this truck?"

"Too big for these Manhattan streets."

Jordan laughs. "What color is it?"

"Blue, why?"

"Amanda, I think that's Seth behind you."

About the Author

Anne-Elise Yadoré Woappi, known as Anne Woappi, is a Christian writer who writes about faith, love, heartbreak, and friendship. Originally born in Douala, Cameroon, Anne immigrated with her family to the United States in 2001. When she's not writing and reading, she enjoys staying active.

How Not To Lose Your Virginity is Anne's first published work. To keep up with the author, go to www.annewoappi.com.